A TALE C

HOK~

HANNAH WALKER

A TALE OF TWO HORNS

Being one of the rarest shifters that exist, Charlie tends to hide his unicorn from the world, choosing to surround himself with what he loves — books. Owning one of the best bookstores in the area, he dedicates his life to his passion, and to spending time with family and friends.

Knox Vaughn is a hero, a larger than life Siberian tiger shifter who has earned the respect of everyone in the paranormal world. Few know the real man, the one who fights for his family and friends and hides who he really is inside.

When a simple mistake thrusts Knox into Charlie's bookstore, he finds himself smitten with the young unicorn. Two lives couldn't be more different on the outside, but Knox has a secret, one he's never shared with anyone other than his family. One that proves he's not so different from Charlie after all.

Unable to ignore the chemistry between them, Charlie and Knox grow closer, but as they do, trouble descends on the small paranormal community, threatening to keep them apart. The two must come together, trusting in what they feel so they can overcome the threats to their union.

When secrets are revealed and truths admitted, bonds form that won't ever be broken. Still, when it comes to tigers and unicorns, it might not be enough to save them.

COPYRIGHT

DEDICATION

FOR MY READERS WHO TAKE THESE JOURNEYS ALONGSIDE MY CHARACTERS.

Emma and Kris, as always, thank you for the sprinting company.

To my Betas, Emma, Tammi, Alyson, Shannon, Debbi, and Jesus. Thank you for all the work you do for me.

Dr. J. Rosado, your medical help has been invaluable. Thank you for everything.

Jessica, thank you for helping make my work the best it can be.

www.facebook.com/JessicaMcKennaLiteraryEditor

liteditor.com

My cover designer, Catherine Dair

https://www.facebook.com/catherine.dair.1

TABLE OF CONTENTS

CHAPTER ONE

Charlie Taylor opened the door to A Tale of Two Horns, the bookshop he co-owned with his sister, Evie. The rich aroma of paper assaulted his senses, and he breathed deeply. There was nothing as comforting as being in his favorite place. Books meant everything to him. They'd been his solace, his escape in his younger years when his parents had forced him to stay home. Oh, they weren't cruel or anything, but as a unicorn shifter, he was rare, *incredibly* rare, and that made him a target for hunters.

Spending so much time hiding in his room, he'd cultivated a love of the written word. How could anyone not enjoy delving into stories of heroic deeds, magical worlds, and incredible romance? They were his escape, his view into worlds he could never hope to visit, worlds that existed nowhere else but in the author's mind. How he longed to experience a love like the ones he read about in his favorite books. To Charlie, there was nothing better than curling up on a lazy Sunday afternoon, reading an epic story of the love between two men while they attempted to save the world.

Flipping the sign to open, he switched on the lights, powered up the till and took a long sip of the raspberry and blackberry Frappuccino he'd picked up on his way into work. Addicted to the things, they were his guilty pleasure, alongside carrot cake. Evie always told him he would get fat, but when things tasted this good, it was so hard to ignore them. Which was why he found himself sneaking his treats in before she got there.

A chime dragged his attention to the doorway, and he grinned at seeing Mitchell, the delivery man. "You're early today."

The rhino shifter carefully set his stack of boxes on the long table beside the till. "I've got a half-day today. The boss is letting me go early seeing as Anna's mating ceremony is tomorrow."

"Is she excited? What about you?" Charlie leaned against the glass counter, the rare and treasured books housed underneath.

"She is. I still find myself wanting to gut Oscar." Mitchell cracked his knuckles.

Charlie chuckled, "You know you don't mean that. You're a gentle giant who adores his sister. You even like Oscar."

"I do like him, but that's my baby sister. If he so much as harms a hair on her head…"

"You know he won't. He adores her. I'd say he follows her around like a puppy, but he's a bear shifter…" Charlie winked.

Mitchell tipped back his head and laughed, long, loud, and soulful. "I always could count on you to make me smile. How's business?"

"Going well. It should be even better with that delivery." Charlie tipped his head to the boxes Mitchell had carried in.

"Oh? Something special?"

"The latest Davidson. You know everyone has been waiting to find out who the serial killer is. I swear that guy has all his fans in a frenzy over this one. I would love to get him to do a signing here." Charlie sighed.

"Is he a para?" Mitchell stole a bite of his carrot cake, winking.

"I don't know. That's why I've not even tried to approach him. I do know he self-publishes his books and that all the big publishers are desperate to sign him. He turns everything down though. He doesn't even go to conventions, so no one knows anything about him."

"That's a shame. Seeing a star around these parts would be good."

Charlie shook his head. "What, are the Vaughn brothers not stars enough for you?"

Mitchell groaned. "Just because they are Siberian tigers, they think they are all that."

Charlie grinned. Most of Corent City, one of the three paranormal cities in the United States, adored the Vaughn brothers, Knox in particular. Knox was the eldest, always stern, deep in thought and imposing. He was big, yet lithe and graceful. Charlie only ever saw him when he was in Corent on business, although what business it was, Charlie had no idea. The man certainly never came into his bookshop.

"Seriously though, having Callum Davidson come here for a signing would attract a lot of attention."

"Maybe you should reach out then?"

"But we don't know if he's para." Charlie slumped. "It's just a pipe dream."

Mitchell patted his shoulder, sympathy oozing freely from him. "I'd best be off if I'm going to finish my rounds before lunch."

"Send Anna my love, luck, and congratulations." Charlie waved as Mitchell walked toward the door.

"I will." With a tinkle of the bell, Mitchell was gone.

Sipping at his Frappuccino, Charlie carefully opened the boxes and ran a hand over the cover of the latest blockbuster. He couldn't wait to read it that night. He had a date— a fruity drink, cozy pajamas, and *A Date with Death*. He couldn't wait.

Humming to himself, he made sure the order was complete, along with the banners, stands, and all the promotional material, and tucked them away in his office. The release date wasn't for another week. Instead, he opened the website with upcoming releases, checking out what he needed to order in. Lost in the list, he didn't hear the tell-tale tinkle of the door. It wasn't until a gentle nudge to his leg had him looking down, that he realized he wasn't alone.

Crouching, he ruffled his nephew's mane. "Hey there, Danny, how're you this morning?"

9

Danny's grumble still sounded adorable as it tinkled with the natural bells of the unicorn speech. He was two, and typically full of energy.

"Aww, did you not sleep well last night, kiddo?" Charlie scooped him up as he smiled at his sister over the counter, the twins in her arms— Faith and Jasper. They were adorable little bundles of fluff at only two months old.

"He had a nightmare. He's missing Lane." Evie blinked a couple of times, pushing tears back.

Charlie leaned over the counter and hugged her. "How long till he comes back?" Lane was part of the Paranormal Assault Force, or PAF, who traveled around the paranormal enclaves chasing after criminals and shifters lost to their feral sides.

"I don't know, the council called him in at a moment's notice. He didn't know how long or even where he was going."

"If you need me to come and stay…" Charlie let the words trail off.

"Thanks, little bro, I should be okay. It was just tough when Danny couldn't sleep, and the twins needed feeding."

"Take a nap in the office later. You know I'll look after them. Besides, Sam and Alfie will be at the café as always. If they do venture outside, they'll keep an eye on them."

Sam and Alfie were both retired. Sam was a bear shifter who doted on the little shifters around, no matter what species they were from. Alfie was a mage who protested he hated all things little, but secretly loved the cubs and kitts who often played in the square.

A Tale of Two Horns was on Cavendish Square, a cobbled pedestrian area in one of the magic districts. There were cafés, magical toy shops, and even a small self-defense studio. The shops sold everything and anything, from wands, spells, potions, to cakes and books, you name it. With a real community vibe, it was a home away from home to Charlie.

"You sure?" Evie's gaze was full of hope.

"Of course, what are little brothers for?"

Evie buzzed a kiss on his cheek and took the twins to the playpen set up behind the tills. Faith was fast asleep within seconds. Jasper, staring up at his mama, twirled one of his blond curls between his fingers and sucked on his thumb. It wouldn't be long before he was asleep as well.

"Why not go now? It's quiet, the twins are almost asleep, and Danny here will keep me company, won't you?" Charlie ruffled his mane, receiving a small nudge on the forearm from Danny's horn, which, like all unicorn shifters at that age, was a little, rounded nub, incapable of doing any damage.

"You sure?"

"Go, Sis." Charlie shooed her out of the room. Grabbing the kiddie-sized table and chair, he waited for Danny to shift back to human, and set him into his seat, coloring gear ready. He grinned as Danny stuck his tongue out, concentrating on the colors. Finally, he held up a gorgeous purple crayon triumphantly. Charlie gave him a thumbs up, and they both settled into the peaceful morning.

Walking around the store, Charlie smiled as he came across the section with all of Davidson's books displayed. Running a finger down one of the spines, he pushed back the sadness welling inside him at knowing he could never meet his favorite author. That was the frustrating thing about living in Corent, a para city. The humans of the world didn't know they existed. A magical barrier surrounded the city, and every other enclave like it. Not only were people persuaded to change direction anytime they came close, but they were also convinced, magically, to forget anything they might have seen. It was what kept the paras in Corent safe. Charlie was thankful for that, but at times like this, he almost wished he was human… almost.

The tinkle of the doorbell, modeled on Danny's laugh in his unicorn form, broke him out of his musings and he walked back to the front.

"Are they here?"

Charlie ran the last few steps and flung his arms around Matt, his best friend. "I missed you. How was your weekend away?"

11

"Forget my weekend. Is *A Date with Death* in yet?" Matt was almost bouncing his excitement was so great.

"It is, but you're not getting a copy until I hear about your weekend." Charlie crossed his arms.

"Urgh." Matt threw up his arms. "It was about what I expected. They can't find any logical reason why I can't cast spells, other than to say there is some sort of block there, but it isn't static. It keeps moving about, so they can't treat it."

"Surely they must have some idea what it is? You went to the doctors at the Mage Council. If they have no idea, what can be done?" Worry rippled through Charlie. Matt hadn't been able to cast properly for a couple of weeks, and no one could find out the reasons why.

"They're researching until they find something. I have lots of exercises to do, and we have to hope that will help. In the meantime, I'm staying active and about to throttle my best friend if he doesn't hand over the goods." Matt made a throttling motion with his hands.

Charlie stepped around the counter, and lifted a small package, holding it above his head. "Is this what you were after?"

Matt jumped up, trying to reach it. Danny, happily coloring at his table, giggled away. "It's not funny." Matt pouted. "Please, Charlie Choo?" He used his old nickname for his friend.

"You're still Matt the Minx, even after all these years." Charlie retaliated with Matt's own nickname. Taking pity on his friend, he handed the parcel over. "Why do I feel like I'm a dealer, passing over some shady substance?"

Matt chuckled as he clutched the package to his chest, stroking it lovingly. "My beauty, you're safe, you're with papa now."

"Maybe I should be worried about you," Charlie teased.

Matt sent daggers with his eyes. "Don't try and pretend you haven't already set up your evening with this book. I know you too well."

"You know I have. You're welcome to come around…"

"Nope. I plan on reading in bed. That way when I eventually pass out, unable to keep my eyes open, I'll already be in bed and don't need to worry about waking up in odd positions."

"Do you plan on getting any sleep?" Charlie shook his head.

"Not until I finish the book, no."

"What about work?"

"Mama is letting me take the late shift at work." Matt's family owned one of the spell shops in the square where A Tale of Two Horns was.

"Lucky. I still have to open in the morning." Charlie slumped.

"I'd offer to bring you coffee, but I know you hate the stuff." Matt shrugged, picking up his espresso from where he'd left it on the counter.

"It smells good, but there's something about it…" Charlie scrunched up his face. "I'll stick to my Frappuccinos."

"You and your fruity drinks. Admit it's because you're a fan of rainbows and you just like the colors," Matt teased.

Charlie's hand went to his hair. While his hair was naturally such a pale blond it was almost white, he'd added streaks in it, pink, purple, green, red, orange, and blue. He narrowed his gaze at his friend. "Sue me, I'm a typical unicorn who loves rainbows."

Matt grinned. "And I love you just the way you are." A knock at the window drew their attention.

"You'd better get going. It looks like your mama is in a bad mood." Charlie patted Matt's shoulder.

"She wants me sorting out the spell parchments today."

Charlie winced. The parchments were old, and for some weird reason, Matt always seemed to end up with dozens of paper cuts anytime he had to sort them out. With a quick hug, Matt raced out the door.

CHAPTER TWO

Standing at the door of his bookshop, Charlie smiled as he watched Faith, Jasper and Danny chase after bubbles Alfie was casting around the tables of the café next door. The twins may only have been a couple of months old, but like all unicorns, in shifter form they were on their feet shortly after being born. Sam was keeping watch, making sure no one got too close and they weren't bothering anyone. Leaving the door open, he went back to work, pouring over the accounts. His least favorite task, he typically left them up to Evie, but she'd been so exhausted lately, he needed to help as best he could. With one ear trained on the younglings outside, he slowly made his way through the papers.

A sudden high-pitched squeal had him slamming his pen down and racing to the door. His mouth dropped open at what he saw.

Danny was cowering on the ground, his front legs covering his eyes, wrapped up in as much of a ball as he could. Standing over him was none other than Knox Vaughn. Alfie was cuddling the twins and Sam was down on bended knee trying to coax Danny to go to him. "What happened?" he cried as he raced forward.

A deep voice washed over him as he crouched down. "I am sorry, I was walking through the square when something slammed into my ankle. It hurt, so I whirled around and roared on instinct." Knox frowned down at him. "I had no idea it was this little one. I think I scared him. I didn't mean to." Knox was running a hand through his deep brown hair. "I know I have a reputation of being fierce, but never with the cubs." He dropped into a squat beside

14

Charlie and held out a hand, palm up to Danny. "Young one, I'm sorry, I didn't mean to scare you. Your horn slammed into my ankle, and it took me by surprise."

Danny peeked out before quickly covering his eyes once again.

"How could you not see them playing?" Charlie demanded, looking between Sam and Knox.

Sam reached out and ran a calming hand over Danny's head. "Actually, Danny here made a flying leap for one of the bubbles at the same moment that Knox here walked out of the café. There wasn't enough time to warn either of them. When Danny landed, he skidded on something spilled on the floor and slammed into the back of Knox's leg. It wasn't anyone's fault."

"Danny?" Charlie called softly. "Let's get you inside. Do you want some hot chocolate as a treat?"

Danny's ears twitched, and he looked plaintively at Charlie.

"Yes, you can have marshmallows as well." Charlie held out his arms and Danny bounded into them, snuggling close.

"I'll put the twins in the pen," Alfie called. Charlie looked down at the babies and grinned at seeing them fast asleep again.

"I'll get the hot chocolate," Knox offered.

Charlie smiled his thanks, surprised at this tender side to Knox. He'd never imagined one of the Vaughn brothers could be this caring. Not when you considered their reputations for being gruff.

As he walked back into the shop, the sight of Evie fussing over the twins greeted him. They'd woken up as soon as they sensed their mother. She looked torn.

"They need feeding, but Alfie explained what happened."

"Go deal with them, I have Danny here, don't I, buddy?" Charlie looked down at his nephew in his arms, now back in human form.

"You sure?"

Charlie nodded and shooed her out of the room.

Sitting Danny in his chair, Charlie checked him over, making sure there were no injuries. There weren't. It looked like he was merely shaken.

A shadow made him turn, seeing Knox there with a couple of drinks. He set one in front of Danny, who grinned. Charlie couldn't help but laugh. The hot chocolate was tall and there looked to be way more marshmallows than normal.

"I asked for extras," Knox's deep voice whispered in his ear. "I thought he deserved it." Knox stood again, Charlie joining him as they both watched Danny pick at the mallows first. "I really am sorry."

Charlie turned, taking in Knox's contrite expression.

"I would never do anything to hurt a cub. I feel terrible for it. My mind was on a meeting. I wasn't paying close attention when I should have been."

"Oh! Don't let us keep you from something important." Charlie stood back and gestured to the door.

Knox laid a hand on his arm. "You're not. I'd finished the meeting and was mulling things over. It was why I was distracted." He looked around the shop. "I don't think I've ever been in here."

Charlie resisted the snort he wanted to give. No, Knox Vaughn did not look like the sort of man who frequented bookshops. "We've been here about a year."

"Ah, that makes sense then. I've only been back in Corent properly for a month or so."

"Oh?" Charlie asked.

"I was in Jenvia before that." Knox smiled. Charlie was stunned at the transformation on Knox's face. Gone was all trace of seriousness, in its place were… dimples? How did someone who looked as dangerous and intimidating as Knox Vaughn have dimples?

Jenvia was one of the other para cities, in Alaska. Charlie didn't mind the cold, but Alaska was a bit too much in his opinion. Corent was in Utah, near the mountains. They had their fair share of snow and ice in winters, but at least the trade-off was warm summers. Taking a quick look at Danny, he snickered. Chocolate coated his lips, and there was a sticky smear on his cheek. "You having fun there, Danny?"

"Uh huh." The little boy didn't even look up, his concentration fully on his drink.

"Thank you for getting that for him. Of course, I may not be thanking you later when he's bouncing off the walls." Charlie grinned.

"At least it's still morning. You have all day to tire him out. Besides, once I realized what was going on outside, it looked like they were having lots of fun."

"Alfie loves sending bubbles around them, letting Danny, and the twins when they're awake, pop them. He often fills them with glitter. They love it, but getting glitter out of a unicorn's tail is no easy feat." Thoughts of the dreaded bath time plagued Charlie.

"I'm sorry, will your wife forgive me?" Knox nodded to where Evie had taken the twins.

"Wife?" Charlie's nose wrinkled. "Oh! No, that's my sister. Danny and the twins are hers, hers and Lane's, her husband. I've got them at the moment as she catches up on some sleep. They had a bad night, and with Lane away it's been hard."

"Lane?"

"My brother-in-law. He works for the PAF. He's on assignment at the moment."

"Lane Dellon?" Knox's eyebrow shot up.

"Yes, why? Do you know him?"

"He works with my brother, Carter."

"In the PAF?" Charlie checked.

"Yes, and from what I know, they're coming home soon." There went that smile again, the one that was doing funny things to Charlie's tummy, no matter how much he wished otherwise.

"Really? You're sure?" Charlie's eyes lit up. Evie would be incredibly relieved. She always worried when he was away. Not that she ever told Lane. It was one of those things she was getting better at the more Lane went away, but it would never be easy for her. Seeing her husband, her mate, leave and walk into danger was hard. Charlie saw it second-hand, and it was stressful enough for him.

"I spoke to Carter before I went into my meeting. They were escorting their target to PAF headquarters."

"How come you spoke to him? I thought they were always on a comms blackout until they got back to base?" Charlie stared at Knox with narrowed eyes.

Knox winced, his eyes darting about, looking anywhere but at Charlie. It was evident he hadn't thought his words through. "I, uh... that is... I..." He slumped. "He shouldn't have called me. He does it though, because he knows I worry too much. It's hard to watch one of your baby brothers race off to fight some of the worst the para world has to offer. We're tigers, we're one of the strongest breeds out there. That doesn't mean we have a defense against magic." The look he sent Charlie was haunted. "There are days I wish they did something else. But, it doesn't stop me being proud of them."

Charlie smiled at Knox, taking in the surprised expression. It looked like Knox didn't mean to actually say all that. "I understand. It's no different for Evie when Lane goes. She'll be happy that he's on his way back to base."

"She does know there are support groups? I mean there are several ones for mates, spouses, children, and a general family one. She isn't alone in feeling adrift at times." Knox was digging about in the pockets of his suit, coming up with a handkerchief, a rich purple cotton, and squatting down, he started to gently clean Danny up with a wink.

Charlie blinked a couple of times before turning to help the young witch who was stacking books on the counter. With one ear on the conversation behind him, he quickly rang everything up and waved to the woman. Turning, he grasped the counter behind him. Knox was sitting on the floor, back braced against one of the walls, Danny in his lap. Danny was chatting away, telling Knox about the latest twins' disaster— something about blueberry puree and a white shirt.

As Danny talked, Knox was carefully cleaning his face and hands of chocolate and marshmallow. The sight of such a strong man so comfortable in his own skin, helping a different breed of shifter, hit him in the feels. He coughed, but both Danny and Knox were thoroughly intent on each other.

Shaking his head, he went to peek in on his sister and the twins.

"How is he?"

"Drinking hot chocolate, or rather wearing it, and talking to Knox."

"Knox is still here?" Evie's voice was full of incredulity.

"I know," he whispered, "he was talking about support groups for you."

"Support groups?"

"Because Lane is out with the PAF. Apparently, there are groups of mates and spouses who get together to support each other."

"How did I not know this?" Evie hissed when Faith managed to clock her around the nose.

Charlie gently reached out and tapped Faith on the nose. "No punching your mamma." They both chuckled when Faith's nose wrinkled. He was rubbing Jasper's back when the little boy let out an almighty burp, rainbow bubbles forming at his mouth.

Through the partially open doorway, Charlie heard Danny explain. "That's Jasper. He's always noisy."

Knox's deep bass swiftly followed. "I'll let you into a secret— that's one of the things babies always do. You know I have four baby brothers?"

"Four?" Danny sounded horrified. "That has to be really loud."

"It was. They are all big now. Max is the youngest boy, then there's Carter, Tyler, and Nate. I'm the oldest."

"Are there any girls?" The way Danny said girls, as if they were the worst things in the world, had Charlie and Evie chuckling.

"One girl, Cora Grace. She's the baby of the family," Knox explained.

Charlie shared a smirk with Evie. "Rather her than me. Can you imagine having five big brothers? I wonder how she manages to date?"

"She doesn't!" Knox snarled through the doorway making both of them giggle. "She's only eighteen. Far too young to be interested in boys."

Evie tried to smother her laughter with her hand, the other one helping Faith to burp.

"Mamma?" Danny called.

"Coming, sweet boy."

Charlie stood, Jasper secure to his shoulder, and held out a hand for Evie, hauling her up and leading her back into the shop. He quickly looked around, seeing people browsing, but no one waiting at the till thankfully.

"How did you not get messy with the hot chocolate? I thought you said he was wearing it?" Evie quirked a brow in his direction.

"He was but…" He waved a hand in Knox's direction.

Knox held up the once purple hankie, now completely covered in chocolate. "I didn't think you'd mind." He chuckled at the mess.

"Oh my gosh, I am so sorry, please let me take it and clean it for you?" Evie stepped forward, but Knox waved her away. "It's no problem. I've dealt with worse things than sticky chocolate over the years." He gently set Danny back in his chair, and gracefully pushed up to standing. "Now, if you're all settled, I'd better be on my way. Once again, I'm sorry for what happened earlier."

"It's fine, they're good." Evie grinned at him, nudging Charlie in the side.

"Uh, thank you for the hot chocolate," Charlie muttered.

With a wink, a ruffle of the babies' hair, and a wave, Knox disappeared out the door.

Evie ran up and peeked out, making sure no one was nearby before she turned around and fanned herself. "Hot. That man is damn fine, with an ass I would…" She frowned at the young ears. Instead, she mimed biting, while tapping her own ass.

Charlie snorted, but nodded anyway.

CHAPTER THREE

The click of the lock behind him was a sign for Charlie to let his happy mask drop, kick his shoes off and relax. Dropping everything but his carefully wrapped copy of *A Date with Death*, he walked through his house, letting his toes curl into the soft carpet. He carefully laid the book in the nook of his reading chair and moved to the bedroom, stripping as he went. By the time he made it to the bathroom, he was completely naked and ready to wash the grime off from the long day. He sighed as his shower started. The one way he'd treated himself was remodeling the bathroom to have everything he could desire in it. There was a whirlpool bath in one half of the room, big enough for two people, and off to the other side was a large wet area, with shower. It wasn't a typical shower, oh no, he'd splurged up for the magical one. There were five showerheads on different walls, all set to cover every area of the wet room. The shower could be controlled by voice commands. He could choose scented water, different temperatures, the power of the stream, hell, even the color if he wanted. He could have music, videos, anything piped into the room. If he called out for shampoo, some would appear from a recess in the wall. He didn't know the mechanics of it— he wasn't a mage, after all— he was just happy with the results.

Setting the water to a warm, steamy mist, scented with lavender and bergamot to relax, he leaned against the wall, letting the water roll over him. He soon found his mind drifting towards Knox, and as the image of the man popped into his head, his cock perked up. Damn the man, he'd even smelled good. Unicorns didn't have the best sense of smell, but it was still better than most humans. Charlie swore the smell still lingered around him even now. Not that it would do any good. As gorgeous as Knox was, Charlie was definitely not his type.

Why would a man like Knox, all grace, beauty, and broodiness, go for someone who was light, airy and literally full of rainbows? It didn't mean Charlie wasn't attracted to him though. The whole idea of 'want him, can't have him' was predominant in his mind. Oh, but what would it be like to kiss Knox? Intense, captivating, and mind-blowing. His cock hardened, and his hand slipped down to squeeze. A bolt of lust arched through him as he imagined it was Knox's hand. The strength, grace, and power the man exuded were incredible. He could just imagine it was them in the shower, Knox kissing him, then pushing him back and down.

He would happily drop to his knees and swallow Knox down. It certainly wouldn't be a hardship. Would Knox be a screamer? Shouting out his pleasure? Or would he carry on his persona of the strong and silent type, not saying a word, just fisting his hands through Charlie's hair and tugging? Charlie wasn't sure which was hotter, but one, if not both, certainly made his cock react. A bead of precum oozed from his tip. Dragging it with his thumb, he smeared it over the head of his cock, groaning. Grabbing the shower gel, he squeezed some into his hand and lathered up his cock, quickly pumping. With each pump into his fist, the muscles in his ass clenched, and a desperate need to be fucked slammed into him. Eyes shut, visions took over of Knox bending him over, hands flat against the bathroom wall, pushing his feet apart as he slid his cock inside him.

Charlie groaned as his fist sped up. It wasn't enough. Blindly reaching out a hand, he roughly commanded body wash to appear. Fumbling, he managed to reach around and slide one finger inside himself, even as his other hand continued to pump himself. The combination was too much, and he cried out, cum spraying the walls of the shower. Knees buckling, he dropped to the floor, letting his head rest against the tiles as he fought to get his breath back.

"Fuck, if it's like that just thinking about him, it would probably kill me to be with him," Charlie muttered into the empty air around him. Eventually, his legs were strong enough to hold him up, and he pulled himself to standing. Remembering what was waiting for him in the other room, he grinned and briskly washed up. Jumping out the shower, more invigorated than he ever remembered being, he quickly dressed in a pair of super-soft flannel pajamas with cartoon zoo animals on and went to the kitchen.

Grabbing the small savory pies he'd made the night before, he spread them on a baking sheet and set them to cook in the oven. Dancing about the kitchen, he prepared his favorite fruit drink, a cinderfella as he liked to call it, because it tasted like a dream. With lemon, orange, pineapple, grenadine, bitters, and ginger ale, it was the perfect pick me up.

Pulling the small pies out of the oven, he scowled when his phone rang. He wanted to ignore it, but that was Matt's ringtone. Thankful he'd sprung for the magic-enhanced phone, he snapped rapidly three times, and the line connected. "This better be good, Matt."

"Have you started yet?"

"I just got in. Getting all my snacks together, then I'm diving in."

"It's so good." Matt sounded so excited. "Just wait until you get to the bit that—"

"Lalalalala, don't you dare finish that sentence. I'll never talk to you again, and I'll subject you to my singing every day."

"Oh man, you would, wouldn't you?" Matt complained.

"You damn well better believe it if you start trying to give me any plot details."

"Then let me just tell you, Detective Callohan is damnnnn fine." Matt exaggerated the words. "He's all hot and full of alphaness, and I want to climb him like I'm ivy and he's a tree."

"Alphaness?"

"You know what I mean, broody, big, almost intimidating with that stare that can pin you in place and turn you into goo."

"Mmm," Charlie sighed, his mind going to another alpha he'd seen. His earlier shower fantasy was still playing out in his mind.

"Spill," Matt demanded.

"What are you on about?"

"You think I don't know every variance in your voice? What, or rather *who*, is on your mind?"

"How do you do that? Work out what I'm thinking, even when we aren't in the same room?"

"I'm just that gifted. Now stop trying to change the subject and dish the gossip. Who has grabbed your attention?"

"Knox Vaughn." Charlie couldn't stop the sigh that escaped as he mentioned Knox's name.

"When did you get to see one of the infamous Vaughn brothers? It's not like they're seen around our part of Corent."

Charlie quickly rattled off the story, explaining what had happened. "Are you fanning yourself?" he asked Matt, slightly stunned.

"What? Knox Vaughn is one damn fine specimen. Plus, an alpha who is like that with kitts? What's not to love. You know, the only way to improve someone like that is if they have dimples."

Charlie whimpered.

"He doesn't!"

"He does." Charlie groaned.

"Does someone have a crush on the big scary tiger?" Matt teased.

"Oh, shut it," Charlie snarled, but wasn't really angry. This was his best friend talking. "Just wait until someone catches your eye. I'm not going to shut up about it."

"Not going to happen, I've sworn off men for the moment. Unless it's a real-life Detective Delicious that is." Matt's voice was dream-like.

"Well, how about you let me go and sample Detective Callohan's delights," Charlie teased.

"I'll pop in for coffee, or in your case Frappuccino, tomorrow."

"Night, Minx."

"Night, Charlie Choo."

As Charlie hung up, he carried all his snacks over and settled into his reading nook. With a sigh, he lost himself to the world of Detective Sam Callohan and a serial killer.

Charlie cast a quick look at the clock. Shit, it was almost four in the morning. He really should put this book down, but it was so damn hard. This story was better than every other book Callum Davidson had written. Looking between the clock and the book, he hummed. *Screw it, it's time for hot chocolate.* Within minutes, he was curled back up, lost in the world of handsome detectives. When his alarm went off two hours later, he shrieked, stunned. Where had the last two hours gone? He looked at the book, there were two chapters left. Did he have time? He grabbed his phone, reset the phone for an hour later and dived back in.

CHAPTER FOUR

Despite how much he hated coffee, Charlie was almost prepared to drink a mug. Exhaustion hung heavily like a cloak around him, but it had been worth it. A whole night with Sam Callohan? Yup, he'd give up sleep every time for that. Daydreaming as he walked to the bookshop, he startled when he slammed into something rock hard and dropped back onto his ass in a heap. "What the?" He looked up, blinking away the harsh sunlight that streamed around the head of whoever he had crashed into, creating a halo-like effect. He couldn't make out who it was, other than the fact they were large, and incredibly intimidating.

"Shit, are you alright?" The silhouette leaned down towards him until Charlie saw a hand outstretched in front of him.

Grabbing it, he was hauled up so fast he once again slammed into a solid wall of a chest. "Ooft."

"Sorry." The voice sounded vaguely recognizable. "Charlie, is that you?"

He looked up, finally able to see now the sun was blocked and promptly wanted to hide. "Knox."

"I seem to be making a habit of this." And there the dimples were. That damn stupid smile of Knox's did crazy, twisty things to his stomach.

"This was my fault," Charlie confessed. "I'm not with it. I didn't get any sleep."

27

"Oh? Why's that, nightmares?"

For some reason, Knox wasn't backing up, and it was making Charlie's head swim. "What? Oh… no, I was reading. I didn't go to sleep."

"That must have been one hell of a book to keep you up all night."

"It was. Promise me you won't tell anyone?" Charlie grinned as Knox looked about conspiratorially, making sure the coast was clear.

"Your secret is safe with me."

"I was reading a book we had delivered yesterday. It's not on sale yet, but I couldn't resist it. The series is just that good." Charlie knew he was blushing, but he shouldn't have read it. He just needed to find out what happened to the hotshot alpha detective.

"What book is that?" Knox took him by the arm and led him off to one side of the pavement, turning them both in the direction of the bookshop.

"It's called *A Date with Death*. It's the latest Callum Davidson, and it's so good. He's such an incredible writer, I get lost in his worlds. The way he describes things, the way the main character, Detective Callohan, investigates crimes, it's amazing." Charlie looked up and saw amusement dancing in Knox's eyes.

"It sounds like you like his work then." Knox gently pulled on his arm, making sure he didn't crash into a bin on the edge of the pavement.

"I love it. I would love to have him come to the bookshop for a signing, but like most things, there's no way to know if he's para." Charlie looked around, realizing they'd stopped outside the entrance to the bookshop. "Oh, we're here. Uh, thanks for walking with me."

"You're most welcome. Sorry I bumped into you." Knox grinned as he stepped back. "You have a beautiful day, and hey, why don't you email that author? You never know until you try!"

With a wave, Knox was gone, leaving Charlie staring blankly at the door. A tap on his shoulder jolted him.

"You okay, son?" Alfie chuckled.

"What? Oh, uh, yes, I guess?"

"Are you asking me?"

"I don't know." Charlie looked off in the direction Knox had walked away.

"Hmm, I'm thinking something has you distracted. Or is it someone?" Alfie pushed.

Charlie blushed, cursing his naturally fair skin.

"Oh, ho, someone has caught your eye." Sam chuckled from beside Alfie.

Charlie wanted to groan at being caught by both of them, but it didn't surprise him. Where you saw one, you saw the other. Sam and Alfie had been the closest of friends since they were Charlie's age.

"Dare I guess that it is our young Mr. Vaughn?" Sam probed.

Charlie turned his head, scowling at the two old gossips, and unlocked the bookshop.

"I'll take that silence as a yes then!" Alfie called, cackling as Charlie ignored them both and went into the shop.

The moment he closed the door and the rich aroma of books assaulted him, his jangled nerves settled and a sense of serenity washed over him. The familiarity and peace of the shop soothed him like a balm. It was enough to shake loose the cobwebs in his mind, and he quickly got to work, opening the shop exactly on time.

With no customers around, he found himself staring at the contact me section on Callum Davidson's website. Clicking on it, vaguely aware of a shake to his fingers, he typed up an email asking if the author might be free for a signing. Being careful, he was deliberately ambiguous as to where the signing would be, simply stating it was in Utah. He made sure to include the contact email as ataleoftwohorns@pmail.com. The pmail service was only used by paranormals and was rigorously vetted. Any paranormal receiving an email from such an address would know instantly that they were dealing with another paranormal. If, by some miracle, Davidson was a paranormal, he would recognize it immediately.

His finger hovered over the send button, but he couldn't do it. If he was honest, it had nothing to do with whether Davidson was para or not, that was easily solved, he'd just used it as an excuse. He was nervous, his anxiety getting the better of him. Why would such a famous author, even if he was para, which was unlikely, want to come and sign books at his little shop? Why would he? There were five other bookshops in Corent alone, two of them a lot bigger than his. No, the chance of Davidson coming to his shop was slim.

Bracing his hands against the desk, he pushed back his chair, rolling away. Briefly hiding his face in his hands, he let his arms drop, his elbows resting on his legs. Why did he have to overthink everything? Wasn't it about time he was brave? Screw it. He wheeled back till he was in reach of his keyboard and hit send before he could change his mind.

Letting out a deep breath, he moved to the shop floor, tidying up, determined to keep busy. So lost was he in his work, he never heard the door chime, and the first he knew of someone in the shop was when something tapped on his shoulder. Letting out a scream, he whirled, brandishing the book he held in his hand like a weapon.

"What, you plan to hit me over the head with… *Berrick's History of the Flora of the Paranormal World*? Although, that's been known to put many a student to sleep." Matt grinned at him.

"Holy fuck, you scared me." Charlie took a series of rapid breaths, trying to regulate his panic. "What were you thinking, sneaking up on me?"

"You were lost in your own little world. Didn't get any sleep last night?" Matt chuckled.

"No, literally not a wink. I finished *A Date with Death* though. It was so damn good, why did it have to finish?" Charlie moved back to the counter, where he spied a blueberry smoothie. "Oh god, I love you!" He grabbed hold of the smoothie, taking a big sip.

"You love me or the smoothie?" Matt drawled from beside him.

"Both?" Charlie grinned. "Seriously, thank you, this is the perfect pick me up."

Matt chuckled as he sipped his own smoothie. "I can't believe Detective Delicious and the hottie fireman haven't got it together yet. Their chemistry leaps off the pages."

"They were so fucking close," Charlie groaned. "I honestly thought they were finally going to at least kiss, but no, Callohan's radio just had to beep at that exact moment. I could have throttled Davidson for writing it that way." He looked back at his computer before he caught Matt's gaze. "So, I took the chance and emailed Callum Davidson."

"Are you serious?" Matt squeaked out. "Holy shit, I didn't think you'd do it. Has he replied yet?"

Chuckling at Matt's enthusiasm, Charlie shook his head. "I only emailed an hour ago, and I had to keep it vague in case he isn't para. I doubt he'll respond."

Matt grabbed Charlie, pulling him into a hug. "Even if he doesn't respond I'm proud of you for emailing. I know it wasn't easy. Have you thought about what sort of event you'll put on if he does turn up? I mean, I know you have the whole release day party planned. I'm looking forward to the cop uniforms."

"You just have a uniform kink." Charlie chuckled as he pulled away when a customer walked through the door.

"Mrs. Braham, do you agree with me that men in uniform are absolutely gorgeous?" Matt batted his eyelashes at the older woman.

"Nothing beats a uniform. When I was a young witch, we used to go out dancing near the PAF base just so we could watch them. Those men were almost as delicious as the firemen." Mrs. Braham winked. "But I have to say the firemen win. After all, Bertie was one in his days."

Matt chuckled as Charlie gaped.

"Close your mouth, dear. You won't attract any beautiful young men if you go around looking like that. Now, what time is your event starting?"

Charlie narrowed his eyes. "Are you coming for the new Davidson book or because you hear we'll have hot young men dressed in cop uniforms?"

"Why can't it be both?" Mrs. Braham chuckled. "I may be old, but I can still appreciate a prime bit of tushy, especially if I can sneak in a chance to grab one, accidentally you understand. I am senile after all."

Charlie choked on his smoothie. Matt tried slapping him on the back, but he was laughing so hard it was like a gentle pat.

"You young boys, we said and did plenty in my day. Now, why don't you ring up my books so you can get back to gossiping about handsome young men?"

Charlie blinked back the tears from his coughing fit and pulled the stack of books towards him. He grinned at the covers. "Are you liking these?"

"What's not to like? Two hot young men finding love and happiness. Of course, the sex doesn't hurt either." Mrs. Braham fanned herself.

This time, Charlie snorted and Matt spluttered.

"You—" she pointed at Matt— "young man, need to remember your generation aren't the ones who invented a little bit of loving. You should have seen us back in the day…"

Charlie grinned at Matt and wrapped up the books. "You enjoy these, Mrs. Braham, and come back when you need some recommendations."

"Oh, I will. In the meantime, find me some more books with men in uniform. None of that mushy girl stuff, I want real men together." She handed over the cash, waved away the change, grabbed her bag of books, and sauntered out the door.

Charlie plopped down into the chair, shaking his head. "Remind me to be exactly like her when I grow up."

"Me too. I plan for us to grow old disgracefully." Matt's brow furrowed for a minute. "How long has she been into the gay romance world?"

"For as long as we've been here. She's one of our biggest supporters. She runs a book group where they choose one book a week to read and talk through. She got them all into gay romance at the end of last year. Detective Callohan is a firm favorite, being gay romance, mystery, and suspense, all rolled into one. I had no idea she planned to be here for the release party though."

Matt shook his head. "I never for one minute imagined she would like the books."

"I think you'd be surprised who comes in to buy them." Charlie shrugged. "There are a couple of cops, firemen, a doctor, and even PAF members who come in for them."

"Really? How have I not noticed them coming in?" Matt's eyes shot to the door and back again.

"You've probably seen them, just not imagined they were buying these books." Charlie shrugged.

Matt was shaking his head. "How have I missed hot men in uniform? There's got to be something wrong with me."

"They weren't in uniform when they came in."

"Why didn't you say so?" Matt huffed.

Before Charlie could respond, the door chimed and in walked Matt's mom. Matt let out an unmanly eep and looked around as if he was hunting for somewhere to hide.

"Matthew, get your ass back to the shop, you have more stock to go through. You can gossip on your own time."

"Yes, Mama." Matt leaned down and brushed a kiss on her cheek and ran out the door.

Alice walked over, patted Charlie's cheek, and stole Matt's smoothie. "Say hi to your sister for me!" She waved as she walked out the door.

With a sigh, Charlie went back to work.

CHAPTER FIVE

Groaning as he locked up, Charlie slumped against the door, his feet on fire and his head thumping. He both regretted and didn't staying up the night before. It had been worth it, because a night with Detective Delicious, even if it had just been on paper, was a dream. However, following it up with a full day at work, and with young unicorn giggles, it had felt like a year. He looked towards the entrance to the square, and wondered if he had the strength to walk for the tram. He really didn't like the idea of paying for a magical transport, but it might be worth it. His feet really were on fire.

"You alright there, lad?" Sam called out as he was walking along the square.

Charlie opened his eyes. "Trying to work up the energy to walk to the tram."

"Long day?" Sam chuckled.

"And night."

When Sam lifted an eyebrow, Charlie groaned. "Not like that. I was up reading."

"Is that a good thing?" Sam reached out for him and took his arm.

"Yes, although I'm paying for it now."

"Alfie!" Sam bellowed across the square.

"What do you want, you old fool?" Alfie grumped as he walked over to join them.

"Charlie here is exhausted. I'm going to help him to the tram."

Charlie groaned. If Matt ever found out, he would never live down being supported by the two old men. "It's okay, I'll be fine," he insisted.

"Oh, hush." Alfie waved him off. Taking both Sam and Charlie by the hands, Alfie chanted.

Seconds later, Charlie found himself outside his front door. Blinking away the light fog from the transport spell, he grinned. "You shouldn't have expended the energy, but I can't thank you enough for this." He grabbed his keys out of his pocket and looped them over his finger.

"You were exhausted. Besides, it's good to feel useful again." Alfie shrugged.

"You are useful. Those little minxes of my sister's adore you. You are a godsend, watching them outside, letting them play while we work. Never, for one minute, think you aren't helpful. Not only that, but I'd like to believe that we are friends. Besides, who else is going to tease me?"

Alfie tipped back his head, laughing away. "You're right there, lad. Go on, get in, grab some food, and sleep, by the gods, you're dead on your feet. I'll have one of those fruity things you love so much ready for you in the morning."

"I might be persuaded to have your secret treat ready for you, if you're good and get some sleep." Sam slapped him on the shoulder. It should have been a light tap, but Sam was a bear shifter, big, and burly. While he was old enough to retire, he still held plenty of power, especially compared to Charlie, seeing as he was a unicorn shifter, who were more graceful and speedy, and nowhere near as muscled.

Alfie grinned as Charlie staggered back slightly, and gently steadied him. "Go on, in you go." He pushed him towards the door, grabbed Sam's hand, and disappeared.

Within moments, Charlie was through the door, shoes off, and pants halfway down his thighs. Kicking free of them, he shrugged out of his shirt and aimed straight for his shower. Thanking his foresight on paying for a top of the range unit, he stepped in. The water was immediately the perfect temperature, and beat rhythmically against his weary muscles. The lights dimmed, and a gentle, soothing, lavender-infused mist swarmed around him. Leaning against the wall, he let the jets beat down against his aching body, letting out all the pent-up tension from the day.

Eventually, his stomach demanded he eat. With a sigh, he got out, quickly drying off and getting into lounge pants. He smiled at them. These were of cartoon baby dragons freezing warriors and always made him laugh. Making his way into the kitchen, he looked at the sad state of his cupboards; he really needed to shop properly. With a sigh, he slung one of the ready meals into the zapper, and went to the table. He'd forgotten he'd left his laptop on standby and the indicator was flashing. Did he really have the strength to check his pmail? With a sigh, he rested his hand on the lid, waiting for the security to check his biometrics. He should check it. After all, what if there was a problem with the release day party? He needed it to go well. While the bookshop wasn't doing badly, it could be doing better. As the email program booted up, he grabbed the stew from the zapper, and made himself a cinderfella. It truly was his go-to drink to cheer himself up. Setting both on the kitchen table, he sat, pulling the laptop close.

Taking his first bite, he looked at his pmail program. His spoon dropped from his hand, back into the bowl with a splash. His heart thundering, he reached blindly for his phone. Three taps of his hand on the table and it was dialing Matt. He switched to speakerphone and laid the phone down, not trusting his shaking hands.

"You not asleep yet?" Matt's voice came through laughing. "Charlie?"

"He replied…" Just saying those words were freaking Charlie out as he stared at the unread messages. There, at the top, was one from Callum Davidson.

"Who did?" Matt's voice sobered, picking up on Charlie's unease.

"Davidson." Charlie was struggling not to panic.

"What did he say?"

"I don't know. I can't open it. I'm scared." Charlie confessed.

"Hold on." Matt hung up on him.

Two minutes later, Matt came racing in the door, his large bundle of keys hanging from his finger. They'd always had keys to each other's houses from the moment they'd moved out of home. "Charlie?"

"In here." Charlie was still staring at the laptop, the pmail unopened, his dinner abandoned.

Matt came storming in, and had it been any other time, Charlie might have teased him.

"I know it's bad if you aren't mentioning what I'm wearing." Matt grinned and struck a pose. He had on a mismatched pair of slippers, one a unicorn, the other a witch's hat. They'd both bought each other the pairs as a joke last King's Day, one of the most important holidays in the paranormal calendar, and similar to humans Christmas. On his legs, he wore thermal rainbow long-johns, a thermal red grandad top, and over that, he wore his ceremonial witch's cape, with a fluffy pompom hat.

Charlie managed a grin. "You look ridiculous, you know that, right?"

"What? I could tell it was an emergency, I grabbed what was at hand. Now—" Matt took the seat beside him, and grabbed Charlie's hand— "You want to explain to me why you haven't opened the pmail?"

"I'm scared."

"Of what? Him saying no? Oh, Charlie." Matt reached out and drew Charlie into his arms, running a soothing hand down his back. "You won't know what he says until you read it. Yes, he might say no, but you know what?"

"What?" Charlie mumbled against Matt's shoulder.

"He's never done a signing before, has he?"

"Not that I know of. I know lots of the big chain bookstores have asked him, but he's always said no. Plus, because he's self-published, he doesn't have a publisher forcing him into these things."

"Well, there you go. If he says no, it's probably just the same as every other time. I don't want you to take it personally if he does. It's not you."

"What, it's him? Bit of a cliché, isn't it?" Charlie snorted.

"Yes, but in this case, it's true." Matt pushed him back, so he could look into his eyes. "Now, how about we open the pmail together and see what he actually says, rather than worrying about it, hmm?"

Charlie took a long breath and pushed back from Matt. Squaring his shoulders, he pulled his chair in and woke the laptop back up. Moving the cursor over the pmail, his hand trembled slightly. With a supreme force of will, he clicked the button.

Dear Mr. Taylor,

Thank you for your pmail. I have to say I was delighted to read some mail from a pmail address. It's the first I've received. Now, as I'm sure you are aware, I typically say thank you, but no thank you to all event invitations. That being said, you are the first one I have received from a pmail address. Therefore, it's my absolute pleasure to agree to attend your release day event for 'A Date with Death.' I am presuming you mean in Corent City? Please let me know the exact details and whether you need me to bring any stock. I look forward to seeing you soon.

Regards,

Callum Davidson.

Charlie slumped back into his seat, and simply stared at his laptop screen. Beside him, Matt was just as speechless. "I never expected…" He shook his head. "I mean, even Knox told me I should pmail him, but I thought there was no point. I didn't think he'd reply, let alone agree to come."

"Wait a minute, when did you see Knox again, and why is this the first time I'm hearing about it?" Matt reached out and smacked him on the hand. "You know better. You're supposed to dish the details on any interaction with a hottie. You're failing in the friend department here, Charlie Choo." Matt was shaking his head sadly.

"Aww, Minx, don't be like that. I literally bumped into him this morning." Charlie quickly filled his friend in as he looked at the congealed remains of what had been an unappetizing dinner to start with.

Matt rolled his eyes and grabbed his phone. A couple of clicks later, he looked up and smiled. "Pizza is on the way. I think a celebration is in order, don't you?"

"You're the best friend ever." Charlie gave Matt an over the top kiss on his cheek.

"I know I am. Now, you have lots of planning to do. This, my friend, changes everything about your event."

"Oh, shit. What am I going to do?" Charlie's wild-eyed expression betrayed his nerves.

"You're going to sit there, let the news soak in, eat some pizza, and think. You've got this— your events always rock. We'll come up with something extraordinary. Be warned though, I've texted Mama and told her I'm staying here for the night. You need help."

"Thanks, Minx, I love you."

"Love you too— ooh, pizza!"

The unmistakable chime of an incoming magical delivery sounded out from Matt's phone. Thirty seconds later, two steaming hot pizzas appeared on the table, fresh from the oven. Charlie let loose with a loud groan. The smell of his favorite ranch pizza drifted from the box, and he grabbed it. The barbecue chicken and bacon mix was heaven in a slice. Add in the gooey stuffed crust, and there wasn't much that was better. Well, unless you counted sex, and seeing as that wasn't on the menu anytime soon, he would just have to rely on pizza to get his high.

Charlie took a bite and sat back with a contented sigh. He grabbed a pad and pen, ready to take notes as needed. They brainstormed as they ate. "So, we have the servers and staff dressed as cops, both in uniform and in copies of the suit Detective Delicious likes to wear. Some will be dressed as a shadowy figure, aka our serial killer. I'm thinking of having one or two in turnout pants. We have a raffle with the cardboard cutout of the cover, winning the book series, and so on. I've already organized with Whisps and Whirls to have mini cakes with edible mini handcuffs, police badges, firemen insignias, and fire hoses on them. They're making EMT themed drinks, alcoholic, non-alcoholic, and magical. Casper at the blood bank has donated a pint of synthetic blood, and we're doing a mock crime scene. Guess the weapon that did it, and you win gift vouchers. So, what else can we do?"

Matt whistled. "Nothing else, because damn, this is going to be one hell of a release party. You're going to need to section an area off so that he can sign books. You'll need to work out how long he's prepared to sign them for. You should make sure you have plenty of stock of all the series. When people find out he's going to be there, I can see them getting the complete set."

"Shit, good point. I can order them on a rush forty-eight hour delivery. I'll need to check if he wants to bring his own stock for that though, or how he wants the sales to be split if he brings his own." He was scribbling notes as fast as possible. "Anything else?"

"Well, you have the original party set for eleven to one in the morning. What about extending it from nine to one? That way you can give him time to sign and chat with people if he wants. You're going to need to see what he's comfortable with, though. He might not want to do lots. But if you could get him to do a reading, that would be amazing."

Charlie snorted. "At least he won't have to read out a sex scene. Oh, I can beg him to let me know when Detective Delicious and the hottie fireman are going to get it together. It had better be soon. I'm getting sexually frustrated on their behalf!" He shared a look with Matt and they both burst out laughing.

"You're frustrated full stop. You'll have to try and flirt with our mysterious author. Can you imagine getting an in with him and reading advanced copies, or ARCs?" Matt's eyes widened. "Oh, we have to ask if there is such a list. I'd have his baby for that."

"Uh, Matt, you can't have babies, you don't have the right equipment."

"Minor detail." Matt grinned around the slice of cake he'd found, the pizzas long since demolished as they'd brainstormed.

"That's gross." Charlie's nose wrinkled as Matt just laughed. Catching sight of the clock, Charlie groaned. "I need sleep."

Matt was suddenly a whirlwind, getting rid of the trash and tidying up the kitchen as Charlie shut everything down. Within a few minutes, they were both up the stairs, Charlie in his room, Matt in what Charlie referred to as Matt's cave. As soon as his head hit the pillow, he was asleep.

CHAPTER SIX

Yawning, Charlie walked down the street. He could have done with more sleep, but he still had a spring in his step and a smile on his face. He'd jumped out of bed, full of hope and happiness. He'd typed up his notes and returned Callum's pmail. As well as outlining his plans, and making other suggestions, he'd asked for Callum's input. He wanted it to be good for the author as well as for him. He knew some bookshops only ever cared about their bottom line, but he and Evie weren't like that. They wanted the readers, the customers, the authors that visited, to come away from any event happy. It wasn't all about the money. For him, it was about the love of books.

Waving at Sam and Alfie, he grinned when they beckoned him over.

"Here, lad, I think you might like these." Sam gestured to the drink and bag on the table.

Picking up the bag, he sniffed, his eyes widening. "Carrot cake?"

"That's the one you like, isn't it?" Sam lifted a brow.

"It is. Thank you, this is the perfect start to the day." Charlie cradled the bag to his chest. "This will keep me going."

"You look better this morning," Alfie commented dryly.

"I had some good news. The event I'm hosting next week, well, the author, Callum Davidson, has agreed to come." Charlie bounced slightly on the balls of his feet. He caught a look pass between the two old men. "What?"

"Have you ever met him?" Sam narrowed his eyes.

"No, why? I don't think anyone has." Charlie looked back and forth between the two men. "Or do you know something that I don't?"

"No, no, just me being old." Sam shrugged. "Now, where are my gorgeous babies? Is your sister late today?"

"Is she not in?" Charlie looked towards his shop, seeing it all fully locked up. "I hope the twins didn't keep her up again. She's been so tired lately."

"Evie still worried about Lane?" Alfie's face fell.

Charlie really wanted to say something about Lane coming home soon, about what Knox had told him, but some inner instinct kept him silent. The last thing he wanted to do was to get Knox into trouble. Especially because Alfie and Sam were ex-PAF and they still had plenty of contacts. He didn't blame Knox at all for talking to his brother. Shit, if he had a chance for Evie to talk to Lane, he'd do anything to arrange it. Pulling himself back into the moment, he looked at Sam and Alfie, sadness in his eyes. "She is. It's hard on her, especially with the kittlings so young."

Alfie reached out, patting him on the hand. "Being PAF is always hard on the family, but she has you, she has her babies, and she has us. That will help. You know she can always talk to us if she would like. We'll need to be careful, make sure that we don't say too much, but we can reassure her about certain things that are in place to ensure the safety of those working in the groups."

"You would?" Charlie smiled. "I'd really appreciate that."

"I'll come by and see her later. Now, you'd better get to work and start getting yourself sorted for your event. If you need any help, just give us a shout. Make sure we get our invites."

"You're coming?"

"Of course we are. Why wouldn't we be here to support you?" Sam looked genuinely confused.

A flash of respect and admiration swamped Charlie. He was surrounded by people who cared, deeply. "Thank you." He reached out and squeezed Sam's hand, trying to communicate without words just how grateful he was. With a final wave, he unlocked the door with his free hand, hip-checking the door open.

Smiling as he shut the door behind him, he looked around his shop. A thrill went through him, the same as he always felt whenever he considered the fact this was his baby, his and Evie's. Humming to himself as he set up for the morning, he raced for Evie the moment she came in. Pulling her away from the babies' stroller, he lifted her and spun her around and around. She tipped her head back laughing.

"Let me go, you pest. What's got you so happy this morning?"

"Do you never check your messages?" Charlie tsked. "He said yes!"

"Who said yes? To what?" She waved at Danny, Faith, and Jasper, who were all giggling at their uncle's antics.

"Callum Davidson said yes! He's coming to the release party." Charlie finally put Evie down, but started to dance her around the shop, reaching for Danny's hand as he gestured he wanted in.

Evie's eyes widened for a moment before she let out a whoop of delight. "Oh, my gods, are you serious?"

"Yes!" Charlie cried out, doing a shimmy across the floor.

"Holy shit, that's… I'm speechless. I never expected him to agree. How the ancestors did you manage to pull that one off?" She picked up the twins and started to dance with them as Charlie took Danny by the hands.

"I have no idea, but I'm happy. This is big, Sis, I mean *really* big." Charlie turned to try and look at her, but Danny wanted more dancing, something he was happy to oblige in.

"Let me get these two into their playpen and you can tell me everything," Evie called, managing to dodge the flying stuffed unicorn flung in her direction energetically by Jasper. "Little terror." She softened her words by kissing him sweetly on the forehead.

A more upbeat tune came over the radio, and Charlie bent at the waist, dancing around with Danny, who was singing at the top of his voice, happy as anything. It had been a while since he'd seen his nephew this happy. He was missing his daddy, so Charlie didn't have the heart to do anything other than smile widely and encourage him. Shimmying his ass back and forth, he sang with Danny, living in the moment, and loving every minute of it. Picking Danny up, he spun as Danny giggled.

"Wheeee!"

Round and round they went, slowing down until Charlie fumbled to a stop, eyes wide, mouth open, a blush spreading across his cheeks. "Oh, umm, sorry? I didn't hear anyone come in."

Leaning against the wall by the door, legs crossed at the ankles, stood Knox, one side of his lips tipped up into a smile, dimples on full display. "I could tell." Knox pushed off from the wall and strode towards them, exuding a sexy confidence that Charlie could never hope to achieve. "What are we celebrating? There has to be good news to be this happy first thing in the morning?"

Danny started to slip down as Charlie's grip on him loosened. Knox reached out, plucking Danny from Charlie's arm, and setting him on his hip, while tickling him under his chin. "And how are you, Master Danny, on this beautiful morning?"

Danny's eyes lit up. "Hot Choc Man! Mallows?"

Knox chuckled. "As much as I would love to get you a hot chocolate with marshmallows, I think both your mom and uncle wouldn't be too happy. It's a little early. I tell you what, if I get a chance to pop in later, I'll see if I can sneak you in a treat."

Danny pursed his lips, considering Knox's words. "Okay," he finally conceded, wriggling to get down. Knox let him go.

"Good morning." Knox's full attention shifted to Charlie. "You look especially happy today. You didn't say what you're celebrating?"

"You remember telling me to send that author a pmail? Well…." Charlie's eyes danced with happiness. "He responded." Knox went to reply, but Charlie held up a finger, stopping him as a customer walked in. "Give me a minute?"

"Of course." Knox resumed his position leaning against the wall as Charlie helped the customer.

"You're having that party, aren't you?" Freddie, a vampire, checked.

"We are, next Friday night. Are you coming?" Charlie asked.

"You bet, I want a crack at the crime scene. I'd like to think I know blood patterns," Freddie winked, making Knox laugh. "Besides, I want to get my hands on a certain detective as soon as possible. I'm hoping he finally gets it together with Teaks, the fireman. I swear if they don't get it together soon, I might combust."

Charlie grinned. "It's not fair, is it? How can they not be together yet?"

"If it doesn't happen soon, we need to club together, find out who and where Callum Davidson is, kidnap him, and hold him for ransom until he agrees to make them kiss," Freddie growled, his long fangs dropping from his gums. "It's so bloody frustrating!"

Charlie caught sight of Knox, who was smirking away at the pair of them. He narrowed his own eyes, making Knox's smile deepen, flashing those damn dimples again. Charlie forced his attention back on Freddie. "I take it you want me to reserve you some books?"

Freddie rolled his eyes. "Of course."

"Want to hear some news? You're the first to know."

"Does blood taste delicious?" Freddie rolled his eyes. "Of course, I want to know."

"I just heard last night that a certain author will be coming to our release party." Charlie waited as the news sank in.

"Are you freaking serious?" Freddie suddenly shouted.

"I am. I just found out last night."

"He's signing books?" Freddie checked.

"We still have to work out the details, but I imagine he will be."

Freddie did a fist pump. "Yes! This is going to shut the coven in Jenvia City right up. Put me down for two complete sets of the series, signed."

"I'll add yours to the top of the list seeing as you're the first one to know." Charlie grabbed a pad and pen, making a note of Freddie's order. "Are you wanting any books in the meantime?"

Freddie sighed dramatically. "There isn't much that can match up to Davidson's books, but this will have to do." He picked up *Dancing with the Marine* and pushed it towards Charlie.

Charlie rang it up. "It's a great one, that. Different from the Callohan series, but that's not a terrible thing. There aren't many authors who can match Davidson's writing and talent. His stories have everything— drama, intrigue, romance, flirting, and nail-biting tension. The *Dancing* one is light-hearted and fun, plus, it's pretty damn hot." He winked theatrically, making Freddie grin.

"I'll let you know what I think." Freddie grabbed the book, waving off his bag, and sauntered out the door with a wave.

"You really do like Davidson's work that much?" Knox walked back to join him.

Charlie snorted. "You should read one, then you'd understand."

"Oh, trust me, I know all about Detective Callohan."

"You do?" Charlie blinked a couple of times.

"Why do you seem surprised? What, I don't look like your typical reader?" Knox leaned on the edge of the counter.

"Uh, no?" Charlie swallowed as the smell of a snow-covered forest drifted to his senses. It obviously wasn't aftershave, which meant that it was Knox's natural shifter scent. It was peaceful, calming but with a hint of the predator underneath, a lurking danger that was just waiting for the moment to strike.

"Hmm, you're partly right. I haven't read the Callohan books."

Charlie wasn't sure why, but that disappointed him.

Knox leaned over the counter, leaning in close to whisper in his ear. "I've written them instead." He pulled back and waited.

47

Charlie replayed the words in his head, they seemed just as crazy that way as they did when he heard them the first time. He opened his mouth, and promptly shut it again. Staring at Knox, who was waiting patiently, he shook his head, struggling to compute the words. Knox was saying he was Callum Davidson? Sure, lots of authors used pen names, but *Knox Vaughn* was Callum Davidson? The author of his favorite series? His mind spun out.

"Forest Moon to Charlie, is anyone in there?" Knox waved his hand in front of Charlie's face. He saw it, but didn't react. "If you don't say something soon, I'm going to do something drastic."

"Kiss him, that will work," Evie called from the other room. "He'd like that."

Now that provoked a response from Charlie. "Evie!"

"What? Who wouldn't want a kiss from Knox Vaughn? I may be mated, but I'm not dead!" She clucked her tongue at him.

Charlie blushed like crazy, but Evie's intervention had been enough to pull him out of his stupor. "I am so sorry about her."

"Don't be, she's making me smile."

"Are you telling the truth? You're Callum Davidson?" Charlie struggled to say the words.

"I am. You know, I would have refused any other invite, but something compelled me when you mentioned it to agree. I've hidden long enough behind the name. Besides, while it might become common knowledge in the para world, it won't anywhere else. We all guard our secrets too well for that."

Charlie plonked his ass down into his chair. "Sorry, you've stunned me. I can't believe you're him."

"Which one is getting to you more? The fact I'm him, or seeing what sounds like your favorite author?" Knox teased.

Charlie's blood rushed south and his head started to spin. His breathing sped up.

"Uh, Charlie, you don't look so good." Knox spun slightly. "Um, Evie? If you have a minute?"

Evie raced out. "What the fuck? Charlie?" She dropped to her knees beside him. "What's going on?"

Charlie tried to hold her gaze. "That's Callum Davidson!"

"Yes, we've established that."

"I love his work!"

"I know," Evie chuckled.

"He's Knox Vaughn!" Charlie hissed.

"Yes," Evie drawled, "We've worked that out as well."

"I'm trying not to fanboy on him," Charlie hissed.

"Too late, brother, I think he's getting the picture of how big a fan you are." Evie grabbed hold of the water bottle Knox was holding out and helped Charlie take a sip.

Inwardly, Charlie was cursing himself. He'd gone and made a total fool of himself in front of his favorite author, the one he had managed to persuade, somehow, to come to his event, and the man he was attracted to. Oh man, Matt was never going to let him forget this.

"I've got this if you need to keep an eye on the kiddos?" Knox squatted beside Evie.

Charlie's eyes silently pleaded with Evie not to leave him. She smirked.

"That would be great, thank you." She leaned forward and hugged Charlie. "Stop worrying," she whispered in his ear. With a smile for Knox, she left them to it.

Knox rested a hand on Charlie's knee, his other hand holding the bottle of water. He shifted so he was kneeling on one knee. "Hey," he whispered softly. "Sorry, I didn't mean to spook you."

Charlie studied Knox, seeing the genuinely apologetic look on his face. "No, it's my fault. You took me by surprise. Even after the email, it never really settled in my mind that I would be meeting you. It was just…"

"You're that big a fan of mine?" Knox was smiling away.

49

Charlie nodded. "Your world transports me to another place. I can lose myself in them. I don't worry about the shop, Evie, the family, Lane being away, Matt, or any of the million other things that occupy my mind. All that vanishes, and I can just live through Detective Delicious' eyes."

Knox chuckled. "I've seen that nickname on some of the forums. You think he's hot?"

Charlie nodded enthusiastically. "Oh yes, he's alpha and commanding. He's strong, yet, every now and then, you get this flash of vulnerability. You see just how much his cases affect him. That scene, where he's so close to breaking down, and he leans on Teaks' shoulder, just for a moment… that scene had me sighing. It was romantic and showed the side of him I always knew existed. I love books which have gay romance in them, but sometimes, the alpha men you see are simply assholes. Detective Callohan shows you don't need to be a bastard to still be strong. That you can be strong and powerful and still care. He's flawed and yet perfect."

Knox's smile was blinding, his dimples out in full force. "I'm glad you see him that way. I see the men in the PAF, I see my brothers, I see how they sometimes struggle with life. Then, I see them go about their lives with this stoic outer layer. I wanted to show that men aren't weak when they have flashes of vulnerability."

"You succeeded." Charlie realized that rather than making him freak out more, Knox's presence was having a calming effect on him. "Thank you, by the way, for agreeing to the event. I sent… you… a pmail earlier with some details."

"You did. That's why I'm here. Your ideas are amazing. I didn't want this to become a massive thing, where I didn't tell you until the event who I really was. I thought it would be best to come around today, and confess as it were, and talk through some of your amazing plans."

"You think my plans are amazing?" Charlie drew back slightly, stunned that a man he admired, liked his ideas.

"I really do. I've seen some release parties, and they are all the same. Not yours. Your ideas are unique and refreshing. I'm actually

50

looking forward to coming out as Davidson and talking to fans. Writing can be a lonely life. I've hidden long enough." There were traces of a sad smile on Knox's face.

A sudden desire to hold Knox, to make him feel better, swamped Charlie. "I'd never thought about that before. Is it so terrible?"

Knox squeezed his knee. "Not always, but that's why I moved back here, so at least I can be near my brothers now they're all based here. That's enough people around me. It's my own fault, I should probably get out and about more."

"I've seen you about recently."

"I had a meeting, remember? After that, I suddenly thought there were more reasons to be out a little more."

"Oh?" Charlie's nose wrinkled. He wasn't sure what Knox meant by that.

"It doesn't matter." Knox grinned. "You feeling a little better yet?"

Charlie smiled softly. "I do, thank you, and I'm really sorry about all this."

"Nothing to be sorry for. Maybe I should have told you differently?" Knox winced.

"I don't think it would have mattered, to be honest." Charlie's face flushed. "I would have been stupidly fanboyish no matter what. I'm sorry."

"For what? It's a first for me. Bar you not feeling great, it's been amazing to see how much someone loves my work. You've made me incredibly happy."

"I have?"

"You have. You know what we need?"

"What?"

"Cake. Cake cures everything." Knox looked deadly serious.

"Who are you really, and where have you been all my life!" Charlie burst out without even thinking about his words.

Knox chuckled away. "Now, I fancy a large portion of Whisps and Whirls' Cosmic Delight. You want one?"

Charlie swallowed. "But they are so expensive."

"I think we can grab one each. My treat." Knox pushed up off the floor, his thighs flexing as he moved.

A shiver raced through Charlie at the thought of being at the mercy of all that power. In his deepest fantasies, he loved the idea of being pinned down, letting his man have his wicked way with him. He was strong enough, even though he wasn't bulky, that the illusion of power wouldn't do it. No, he needed someone that actually could hold him down and give him a good, hard fucking.

"Back in two," Knox called from the door.

Charlie blew out a ragged breath. By the time the release party came around, he was either going to be a puddle of goo or spontaneously combust if he kept spending time with Knox. But what a way to go it would be.

He was still in his chair when Knox returned a few minutes later, the tell-tale green and gold box from Whisps and Whirls in his hand. Smiling, he called out, "Evie, do you guys have a moment?"

Evie joined them, her eyes lighting up as she spied the box. "What did you get, and there'd better be something I can eat in there, or I'm stealing Charlie's. You can't tease a girl and not deliver. That's evil."

With a flourish, Knox laid the box on the table, and pulled off the lid. Gasps echoed around them. Three Cosmic delights were nestled in the box, along with a box of cake pops for Danny. "I would have got something for Faith and Jasper, but I know at their age, they can't have anything. I hope that's okay?" Knox looked to Evie.

"That's perfect. You know, Danny's going to fall in love with you at this rate," Evie teased.

Charlie shot her a look. She just grinned. He knew where her mind was, and the little she-devil was match-making, he just knew it.

Oh, his sister may look all innocent, but she was hiding her true nature.

Danny, with some inner sixth-sense, had come toddling out, and was currently trying to climb Knox like a jungle gym. Charlie found himself jealous of his nephew for a moment. Then his heart melted as Knox scooped Danny up, sat him on his hip, and handed him a box of cake-pops.

"Why don't we sit you in your seat?" Knox took him over to his special table and sat him down. Returning to the counter, he grabbed the bag Charlie hadn't noticed, and pulled out a small bottle of milk, opening it and passing it to Danny.

Charlie was reverently lifting out the Cosmic Delights, laughing as Knox produced another three bottles of milk. It was the perfect complement to the cake, after all, nothing would match up to the cake. The cake was deceptively simple, or so it seemed. It was a vanilla sponge with rainbow icing. But what set it apart from other cakes were the small, magically produced shapes baked into the cake. Each one had its own unique flavor. The magic came into play to make sure no mouthful had combinations the eater would hate. If you hated lemon and lime, it would never appear, but if you loved blueberry and raspberry, more of those would be present. Other shapes popped in your mouth, fizzing, and giving your taste buds a small magical zap. Some balls gave you a small burst of happiness, a little pick me up, enough to make you smile. Just occasionally you would get a surprise, one of the shapes would turn your lips blue, or tinge the tips of your hair green. Whatever happened was always a surprise, and the magic in them managed to work out exactly the perfect combination for each person every single time.

Charlie bit into his and groaned. His taste buds were zapped, and a burst of raspberry flooded his senses. He looked up when Evie burst out laughing.

"Your lips are a very eye-catching shade of green there."

He tried to pout and see his lips, in the end, grabbing the mirror Evie dug out from her bag. He burst out laughing. His lips were the green of grass in the spring. He licked his lips, tasting lime, and grinned. The smile died as he looked up, catching Knox's eyes trained on his mouth.

Charlie couldn't look away. There was a delicate cough, and he heard Evie leave the room quietly, taking Danny with her. Without realizing he'd done it, he licked his lips, a thrill racing through him when he saw Knox's eyes flare with lust.

When Knox took a single step towards him, he suddenly imagined what being a tiger's prey felt like. His heart was hammering, and the flight or fight instinct was riding him. Oh, but he was going to choose fight, or in this case, what he hoped was kiss. He stayed still, not daring to move, or to say a single word.

"Your sister is right." Knox took another step towards him. "Your lips are… they're something, that's for sure. So plump, the way you tease the bottom lip between your teeth when you're thinking. I can't take my eyes off them. I want it to be my teeth nibbling on that lip. I want to pull that lip into my mouth, taste it, trace it with my tongue." He took another step forward.

Charlie's gaze dipped to Knox's lips, imagining everything he'd said.

"Charlie, do you have nothing to say?"

Charlie managed to shake his head.

"If you don't tell me otherwise, I'm going to think your silence is giving me permission to kiss you." Knox took two more steps. He was right in front of Charlie now, their bodies almost touching.

Anticipation thrummed through Charlie, his cock perking up and taking a definite interest in the man in front of him. Knox's gaze was mapping his face. He reached out with a thumb and traced Charlie's bottom lip, pulling it softly down, from where Charlie hadn't even realized he'd been biting it. The gentle pressure on his mouth was setting his nerves on fire, and he leaned into the touch. His fingers were flexing at his sides. He wanted to reach out and touch Knox, but was scared to break the spell they were under.

Slowly the thumb traced from his bottom lip to his top, then moved to run along his jaw as Knox's palm swept along his neck. His pulse was hammering now, every cell like a live wire, waiting to go off at the slightest touch. When Knox's hand swept behind to cup his neck, he pushed back into the touch, giving up every ounce of control to the man. One of his hands lifted of its own accord, hovering at chest height, half pleading, beckoning Knox onward.

"Fuck, you're perfect." Knox's gaze connected with his, desire, power, control, and full on need shining through.

Charlie couldn't stop the whimper of sound that escaped him. Knox's reaction was instant. His head dipped and claimed Charlie's lips. The hand on his neck held him in place as Knox's other arm snaked around his waist and hauled him so he was flush with the hard, muscled body he'd been dreaming of being up against. His hand fluttered against Knox's chest for a moment, before his fingers grasped at the shirt Knox was wearing, holding on, needing it to ground him.

Knox's tongue mapped every curve of his mouth, the hand on his neck moving him as Knox wanted. The other hand slid down his back to grasp his ass. Knox's mouth greedily swallowed his whimper. His cock was rock-hard as it pressed up against Knox's thigh. He could feel an answering hardness pressing into the bottom part of his stomach.

A sudden high-pitched squeal from the other room broke the kiss. Charlie went to take a step back, but Knox held him in place, pulling back just enough to look into his eyes. Charlie was captivated by the deep green which sparkled with happiness and amusement and a healthy dose of lust. He couldn't help the sudden impulse that flared through him, and he gave into it. His tongue darted out and traced over one of Knox's dimples.

Knox suddenly tipped his head back and claimed his lips once again. Glad Knox was man-handling him, it meant he could give himself up to the kiss, stay in the moment, and not care about anything around them. He could happily stay there, kissing this man, all day. Eventually, though, Knox slowed the kiss, and with one last tug on his bottom lip, he pulled back. "You are far too tempting. From the moment I walked in and saw that ass shaking, I was done."

"You liked my ass?" Charlie teased.

"Yes," Knox growled as a hint of canines appeared just underneath his lip. His hand squeezed the cheek of his ass that was still held possessively in Knox's grip. "I could have watched you shake it all day."

Charlie's breath sped up. Before he could reply, he heard the unmistakable sound of the door opening. With a warning look, Knox released him. Charlie quickly straightened his clothes and retreated behind the relative safety of the counter. *Shit, of all the people…* "Hey, Matt."

"Hey, Choo," Matt called out, even as his eyes zeroed in on his lips. "Your lips…" Matt looked from Charlie to Knox, and then down at the counter. "No! You've had a Cosmic Delight. That's not fair, where's mine?"

"Knox brought them." Charlie nodded in Knox's direction.

Matt turned, his smile wide as he looked Knox up and down, darting a gaze back at his friend. Charlie could see the gears turning in his mind. Damn it, Matt knew him too well. He would know something had happened.

"You just randomly bought Charlie a Cosmic Delight?"

"No." Knox grinned. "We were celebrating."

"What are we celebrating?" Matt's gaze was still bouncing between the two men.

"Getting Callum Davidson to be here for my party." Charlie's lips were twitching.

Matt looked at Knox. "Charlie told me you pushed him to send the pmail. Thank you."

Behind Matt, Charlie mouthed, "Can I tell him?"

With a twinkle in his eyes, Knox subtly dipped his head.

"Hey, Matt, I know who Callum Davidson is. I've met him." Charlie laughed as Matt spun around to stare at him.

"Who?"

"In fact, you've met him as well," Charlie teased.

"No, I would have known if I'd met my favorite author." Matt scowled.

"Not if he used a pen name, you wouldn't." Charlie was loving getting one up on his friend.

"Who?" Matt demanded. When Charlie didn't answer him quick enough, he stalked forward. The only thing was, after having a true predator like Knox stalk him, Matt trying it had no effect whatsoever.

"I'm thinking maybe I should keep the knowledge to myself. I can imagine you'd do anything I asked to know who it was." Charlie leaned against the counter, laughing.

"Don't make me hurt you." Matt advanced.

"What do you think you can do? We know each other's weaknesses. We're an even match when we fight." Charlie shrugged. They were as well; they'd been fighting good-naturedly for years.

"Who said I was talking about anything physical? I know all your secrets, remember? What about I tell Knox here some of your juicy secrets?" The grin Matt sent Charlie was full of cockiness.

"You wouldn't!" Charlie's eyes widened.

"You can tell me," Knox called from his position back leaning against the wall.

"You stay out of this." Charlie narrowed his eyes.

Knox smirked.

"You know what you need to do to stop me then, don't you?" Matt teased.

Charlie stared him down. The two friends locked gazes, a silent battle of wills— Charlie trying to decide if Matt actually would go through with it. The thing was though, that he did want to tell Matt about Knox, all about him, but some of it would have to wait until later. Theatrically pouting, he conceded. "You win."

"Yes!" Matt did a fist pump.

"Come on then, tell me. Who is our mystery author?"

Rather than say anything, Charlie gestured to Knox. Knox waved. Matt frowned, looked at Charlie, then Knox, and back to Charlie again. "What are you saying?"

Charlie waggled his eyebrows.

Matt blinked a couple of times. "Holy shit! *Knox* is Callum Davidson?" His voice raised on the last word. He spun and stared at Knox. "You're Davidson?"

"In the flesh."

"Holy shit." Matt drew the words out. "Holy fucking shit, are you serious? Charlie, is he serious?"

"He is, and I'm glad I'm not the only one who reacted to the news." Charlie tapped Matt on the shoulder, trying to reassure him.

"He writes Detective Delicious and the hottie Teaks?"

Charlie grinned. Suddenly, Matt spun and stalked towards Knox, going up on tiptoe. "I've got a bone to pick with you." He poked a finger into Knox's shoulder.

"Uh, Matt, I wouldn't do that if I was you. You need to remember he's a tiger, a predator."

"We're not in the wild, it's not like he's going to hunt me… are you?"

Knox lifted a brow and stayed silent.

"Damn all strong and silent types. I'm sorry, I'm just so mad at you!"

"You let him read one, didn't you?" Knox stared into Charlie's eyes. "You both read it."

Both Charlie and Matt nodded.

"I should punish you." Knox shook his head at Charlie. "Maybe I should say no to your event."

Charlie whimpered, but didn't miss the flare of lust in Knox's eyes at the sound. It looked like the tiger wasn't immune to him. Sudden confidence infused his soul, knowing he had as much an effect on Knox as Knox had on him. "You won't do that though. You know how much it means to me that you agreed."

Knox hummed. "I should though."

"But you won't." Charlie grinned.

Knox muttered something under his breath that Charlie couldn't hear. When Matt's eyes widened comically, he wondered if Matt had caught Knox's words. "We need to sit down and go through all the details."

"Whenever works best for you." Charlie shrugged. "I'm here all day."

"I need to go to a meeting. How about I take you out for dinner instead?" Knox refused to let Charlie look away.

"I'd like that."

Knox opened his mouth when his phone rang. Holding up his finger, he answered. "Vaughn."

Charlie watched him, seeing the emotions play across his face—wariness, fear, trepidation, and then finally happiness. "When? Okay, thank you. Bye." As soon as the phone clicked off, he stalked over to Charlie, picked him up and spun him around, while calling out, "Evie!"

"Yes?" Evie called from the doorway, one of the twins held in her arms as she nursed him.

"I've just spoken to my brother, Carter. Lane should be home in the next two hours."

Evie sagged, and Charlie tapped Knox, wanting down. The minute his feet were on the floor, he wrapped his arms around his sister, being careful of Faith in her arms, and held her as she trembled.

"He's safe? He's coming home?" She looked over Charlie's shoulder at Knox.

"He's pulling into base in the next few minutes. Once he debriefs, I'm sure this will be his first stop." Knox's smile was blinding.

"Thank you, Knox." Evie buried her face in her brother's shoulder.

"We're part of the extended PAF family. We all stick together. Charlie, can I have a quick word?"

Charlie gently eased Evie out of his arms and straight into Matt's before walking and joining Knox at the wall. "Hey." He stepped into Knox's personal space, squeaking slightly as Knox clamped his hand on his waist and hauled him in tight against his body.

"I'm going to have this meeting, go and see my brothers, and then call you and arrange dinner tonight."

"Don't you want to spend the evening with them?" Charlie was breathless.

"I want to spend time with you." Knox held Charlie's gaze trapped. He claimed Charlie's lips in a bruising kiss, then gently pushed him away. "I'll call you." With that, Knox breezed out the door.

When Charlie finally turned around, two intense stares met his gaze. They were not going to leave him alone without spilling. He walked around the counter, retook his seat, and waited for the interrogation to begin.

CHAPTER SEVEN

Evie was smirking at him, but Charlie didn't care. It was like he was dancing among the clouds he was feeling so high. Happiness exuded from every pore.

"I can't believe you've gone and kissed Knox Vaughn," Evie muttered for what must have been the hundredth time.

"I still can't believe it, and I was the one kissing him!" Charlie laughed.

"My baby brother and Knox Vaughn, how the fuck did that happen?"

"You make it sound like it's more than it is. He simply kissed me."

"And agreed to your event, brought us Cosmic Delights, asked you out to dinner, can't take his eyes off you… do I really need to keep going?"

"I feel like some love-struck teenager asking this, but… he couldn't take his eyes off me?" Charlie's finger touched his lips for the umpteenth time that day.

"No, he couldn't. From the first moment he saw you, he tracks your moves, there's an intensity there. It's like he always knows exactly where you are when you're in a room together. He reminds me a lot of Lane. Knox may not be PAF, although I think he was, but he has the same traits."

"He was." Charlie's smile faded. "He dropped out to stay home and look after the others when their parents died in the last onslaught of ferals."

Evie's hand went to her mouth. "I didn't know."

Charlie looked out the door as if looking for Knox. "I know the PAF family rallied around them. His parents had gone out to help, even though they'd retired. They'd responded when the call went out that the city was being overrun. They paid the ultimate price. Knox was wounded, and would have carried on from what I know, but someone needed to look after the others, so he left. I don't know what job he took, but it was what his family needed. I'm guessing that's why his brothers are always calling him."

Evie sniffed, and Charlie hugged her. "No tears today, it's a happy day. Lane will be walking through that door any minute."

"Or… he could already be here," a deep baritone called from behind them.

They both spun, Charlie standing with a massive smile on his face, Evie launching herself across the room, jumping up and wrapping her arms and legs around her mate. Charlie went to retrieve the kiddies as they kissed. "Hey, Danny?"

Danny looked up from where he was dancing Jasper's toy unicorn in front of the twins.

"Your daddy is home."

Danny launched the toy into the twin's playpen and ran out the room. Charlie picked up Faith and Jasper, putting one on each hip.

Charlie watched Danny slam into his daddy, arms raised high, trying to attract his attention. "Lane, look down!"

Lane looked at him, and Charlie gestured down to Danny. Lane gently pushed Evie back a step and scooped his eldest son up. "Hey, buddy." He held him tight to his chest.

"Daddy!" Danny burrowed into Lane, refusing to let go.

Charlie walked forward with the twins, smiling at Lane as he leaned down to kiss each twin.

"I missed you guys."

"Why don't you all go home?" Charlie passed Faith to Lane, but kept Jasper in his arms. "I've got everything here. Go be a family. Take tomorrow off."

Evie didn't object. "Thank you." She was a whirlwind as she got all their gear together.

"Charlie, thank you, again, for always looking after my family while I'm away." Lane locked gazes with him. "You have no idea how comforting it is to know that you're here for them, looking after them. It's one less thing to worry about every time I leave."

"They're my family, you're my family, I'll always be here for all of you. It's good to have you back though. There's always a hole, this empty space when you're away. I'm not saying that to make you feel guilty, but you mean the world to them. They miss you, but I know you miss them just as much."

"I do." Lane's voice cracked slightly.

Charlie actually looked at his brother-in-law. Lane looked tired, and there was a large bruise on his cheek, which he didn't think Evie had noticed. While it was evident he'd showered and changed at the PAF compound, it hadn't taken away the other effect. Tracking over Lane, he saw bloodied knuckles and a large scratch on his forearm. When he lifted his gaze again, he saw Lane dart a gaze to Evie and back. Charlie knew Lane was silently asking him not to say anything, not to make an issue of things. "I won't mention it." The relief on Lane's face was palpable. Whatever had happened on this latest mission, it had been physical.

"Thank you. You know how she can get," Lane whispered, his blue eyes full of humor.

"Only too well." Making sure no one else was in the shop, Charlie leaned forward. "I knew you were coming home though."

"How?" Lane demanded.

"Knox Vaughn told me."

"Since when do you know one of the Vaughn brothers?"

"Since Danny here managed to try and take him out with his horn." Charlie tickled Danny. "Long story short, Knox got Danny here a hot chocolate."

"With mallows," Danny interrupted.

"With mallows." Charlie laughed. "And he mentioned that he'd heard from Carter. He didn't mean to, but it was reassuring for Evie to know you were safe."

"Huh, small world." Lane handed Faith over to Charlie, and reached out for the bags Evie was carrying, looping them over his shoulder. He reached for Jasper, kissing him and resting him on his hip.

Evie grabbed Faith and brushed a kiss along her brother's forehead. "I adore you."

"Love you too, Big Sis, now go and be a family. If you want me to take them tonight, so that you two can have a night together, just let me know."

"Oh, Charlie, no, you can't pass up your plans for tonight." Evie was shaking her head like crazy.

"I don't mind. You guys come first."

"No. We'll stay tonight as a family. Lane needs some time to decompress, and you need to go out on your date."

"Charlie has a date?" Lane raised an eyebrow.

"With Knox Vaughn," Evie said smugly.

Lane did a double take. "You've got a date with *Knox Vaughn*? What the hell have I missed."

Evie burst out laughing. "I'll explain it all at home."

"You'd better." Lane leaned forward and nipped at her ear. With a wink at Charlie, he nudged Evie towards the door.

Charlie's smile was the widest it has been in a long time. Between Knox kissing him, revealing himself as Davidson, agreeing to his release event, and now Lane coming home, things really couldn't get any better.

The afternoon went by in a happy blur. In-between serving customers, he finished up designing his invites and everything he needed to show Knox. He blew out a breath still stunned that Knox was Callum. He wondered if Knox had any ideas about the party, wondered if he planned on kissing him again.

"Is that smile for me?"

Charlie's head snapped up to see Knox standing in front of him. "Part of it."

"Only part of it? I have to be doing something wrong, then." Knox stalked around the counter, his hand going straight to Charlie's neck, cupping the side of it, with his thumb rubbing across his jaw.

"I'm happy for Evie, with Lane being home. And for you with Carter."

"Ah, thank you, it was good to see him."

There was more emotion behind Knox's eyes, and Charlie wondered what Carter had looked like. "Did Carter show the same signs Lane did? Bruises and so on?"

Knox nodded brusquely.

"Is he alright?" Charlie stepped in closer to Knox, shaking slightly as he laid a hand over Knox's heart. Knox's hand immediately laid over his, holding him there.

"He will be. I hate seeing him with so much as a bruise. I know they're all grown men, but…"

"You're still the big brother," Charlie finished off.

"Exactly."

Charlie lifted his hand and traced over Knox's jaw, feeling the scrape of stubble underneath his fingers. He couldn't resist tracing over where his dimple was. When he looked up and into Knox's eyes, they were dancing with laughter. "You have a thing for my dimples, don't you?"

"Uh huh." Braver than he'd felt in a long time, Charlie continued on and traced over Knox's lip.

"You're playing with fire." Knox's eyes locked onto his.

"What if I want to get burned?" Charlie challenged.

"Then that can be arranged." Knox shifted his hand to the back of Charlie's neck and hauled him close. He started to nibble at Charlie's lips, teasing, nipping, and sucking.

Once again, Charlie found himself surrendering, his fingers curling into the fabric over Knox's heart, still held tight by Knox's much larger hand. The kiss was slow, soft, soulful, and full of passion. Eventually, Knox pulled back, resting his forehead against Charlie's. "I needed that."

Charlie just hummed.

"You ready to close up? I never got a chance to call, so I thought we could just go to dinner now, and discuss everything then."

"Sounds good. Give me a couple of minutes to shut everything down."

"Of course." Knox chuckled. "You need to move to close everything up."

"Yeah," Charlie mumbled.

Knox laughed and gently pulled Charlie's hand from his shirt, turned him around and smacked his ass. "Get to it."

Charlie took an unsteady step forward and got to work. "If you want, you can look over my notes. They're on the counter there."

Knox immediately went straight to his notebook. He was so engrossed, Charlie managed to sneak right up to him, and slipped his hand around Knox's back, making him jump. "Sorry." He chuckled.

"I should have been paying attention. But really, these invites—designing them in the shape of police badges, the whole theme you have going, is fantastic. The crime scene idea has captivated me since the moment you mentioned it. I agree with all of this."

"Are you telling me there's no need for us to go to dinner now?" Charlie was aware of how much he was pouting. "I thought we'd get to chat."

"Oh, we're still going for dinner. It just means it's all pleasure now. Order the books, I'm happy for you to earn from them. If you need more, I can bring them in. I have plenty of each of them in the series. I'll provide a couple of signed box sets for your contests. I'm sure I can find some other things as well. I'll dig them out. Right now, I want to learn more about you, Charlie, not about my books, not about work. You."

"As long as I get to learn more about you as well," Charlie insisted. He felt dwarfed at times by Knox's dominance, his self-assured nature, and wanted to be sure, whatever this was, they were on equal footing.

Knox caressed his cheek. "As far as you're concerned, I'm an open book. Whatever you want to know, ask."

Charlie bit his lip. *Screw it.* "Why me?"

"What do you mean, why you?"

"Why are you wanting to take me out to dinner, why agree to the event, why… kiss me?"

Knox turned to face Charlie fully, pulling him flush against his body. "Because when you came out of here all righteously angry about what happened with Danny, I saw someone who was prepared to stand up for those they loved, those they protected, even if it was against a bigger predator. I see someone who is confident in their own skin." Knox wound a couple of strands of Charlie's rainbow hair through his fingers before letting it slide free. "I see someone doing what they love, and being true to themselves, and that's rare. I see someone who is incredibly sexy, with one of the finest asses I've seen in a while."

"You like my ass?"

Knox grabbed the ass in question and squeezed. "That's what you took from that?"

"Among other things, yes." Charlie chuckled.

"Yes, I like your ass, the way it moves, the way it feels in my hands, the way it looks. It's a mighty fine ass."

Charlie pushed up on tiptoes and brushed his lips across Knox's lips, whispering, "I like your dimples."

"I'd noticed. I think I've smiled more for you than I have in years."

"Oh? I make you smile, do I?"

"You do, and you know it."

"Maybe I just like to hear it, to hear I affect you."

"Oh, you affect me alright." Knox thrust his hips forward so Charlie could feel the proof of just how much Knox liked him.

Charlie whimpered.

"Fuck, the things that sound does to me."

The words were torn free from Knox in such a way Charlie couldn't doubt the veracity of them.

"I want to kiss you again."

"Please," Charlie begged, completely uncaring that he was.

"I can't. If I start kissing you again, we'll never make it out to dinner." Knox gently eased Charlie back and stepped away. "And I want to get to know you, Charlie. Yes, I want to kiss you, but honestly, I want to get to know you more. You're someone I can see having a relationship with."

"I am?" Charlie was stunned. "I mean, I feel the same, but I did wonder if you were after something short-term."

"I'm too old for that." Knox scowled. "I refuse to be ashamed that I'm looking for more."

"How old are you?" Charlie finished closing down the till, and started to turn the lights off.

"Thirty-four."

"Huh."

Knox narrowed his eyes. "What? Too old?"

Charlie looked around the shop, checking he hadn't forgotten anything. "No, just that's about what I thought you were."

"You're what twenty-two?" Knox looked almost nervous guessing.

"Twenty-four."

"Close enough." Knox walked to the door, waiting for Charlie. The minute he was in range, his hand went to Charlie's lower back, guiding him through the door, before he took the keys from Charlie's hand and locked up.

"Where are we going?" Charlie waved to Sam and Alfie who were busy smirking at him.

"Trevecki's." Knox's hand went straight back to resting just above Charlie's ass.

Charlie stopped dead. "Trevecki's?"

"Yes, why?"

"Everyone who is anyone goes there."

"And?"

"You're sure you want to be seen there with me? It's going to be all over Corent by the end of the evening. You know people gossip, and that's the best date night spot to go to."

"Why do you think I'm taking you there?" Knox dipped his head to Sam and Alfie as they passed.

"Have a beautiful night, boys!" Alfie called, making Sam laugh.

"Boys?" Knox looked over his shoulder.

"You're young compared to us, so you're boys." Alfie shrugged.

Knox rolled his eyes. "Have a nice night, gentlemen."

Charlie could still hear Sam and Alfie gossiping as they walked down the street. When Knox reached for his hand, he jerked, but threaded his fingers through Knox's before he could pull away. "Sorry, you just surprised me."

"Didn't think I was the type of man to hold hands?"

"Not really."

"I like touching any part of you." Knox winked.

Looking around reminded Charlie just how much he loved living in Corent. The stars were starting to come out as the day darkened into evening, and there were no clouds in sight. The gentle breeze brought a slight trace of honeysuckle. A nudge on his shoulder made him look up. Knox pointed to the park across the road. A family of rare arctic foxes, noticeable for their white coat all year round, were racing around the kiddie obstacle course, being cheered on by what Charlie was guessing were their parents. The pure white foxes gleamed in the light of the rising moon, bright against the backdrop of play equipment. In the large pool, it looked like there was a late-night swimming class going on. It always made him smile to see ducks share their water with the penguins, swans, and stingrays. Chuckling away, he pointed out a young bear who was staring at the water. "What's the betting he dive-bombs them?"

"High. I tell you what, if he doesn't, I'll do anything you want, when you want it. It could be working in your shop, something at home, whatever."

"And if he does?" Charlie checked.

"Then I get to kiss you whenever I want, wherever I want, without complaint."

"I don't see me losing on this. Deal."

"You think that now, but just wait." Knox winked.

"What do you have in mind?" Charlie tried to work out if Knox had played him.

"Time will tell." Knox tapped the pout that was forming on Charlie's lips. "No pouting allowed, we have a bear to watch." He maneuvered Charlie until he was in front of him, wrapping his arm around Charlie from behind, one hand laying over Charlie's heart.

Charlie rested his own hands on top, holding Knox there, liking the connection. Staying silent, they watched the bear planning his attack. He was sneaking in-between the small huts there for shifters to change in. His gaze was darting about the place, making sure no one was watching. The pool guard on duty had his back to the bear, and was oblivious to what was about to happen.

70

Suddenly the bear raced forward, letting out a roar as he jumped. The splash was incredibly impressive, arching up so high it managed to soak not only everyone already in the water, but everyone standing around watching. A chorus of shouts rang through the early evening as the bear lay on his back in the water. Within seconds the other animals dive-bombed him.

"A water-fight, why am I not surprised?" One of the parents on the edge groaned, making Charlie chuckle.

"Sometimes I miss those carefree days," Knox's voice had lost all trace of amusement. "I tried so hard to keep things fun for them. Cora was so small…" His voice trailed off.

Charlie wrapped his arms around Knox's not saying a word, just trying to provide what comfort he could.

A little while later, Knox seemed to come back to himself. "I'm sorry. My mind went—"

"It's okay," Charlie cut him off. "I'm perfectly happy just being here in your arms."

"You seem to bring out all my emotions. I think it's because I feel so relaxed around you, like I can be myself. That you won't think less of me if I show how I really feel." Knox placed a tender kiss on top of Charlie's head.

"I'm glad you feel that way. There's nothing wrong with emotions, and it warms my heart that you feel comfortable enough with me to show me. Thank you." Charlie squeezed Knox's arms tighter.

"Come on, time for food." Knox shifted, wrapping his arm around Charlie's waist and leading him away.

"Can I ask something?" Charlie looked up to Knox.

"Of course." Knox smiled down at him.

"Do you regret giving up being in the PAF?"

"Yes and no. I always wanted to work to protect people. Both my parents were in the PAF, my uncles, most of my family. Being a Siberian tiger, it's normal to go into the PAF. Having to give all that

71

up was hard, but I did it to give my siblings the best life they could have. Me being in the PAF was too big a risk. If they lost me, they would have gone to the lone shifters sanctuary. I couldn't have that. In the end, it wasn't a tough decision to make. They come first, they always have. If anything, they tell me to back the fuck off now." Knox rolled his eyes. "It's hard to step back after all this time, but watching them all move on, go into the PAF, is difficult. In many ways I feel like a father. It makes me worry about what I'm going to do with myself when they all get completely fed up with me."

"You could always take in a younger shifter who is too old for the lone shifter sanctuary. Say, someone who has recently joined the PAF, might be feeling a bit overwhelmed, and could do with having a father-type figure who will understand exactly what he is going through. I don't doubt for one minute your brothers will always come to you for advice, but maybe it's time to be more of a brother to them, rather than a father? Maybe that's what they need more from you right now?"

"You have a wise head on your shoulders."

Charlie sent Knox a cheeky grin. "Fancy telling my sister that? She never listens to me." His accompanying pout was enough to lighten the mood.

"I think that's a lie. I believe she listens to you a lot, just not always what you want her to listen to."

That drew a surprised laugh from Charlie. "There is that."

Knox leaned forward and opened the restaurant door, holding it open for Charlie. "After you."

The maître d' sat them in the middle of the room, clearly visible by everyone, and they were certainly attracting a lot of attention. It was making Charlie feel just a little bit uncomfortable. Thankfully he could hide behind the menu, at least for a little bit. His eyes widened as he took in the prices. Holy shit, this place wasn't cheap. But they had zirafon, the seafood dish that was incredibly rare, and only ever found in the paranormal world. The closest to it was lobster, but it was so much more than that. It was caught by sirens, responding to their call, walking up from the deepest trenches on the earth. The meat was juicy, tender, and succulent. Paired with a creamy peppercorn sauce, it was incredible. Served with seared vegetables in a garlic glaze and he was in heaven. It was expensive, and he groaned, looking at what else he could order.

"You've seen something you like?" Knox pulled the menu down with the tip of his fingers.

"No," Charlie insisted.

"Liar," Knox chuckled. "What have you seen?"

Scowling, Charlie confessed. "The zirafon in peppercorn sauce. It's my favorite, but I never order it in restaurants. I'm lucky I do deals with one of the sirens for some."

"You have a zirafon dealer?" Knox shook his head. "I don't know what surprises me more, the fact you love zirafon, or that you have a dealer."

"Let me guess, I'm a unicorn so you thought I'd go for a fruity type of salad?" Charlie refused to look away, yet Knox wouldn't look at him. "You did!"

"Uh, no comment on the grounds it may incriminate me."

"Oh, you did!" Charlie shook his head. "I'll have you know I love eating something tender and meaty that I… can…" Charlie broke off as his own words registered. His face flamed. "I, umm, didn't mean it quite how it sounded."

Knox was shaking with suppressed laughter and the waiter's face was contorting as he watched them. Managing to get himself under control, Knox looked at the waiter. "Two zirafon with all the trimmings please, and we'll have a bottle of redari wine, please."

The waiter reached for the menus and walked off.

"You didn't have to do that. The zirafon is expensive enough without buying a bottle of redari." Charlie laid his hand on top of Knox's smiling, when Knox turned his over and held his. "I'd have been happy with anything. I'm here to spend time with you, and not to simply get expensive food and drink."

73

Knox's thumb stroked back and forth over the back of Charlie's hand. "I know, but I have a feeling you don't get pampered often, and I wanted to do this. I happen to love zirafon and redari, I'm not ordering them just because they are some of the most expensive items on the menu."

"Good."

"Now tell me more about this dealer you have. I have got to hear this."

Charlie grinned. "Abalia is a siren, works for Zinkie's, the main broker in custom spell work. He's an avid reader and has been coming into my shop since I opened. It turns out he hates eating zirafon, but loves going out into the sea to sing. He used to just let the zirafon go, but we got talking one day, and he offered to do a deal. Once a month he brings me some zirafon and I trade him some of the newest releases. I know I get the better deal, but he says he does, seeing as he doesn't pay for the zirafon. I tend to give some to Evie, have friends over for dinner, or pass some over to Matt's mom."

Knox whistled. "Depending on how many books you give him, you definitely get the better end of the deal."

"Anywhere between five and ten books."

"Definitely the better deal." Knox's thumb was still tracing back and forth over the back of his hand. "Tell me, have you and Matt always been best friends?"

"For as long as I have memories. Our mothers were best friends from childhood, and they bought houses next door to each other when they settled down with families. We've always been close. Mama Alice took Evie and I in when my mother passed on."

"And your dad?" Knox asked gently.

"He lived apart from us. I know there was some reason it was kept quiet, that he stayed away from us, but I never did find out why. I'm not sure if Evie knew either. We do have the same father though."

"I'm sorry."

"I had Matt's dad— Jack, he was a father-figure to me. I had a happy childhood, never lacked for anything." Charlie's eyes were wistful as he reminisced about his childhood.

"What happened to them, if you don't mind me asking."

"Hunters." Charlie's jaw cracked. "She was on a business trip to Jenvia, and they got ambushed. They cut her horn off, and she died before anyone could help her. The trade in unicorns is still as rife as ever. I know some people have questioned Evie, Lane, and I for allowing the twins to be outside, even Danny, but Sam and Alfie are fierce in their protection. They're ex-PAF, they would give their lives for those babies."

"It's obvious how much they adore them."

"It is, no matter how grumpy they pretend to be. What most people don't know is that Sam and Alfie are guardians to all three. They watched us grow up, lived on the same street as Matt's mom when she was little." Charlie leaned back as the waiter set a plate in front of him. "There's no one else I would trust as much with the babies as I do those two."

"I can see why." Knox groaned as he took the first bite. "Holy shit, that really is amazing."

"It is. You can see why zirafon goes for as much as it does."

Knox's gaze became calculating. "I'm going to have to think of ways to get into your good graces and see if I can't gain an invite to dinner the next time you're cooking this."

"Why, Knox, are you just after my food?" Charlie baited him.

"Oh, I'm after your food, alright, but I'm after the guy that makes it a lot more."

"Is that right?"

"Yes, it is." Knox's gaze held his steady.

Charlie thrilled inwardly at the revelation. "I was wondering…"

"Why do I suddenly get the feeling that I'm not going to like this?" Knox teased.

"I'm just wondering if you can tell me anything more about Lane and Carter, their mission? I don't know what Carter looked like, but Lane had scratches, bruises, and scrapes. It was obvious he'd been fighting, but it had me worried. He's been going out on missions more and more. I've seen more units moving about, I hear the gossip about which family members are out. Putting the clues together, there's a lot more feral activity going on than most of us are being told about."

Know was looking around the restaurant as if checking to see who was there. "Let's have dinner, and then talk elsewhere, okay?"

Charlie's heart thumped like crazy. "Of course."

"Now, why don't you tell me more about who you are?"

The rest of the meal was spent going back and forth, learning all they could about each other. Conversation flowed easily, and it wasn't until there was a discrete cough beside Charlie's chair that he realized the restaurant was starting to empty. With wide eyes, he turned to Knox. "How long have we been here?"

Knox looked around the restaurant, his eyes widening. "All night?"

Looking at the table, Charlie saw the bottle of wine and the remains of the decedent chocolate cake they'd shared. "Maybe we should go."

Knox grinned and signaled for the check.

CHAPTER EIGHT

He was falling for Knox, he knew he was, and there was little chance of stopping it. The walk home had been romantic, holding hands as they strolled along moonlit streets. They hadn't rushed, instead, taking their time to look at flowers, animals, and the wonders of Corent City. The experience had infused his soul. Something was building inside him, and he wanted to explore what he was sure could be a budding relationship. He still couldn't quite believe he was in this position, but he was.

"What are you thinking about?" Knox prodded gently.

"Just how comfy I am with you. It surprises me."

"Why?"

"Because you're very alpha, you're ex-PAF, you're older than me, I'm often seen as flamboyant, just for my hair alone." Charlie shrugged. "I just happen to like rainbows. It's a unicorn trait."

"That it is. I love your hair. I don't think that you can be called flamboyant just for that. People see me as alpha, and I guess I am, but I'm also just a man. I have feelings. One thing I've always wanted is a partner I can be myself with. Someone who can sit there and listen to me moan when my characters are driving me crazy, when my family are pushing me to the brink. Someone that is there to bounce ideas around with. I want to curl up on the sofa and talk about our days. Yes, I'm ex-PAF, but that doesn't mean all I am is muscles and fight."

"I do like your muscles, though." Charlie ran a hand along the muscles on Knox's forearm. He looked up the street, seeing his front door. "Do you want to come in?" Charlie bit his lip as he waited.

"I would love to come in, if you're sure?" Knox stopped outside the door, his hand going to the back of Charlie's neck, his thumb stroking over the skin there.

"I'm sure." Charlie licked his lips. "I want to kiss you again."

"I can do that." Knox's eyes flared.

Charlie smiled to himself. He loved seeing how he affected Knox. Leading the way up the path, he stopped so suddenly, Knox slammed into him.

"You step on something?" Knox was trailing kisses over the back of his neck.

"Knox."

The breathy quality to his voice must have alerted Knox that something was seriously wrong, because he was suddenly behind a wall of muscles. "I take it you didn't leave your front door open."

"No, and if Matt were here, then he'd have shut it. Oh, ancestors, what if Matt's here." Charlie's breathing picked up speed.

"Don't call out, don't phone, just wait. Let me go in and check. Take my phone, and call Carter, tell him and whichever brother is closer to get here. Now." Knox's claws burst free from his hands the second Charlie had taken the phone.

Shaking, Charlie found Carter's details in the phone and dialed.

"Did you strike out with your young stud, big brother?" What Charlie presumed was Carter teased the minute the line connected.

"This isn't Knox, it's Charlie."

"What's happened." Carter's voice changed instantly.

"We've just got back to my house. The door was wide open. Knox just went in, he told me to call, get you and another brother down here."

"Stay there! We'll be there in three minutes. Stay calm and wait, Charlie. Don't do anything stupid."

"Okay." Charlie was shaking, worry for Matt and Knox warring for equal dominance in his mind.

"I need to call my brothers. Call me back if anything changes. We'll be there soon." Carter clicked off the phone and Charlie didn't know the last time he'd ever felt so alone, or so worried.

Trembling, he wrapped his arms around his waist, waiting for something to happen, yet hoping nothing did.

When a hand clamped down on his shoulder, he nearly screamed, but managed to bite it back just in time.

"Sorry, didn't mean to frighten you." Charlie turned to see what had to be one of Knox's brothers. Two others jogged past him. "I'm Max, that was Carter and Nate who went by. They'll make sure Knox is okay. It's nice to meet you, even if it is like this."

Max's grin came easy, and Charlie bet it was from being the youngest, and being protected by his big brothers.

"You know, you're cuter than Knox told us you were."

Charlie spluttered.

"That got you. Yes, my big brother is definitely enamored with you, just don't tell him I told you that. Do me a favor? Make him work for it."

"You want me to give your brother a tough time?"

"Hell, yes!" Max waggled his eyebrows. "He deserves it." Max's grin fell.

Charlie took a steadying breath and turned around, relief swamping him to see Knox striding out. Thank the ancestors he was okay. But if he was okay, then why did he look concerned? As soon as Knox was in range, he grabbed Charlie and pulled him into an embrace.

"I don't want you to panic, but Matt's in there."

Charlie tore himself free, Knox unable to stop him, and he charged into the house. He pushed past one of the brothers who tried to stop him and raced into his front room. "Oh shit!" He dropped to the floor beside the other brother, who was kneeling over Matt. Blood was trickling out of Matt's nose. "Matt!"

He fumbled for his phone, needing to call for help. A hand stopped him.

"Nate's already called for help. They'll be here soon." Knox held his hand. "Carter here is a medic. Let him help your friend."

"What's wrong with him?" Charlie trembled.

"I don't know, does he have any conditions?" Carter's gaze flicked up to his briefly.

"He's been seeing the doctors at the mage council. His magic was strange, he's been struggling to cast, and it's been acting wild. They don't know why. He's been going for all sorts of tests. No one has any idea what is wrong with him." Charlie couldn't take his eyes off Matt's face. "Did he collapse, or did something happen? Was he attacked?"

"He doesn't have any obvious injuries, and we can't see any obvious signs of any struggle."

Charlie fumbled for his phone. "Mama Alice. I need to call her."

"Do you want me to call for you?" Knox reached for the phone.

"No, thank you, but no." Charlie dialed. "Mama Alice…" The words broke.

"What's happened?" She picked up on his tone immediately.

"I don't know, I just got home, it's Matt." Before he could finish his sentence, Alice appeared in the room.

"No!" She dropped to her knees beside her son. "Oh, Matt." Her hands started to scan over his body as she fired questions at Carter.

Charlie stayed quiet as the pair of them worked over Matt. Seconds later there was a loud crack as two doctors appeared in the room, bags in hand. Carter rattled off details as he made room for them. As soon as Carter finished, Alice took over, filling them in on his history.

"Let's transport him to the hospital. You coming with us?" The doctors looked to Alice.

"Of course."

"I'll meet you there," Charlie called as she stood beside the doctors.

She nodded as they disappeared.

Charlie stared at the place Matt had been, barely able to comprehend what was happening. He was hauled up against Knox.

"Come on, let's get you to the hospital," Knox whispered in his ear.

Charlie didn't say anything, he just continued staring into space, walking when Knox led him, obeying any instructions, but otherwise, all he could do was think of Matt.

Bright lights suddenly assaulted his eyes, and Charlie looked around, realizing they were in a hospital waiting room.

"Welcome back," Knox murmured softly in his ear.

"Sorry, I hope I didn't worry you." Charlie looked up from where he was laying against Knox's shoulder.

"It's okay, I know you're worried. We all are."

"All?" Charlie lifted his head and looked around the room. There was Knox, Carter, Nate and Max. Sam and Alfie were also there. "Thank you." His voice was wobbling and husky. "Is there any news?"

"Nothing yet." Knox shifted slightly so he could wrap his arms around Charlie fully, holding him tight.

Warmth spread through him and helped eased the terror threatening to consume him. "How long have we been here?"

"About an hour."

"Really?"

"Yup, you've been pretty out of it. In case you're worried, Nate and Max made sure everything was safe and secure at your place before they joined us here. Alice called in Sam and Alfie, and they met us here." Knox gestured around the room.

"Thank you, Sam, Alfie, everyone."

"He'll be alright, Lad. Just wait. We may not know what's wrong yet, but we'll find out," Alfie assured him.

"I hope so." Charlie looked to the brother closest to him. "I'm sorry, I wasn't really thinking when I saw you all. You're Max?"

"I am, the good looking one." Max winked. "On the other side of Knox is Carter, and opposite us is Nate. Tyler is staying home with Cora. We're a protective bunch and don't like to leave her alone at night."

Charlie managed a weak smile. "Thank you all for being here. I'd be in pieces, or more in pieces, if I was here by myself. Where's Alice?"

"She's gone with them, seeing as she knows what's going on with him." Knox's hands were running a soothing pattern over his back.

Charlie suddenly gasped and looked around. "I should have been there. If I hadn't been out, I would have been able to help him. This is my fault!"

Knox stiffened underneath him, and Charlie realized how that must have sounded. Slumping against Knox, he kissed the side of his neck. "I didn't mean that how it sounded. I don't regret going to dinner with you, not for one moment. I'm just feeling guilty because Matt is my best friend and I wasn't there to help him. I feel like I should have been, but even knowing there's something going on with him, I can't stay with him every minute of every day. That's just not possible. Besides, he'd be the first person to tell me that I'm being stupid."

"I'm sorry you weren't there for Matt." Sam leaned forward. "But he would be the first one to kick you up and down this room for even thinking about blaming yourself. Besides, he'll also be the first one cheering you on for going out with Knox here. Now, seeing as we need to wait for news, do you want to tell us how your date went?"

Charlie's face flamed. "No."

"Aww, come on, Charlie, we want to know so we can tease our big brother. We don't get many chances at it." Nate waggled his eyebrows. "There has to be some ammunition in the evening. Come on, do me a favor and dish the dirt."

"You wouldn't do that to me, now would you?" Knox whispered into his ear, his tongue flicking against Charlie's lobe.

Charlie shuddered. "No."

"No fair!" Max called across the room.

Charlie chuckled.

"What do you see in him?" Nate looked confused. "He's nothing more than a giant pain in our asses!"

"I think that's the other way around," Knox drawled.

"Oh, hell no!" The three brothers chorused as one.

Charlie cast Knox an evil look. "So, who wants to tell me some stories, keep my mind busy?"

"What, about Knox?" Nate's eyes danced with humor.

"Yes." Charlie's grin was wicked as Knox's grumble ran through him.

"Please don't," Knox begged, "Charlie will never want to see me again."

"Aww, is big brother all scared?" Max taunted.

"With you three against me, hell yes!"

"We need to get revenge. Charlie, have you any idea how embarrassing it is having to get a sex ed lesson from your brother? I was mortified." Max's overly dramatic shuddering was making Charlie laugh. "I'm serious. He had videos and a dildo. He made us all practice using condoms. That's scarred me for life. I swear I couldn't look at a condom for years without thinking of him. Have you got any idea how much of a buzz kill that is?"

Charlie snorted before dissolving into a fit of laughter. If it was slightly manic, no one called him on it.

"You know," Nate began with an evil grin, "I remember one time when I was about seventeen—" the grin Nate shot his brother was beyond evil— "I was sneaking back in from a party."

"Not this!" Knox begged.

"See, you saying that just piques my curiosity even more," Charlie teased, linking his fingers through Knox's, laughing when Knox grumbled and hid his face in Charlie's hair. He waved for Nate to carry on.

"I was being so quiet. I'd made it past the booby traps that Knox always put in place to catch us, and decided I needed some water before bed. I walked into the kitchen and stopped dead. There was Knox, balls deep in some twink. That would have been bad enough. But no, the twink was yelling… 'ride me, daddy tiger, give me those stripes.'" Nate shuddered. "Knox slammed his hand over the twink's mouth and I don't know if that's because he was just being noisy, or because of what he was saying."

"Because of what he was saying," Knox grumbled. "He was hot, but incredibly odd. I, uh, stopped seeing him after that."

"Oh, wow." Charlie shook his head. "Should I be worried about what your brothers think of me, if that's the sort of people you date?"

"Nah." Carter grinned. "You look sane. His taste has definitely improved."

Charlie theatrically wiped his forehead. "Phew. Tell me, Nate, what did you do?"

"Gagged and ran out the room. My screaming woke up everyone else. Suddenly, Knox here is faced with four brothers and a sister all laughing at him after I explained what was going on. He was as red as a tomato and hustled the guy out the door. The entire time the guy is complaining, going 'but I want my daddy tiger!' That set us all off. I think it took about six weeks for us to stop teasing him about it."

Across the room, Sam was clutching his chest. Charlie cried out, "Sam! Are you okay?" Panic flaring in his chest.

Alfie waved him off. "He's laughing so much he's not got any air left. Nothing more than that."

Sam took a series of sharp, shallow breaths and managed to croak out, "You are so lucky no one in the PAF learned that. You'd never have heard the end of it. Sure, you weren't working on a team anymore, but you were in the office. The teasing would have been merciless."

"Tell me about it," Knox grumbled. "I had to bribe this lot with food and cakes to keep them quiet."

Max high-fived Carter.

"They were little demons. Evil little shits." Knox narrowed his gaze at his brothers.

Charlie turned his head, kissing Knox's jaw. "You know you love them really."

"Sometimes I question my sanity." Knox tipped his head giving Charlie more room.

"What other stories do you have?" Charlie faced the brothers again.

"Well—" Carter broke off as the door opened and Alice walked in.

Charlie was on his feet instantly, racing across the room and pulling Alice into his arms. "How is he?"

"He's stable and resting. He woke up briefly though." Alice soothed a hand over Charlie's back, trying to reassure him.

"Do we know what happened? Was it his problems, or was he attacked?"

"It was his own magic. When he woke up he told us his magic suddenly flared and he couldn't get it under control. That's the last thing he remembers. They're going to run some tests, but are keeping him in a room where they can turn the magical suppression on at the flick of a switch. They don't want his magic to run amok again. There's no telling what it will do. Whatever it did to him, it put enough strain on his mind it caused nosebleeds. That's what you saw." Alice cupped his face. "I know you, Charlie, and you're going to be blaming yourself for not being there. Well, I'm telling you I'm glad you weren't there. If his magic was so out of control it did that much damage to him, it could have killed you."

"But—" Charlie started to insist, but the look on Alice's face stopped him.

"You want to come and see him? You can only stay a few minutes, but it will help you both."

"Thank you." Charlie looked back at Knox. "Are you going home?"

The look in Knox's eyes told Charlie he was being stupid. "No, we're waiting here."

"Okay, thank you." Charlie took a deep breath and followed Alice out the room.

CHAPTER NINE

Trembling as he opened the door, Charlie wasn't sure what to expect. Seeing monitors surrounding the bed, and both a medical nurse and a magical nurse, worried him.

"They're just taking all his baseline vitals. I know the machines look scary, but he's doing alright, I promise." Alice held his hand, leading him to the bed.

"How are you so calm?" Charlie looked over his best friend, trying to ignore the wires and the IV line. A magical orb floated above his head, waves showing up inside it.

"Because I know he's getting the best possible care." Seeing the direction of his gaze, she went on to explain, "That orb is just measuring the waves of his magic, nothing to worry about. Sit and talk to him."

"But he's sleeping."

"He's resting, but his eyes were open a few minutes ago," one of the nurses spoke softly from beside the bed. Charlie guessed it was the magical nurse based on her purple scrubs.

Charlie took the seat close to Matt's head and gingerly picked up Matt's hand, holding it between his. "Hey, Minx. You've given us all a bit of a scare. I need you awake, Matt. Who else am I going to gossip with? Don't you want to hear all about my date?"

Matt's eyes blearily opened, locking onto Charlie's gaze. "You went on a date? Who?"

"Knox." Charlie grinned. "He was walking me home when we saw my door open. He went into alpha mode, making me call his brothers, and went in to see what was going on. He found you. Carter, his brother, was helping you. He's a medic with the PAF."

"I didn't destroy your house, did I?"

"No, you didn't, but I wouldn't care if you had, as long as you were okay." Charlie was quick to reassure him.

"I could feel it spinning out of control. You were closer than Mama's house, so I aimed for you. I ported to the pathway, somehow managed to unlock the door, ran in, thinking you'd be there. I don't remember much else."

"I'm just glad we got there in time to save you." Charlie sniffed back the tears.

"Don't cry, Choo. Tell me about your date instead. Where did you go?"

"Trevecki's."

"Holy shit, he's got to be serious about you then." Matt's grin was weak, but it was there.

"We had zirafon and redari."

Even the two nurses stopped what they were doing to stare at Charlie. "What?" He blushed.

"Sorry, but if your date is taking you there, buying you that, he's serious about you." The male nurse, Orin, according to his nametag, chimed in.

"It was our first date," Charlie confessed.

Orin whistled. "Color me impressed. Who is this bastion of dating heaven?"

"Knox Vaughn," Matt answered before Charlie could say anything.

Orin did a double take. "Dayum, the man looks like a god, is all alpha and mysterious, and takes you there? You are one lucky man."

"It was a great date." Charlie flushed.

"Nope, not jealous at all," Orin mock growled, making them all laugh. "Well, you're all set up here, Matt. If you need me for anything, call my name, or hit the buzzer and my pager will go off," Orin explained. "Otherwise, I'll leave you alone for a few minutes."

"You scared me." Charlie carefully wrapped his arms around Matt, holding him tight. "I thought... I was sure... you were so still. Knox ran in when we saw the open door, demanding that I stay out of the way. We weren't sure if I'd been broken into. When he came out, just the look on his face and I knew something was wrong. Seeing you there, you looked so still, so unlike the man I know..." Charlie choked back a sob. "I can't lose you, Matt. You have to do everything they say you need to do. I don't care what it is, you need to do it. You're my best friend. Life doesn't work without you in it."

"I promise. If I hadn't been serious about what was going on before, I am now. I don't want to go through that again, let alone worry everyone else." Matt leaned into the hug.

Charlie would have dive-bombed the bed, but with Matt so fragile, he leaned in carefully. He wrapped his arms around Matt, closed his eyes, and held his friend tight.

Charlie didn't know how long he stayed in Matt's arms, but when he finally pulled back and looked around, Alice had gone, and Knox and his brothers were in the corner of the room quietly talking. "Sorry." He coughed. "I didn't realize you'd come in."

"You were settled, taking the time to reconnect. The last thing we wanted to do was to disturb you both." Knox walked over, his hand automatically going to the spot on Charlie's lower back that he seemed to favor. "Hey, Matt."

"Knox." Matt stared the man down.

Charlie had to hand it to Knox, he didn't so much as flinch under the scrutiny.

"You're dating Charlie now?" Matt demanded.

"I am, and will be for as long as Charlie allows." Knox held Matt's gaze, while his hand maintained the soothing strokes on Charlie's back.

"I'll be watching you. Make one wrong move… it doesn't matter that you're ex-PAF, a tiger, an alpha, or that my magic is on the fritz… you hurt him, and I will gut you with my bare hands. Do I make myself clear?"

"Crystal clear. But, let me make one thing clear. If I hurt him, I'll be kicking my own ass."

Charlie's head shot up to look at Knox. Across the room, conversation ceased.

"What did I say?" Knox looked around confused.

Max took pity on him when no one else answered. "It's telling that you're saying you would kick your own ass. It gives us an insight into your feelings for Charlie here."

"It does?" Knox looked around.

To Charlie, he looked adorably confused.

"It does." Nate chuckled.

"Huh." Knox scratched at the stubble forming on his chin. "Well, I would. Charlie here doesn't deserve to be hurt."

Charlie tipped up onto his toes and kissed the underside of Knox's jaw. "Thank you."

Knox wrapped his arm around Charlie and pulled him close. "Matt, I want you to know, if there is anything you need, you just need to let one of us know, and we'll be here for you." He looked back at his brothers, daring them to disagree.

Charlie caught the wicked glimmer in Matt's eyes and waited for whatever nefarious plan he was cooking up.

"You'll do anything I need?"

"Of course," Knox was quick to answer.

Behind him, Sam winced, knowing Matt far too well.

"In that case, I need whatever you're working on right now. I need to know what happens to Detective Delicious and Teaks." Matt's lips were twitching.

There was a gasp behind Charlie.

"You told them?" That was Nate.

"I did. I agreed to do the event that Charlie is holding for the release."

"You're coming out as an author?" Carter looked stunned. "I didn't think you wanted to?"

"I hadn't planned on it, but then when I bumped into Danny, met Charlie, and saw the shop, I realized that Charlie was someone who truly cared about the books, not just about the money. It's not like I've come out to the world at large, just this small part of the para world." Knox shrugged.

Charlie's brow furrowed. "Uh, you do realize that once The Sentinel reports it on their web page, that it's going to be all over the para world in minutes? A reporter is coming, and they love getting the scoop." Charlie bit his lip. "If you want to cancel, you can, I won't mind." At the incredulous looks sent his way, he winced. "Well, not too much anyway. I don't want you to feel uncomfortable, or like you're being forced into this. Do I want you there? Yes, without a doubt, but not if it's not what you want to do."

"You would honestly call the whole thing off for me?" Knox turned Charlie, so they were facing each other. He gently cupped Charlie's face, staring into his eyes. "You would really call everything off, even though you've told people, even though you've ordered all these extra books?"

"Yes, I would." Charlie reached out and traced one of Knox's dimples. "Do I like you as an author? Hell yes. But I like you more as a person. I could never force you to do something you didn't want to do."

"And my brothers wonder why I like you." Knox stole a quick kiss.

Charlie grinned.

"Thank you for the offer, but I'm happy to do this. I was always going to confess who I was, this is just maybe a little quicker than I had planned. I decided to consider it, having seen your shop, but when you sent the email, it was a done deal after I read what you had planned." Knox turned to face Matt. "Now, if you do as the doctors and nurses tell you to, you behave and work on getting better, then I will let you read some of what I'm working on."

"Oh, come on!" Max growled. "Even we don't get to read what you're working on."

"If you ever get injured, I might let you. And no, that's not an invitation to do something stupid and get yourself a bed in here alongside Matt." Knox's gaze was focused on his younger brother. "I mean it."

"Would I do a thing like that?" Max tried to pull off an innocent expression and failed spectacularly.

"Yes, you would," the brothers chorused together.

Charlie turned to Matt, about to make a quip about the Vaughn men, when he realized Matt was sound asleep. Reaching out to get everyone's attention, he waved at them, gesturing for them to be silent.

Knox nodded towards the door, and the brothers quietly left. "Are you staying overnight?"

"I want to, but Mama Alice will be, I'm sure."

"I will be." Alice floated in through the doorway. "You go and get some sleep. You have the shop to open in the morning."

"So do you," Charlie protested.

"No, Gemma is going to look after it for me." Alice took up position by her son. Gemma was Alice's daughter, Matt's sister.

"Are you sure you don't need me to open up? Evie can open ours." Charlie moved so he could lean over her chair and hug her.

"Oh, sweet boy, thank you, but we'll be okay."

"Just promise me, if you need me for anything, you call. And you'd better be calling if there is any change with him." He nodded to the sleeping Matt.

"You know I will." She turned and pinned Knox with a ferocious glare. "You'd better look after my boy. And he is my boy, even if it isn't by blood."

"I promise. I'll stay with him tonight." His eyes widened at her scowl. "I didn't mean like that! I meant so he has some company. That's his best friend lying there. The last thing Charlie needs is to be alone right now. I want to make sure someone is watching out for him as you watch over your son. I know how deeply you care for Charlie. The last thing you need is to worry about him as well." Knox dug a card out of his pocket. It was a magical business card, and was attuned to show the best number to get him on. If he was at home, his home phone would ring, his office, that phone and so on.

Charlie watched as he pressed his thumb to one of the corners activating the card. It was a safeguard so if you lost a card, someone couldn't get access to all your numbers. That was one of the things he loved about the differences in the para world, the little advances and spells they had that made a massive difference to life. If the humans knew, they would be sick with jealousy. Tuning back into the conversation, he saw Knox smiling at him.

"You ready there?"

"I am, as long as you're sure, Alice?" Charlie hugged her.

"I'm sure, now scoot."

Charlie gently tucked a stray lock of hair behind Matt's ear and looked up at Knox. "Ready."

CHAPTER TEN

Worrying about facing the chaos that he'd left his house in, Charlie was stunned stupid to see the door open as they walked up the path, a beautiful young woman standing in the doorway. She was around five feet three with waist length strawberry blond hair and freckles dotting her nose. When she smiled, dimples the same as Knox's appeared. This had to be Cora, Knox's sister.

"Hi there." She waved at them both.

"Cora, what are you doing here?" Knox strode forward and wrapped his sister in a hug, lifting her off the ground.

"Carter spoke to Tyler, explaining what was going on, who Matt was to Charlie, who Charlie was to you. We arranged to come here and help clean everything up so that you wouldn't need to worry about it when you came back."

Charlie's eyes went damp. "Thank you," he choked out. "That's one of the nicest things anyone has done for me."

Cora pulled back from her brother and wrapped her arms around Charlie, squeezing him with a strength that surprised him. She was chuckling when she pulled back.

"Stronger than I look, right?" At Charlie's nod, she took him by the hand and led him into his own house. "Those brothers of mine make sure I can defend myself. They take me boxing, running, and to spell defense class. I have amulets, and all the defensive spells a non-magic can use."

"Why does that not surprise me in the slightest?" Charlie's lips twitched as he looked over his shoulder at Knox.

"She's my baby sister. She needs protecting." Knox looked unrepentant.

Walking into the family room, Charlie's jaw dropped. It was tidier than it had been when he left for work that morning. There was no trace of what had happened with Matt. Despite some of the furniture being broken, everything was exactly where it should have been. "How?"

"We had some help." Cora waved towards the kitchen door where Sam stood, Charlie's 'Bitch, I'm fabulous' apron tied securely around his waist and a wooden spoon in hand. Beside him, Knox froze, and they both blinked, stunned, at the sight.

"I told him he looks stupid in it!" Alfie's voice came from behind Sam. "The old fool wouldn't listen though!"

"What? It's perfect, I *am* fabulous!" Sam protested, striking a pose.

Charlie recovered first, raced across the room, and slammed into Sam, hugging him tightly. Sam patted him on the back, as he drew him close. "What, you think we would leave you to come home to things the way they were? Have a little faith in your friends."

"Thank you." Charlie looked from Sam to Alfie, Cora, and finally what could only be Tyler beside Knox.

"Hi, I'm Tyler, the best looking of the bunch." Tyler winked, before choking on a cough as Knox threw a punch into his side.

"Stop flirting!" Knox demanded.

"What, I just said hello."

"No, you flirted." Knox towered over his brother, or at least tried to, he only had an inch on Tyler at most.

"You're just being protective."

The look Knox sent was all 'duh.'

"Anyway," Alfie drawled. "I made some lovely stew and dumplings for you to eat tomorrow. You're going to need all the strength you can get. I know you, Charlie. You'll be at the hospital first thing in the morning, then back and forth constantly as Matt recovers. You'll forget to eat. Now, you'll accept every bit of help we all offer. There will be no complaints, no grumbling, and gracious thanks." Alfie stared him down.

Charlie looked around the room, seeing the smiling faces, the love and support, and it took everything in him not to break down. Between the date with Knox and everything with Matt, his emotions were raw and erratic.

"Aww, come on, have some hot chocolate and relax." Cora grabbed his hand and led him to the table.

Charlie let himself be guided, following along without complaint. The stew smelled divine. Knowing Sam and Alfie, the meat would be tender, the sauce just the right thickness and the dumplings like little clouds of deliciousness. He looked at the two older men, warmth shining from his eyes. "Thank you. You're right, cooking will be the last thing on my mind."

"We'll make sure he eats it." Cora's hands were on her hips, and Charlie got a sense of just how feisty she could be when she wanted to.

Sam placed a steaming mug of hot chocolate in front of him, topped off with cream and chocolate sprinkles. "Drink that, it will help you sleep."

"I don't need to sleep," Charlie insisted, but when Sam refused to look away, he picked up the mug and sipped. The richness of the cream combined with the luxuriousness of the chocolate to blend into a little slice of heaven. The warmth settled deep into his bones, and his body finally began to relax. He was swaying in his seat before he realized it. When a yawn cracked his jaw, Knox gently pulled him from his seat.

"Come on, let's take you to get some sleep." Knox gently pulled him to stand.

Charlie rapidly shook his head. "I don't want to go yet."

"Then how about we curl on the sofa and chat?" Knox walked him into the family room, immediately sitting him down onto the sofa and pulling him to his side, resting Charlie's head against his shoulder.

With a flick of his wrist, Alfie lit the fire, the flames immediately curling around the logs and blazing contentedly. Warmth wormed its way across the room and settled around Charlie. Sam, Alfie, and the others were quietly talking as he stared into the flames, letting them hypnotize him. His mind seemed to focus on the sight of Matt collapsed on the ground, Carter beside him, working at helping him. If Knox hadn't been with him, if they hadn't called his brother… would he have had the presence of mind to call Mama Alice, to call for help? The what ifs were swirling around, taking his mind down dark paths. Life wouldn't be the same without his friend. It simply didn't work. Matt was his partner in crime, his confidant, his lifeline.

"He'll be okay," Knox murmured into his ear. "We won't let him be anything else. If the doctors can't find out what's wrong, I'll reach out to my contacts in other cities."

"The doctors at the Mage Council haven't been able to find anything out." Charlie worried his bottom lip between his teeth.

"That may well be, but they tend to only look for certain things. Some of the medic mages I know have seen all sorts of weird and wonderful things. I promise, I'll not stop helping you look until we find out what's wrong with him and see him better."

Charlie trembled, but held it together. "Thank you, all of you."

Smiles and winks were sent his way. When Knox carefully eased his head back to his shoulder, he let him and listened to his friends talking, the soft voices lulling him to sleep.

The world was swaying gently. Without opening his eyes, Charlie tried to work out if he was still dreaming and on some grand adventure, or something was happening.

"I can see you thinking there." A quiet voice chuckled above him.

"Knox? What's going on?" He forced his eyes open.

"You fell asleep on me in the family room. I sent the others home, and I'll put you to bed."

Charlie whimpered, even if he didn't mean to, and his eyes slid shut again.

"What's wrong?" Knox didn't stop the steady steps up the stairs.

"I don't want to be on my own tonight. I know that sounds like I'm a wimp, but coming home with the door open like that freaked me out, then seeing Matt collapsed…"

"I can stay with you if you want? Not to do anything, but I'm more than happy to hold you all night long."

"You'd stay for me?" Charlie's eyes opened at that.

"Of course, I would. I'll be the perfect gentleman."

"What if I don't want you to be?" Charlie retorted.

Knox walked through the door to his bedroom and carefully laid him on the bed before squatting beside it. "You've had a long night. The last thing I'm going to do is take advantage of you." He reached out and ran a hand gently over Charlie's cheek. "I can think of nothing better than spending the night in bed with you, making love to you. But I don't want it to be because you're just looking for comfort." Knox gently laid a finger over Charlie's lips, silencing him. "No matter what you say, it would be part of the reason. It's natural to seek out comfort at a time like this. Instead, I'll hold you in my arms all night long and maybe steal a couple of kisses. If you still want me to take you to bed in a day or two, then trust me, I will be delighted to oblige." Knox lifted his finger and replaced it with his lips.

The kiss was languid and full of comfort, and without realizing it, precisely what Charlie needed. When Knox pulled back, his dimples were showing. "Now why don't you get ready. I would ask to borrow sleep pants, but I imagine they might be a bit small for me."

Charlie grinned at the mental image Knox's words gave him.

"If you have no objection, then I'll just sleep in my boxers." Knox's hands hovered over the buttons on his shirt.

Charlie shook his head. "No, no objections here." He watched, mesmerized as Knox started to undo the buttons, a tantalizing hint of skin peeking out from between the layers of fabric. Without conscious thought, he licked his lips.

"Behave." Knox shook his head.

"I didn't do anything!" Charlie protested.

Knox leaned forward and gently tapped Charlie's lips. "You think I can't see you licking your lips? Liking what you see, are you?"

"Uh huh." Charlie's gaze was riveted as Knox pulled the shirt from his shoulders, his upper body on full display. Knox might not be PAF anymore, but he was still in the same shape as if he was. There was a light smattering of dark hair on his chest. Just enough for Charlie to tangle his fingers in. His pecs, stomach muscles, everything, perfectly defined and Charlie had the sudden urge to run his tongue over every groove he could find.

When Knox's hands went to the button of his pants, Charlie bit the inside of his cheek. He refused to even blink as Knox pushed the pants down his legs and stepped out of them. It was by sheer force of will that Charlie didn't whimper at the display Knox was putting on. His thigh muscles bulged and rather than boxers, Knox was wearing boxer-briefs. Seemingly skin-tight boxer-briefs. They lovingly outlined and cradled his sizeable package and Charlie really wanted to reach out and push them down.

Suddenly there was a snapping sound in front of him. Charlie blinked a couple of times and focused on Knox's fingers as he was clicking them together in front of Charlie's face.

"Focus, Charlie!" Knox flicked his nose. "Get changed."

Charlie mindlessly obeyed orders, quickly stripping out of his clothes, glad to get out of them. It had been a long-ass day. Without thinking, he reached into his drawers and grabbed the closest pair of pajama sleep pants. It wasn't until he stood, stripping down to his own boxers that he realized Knox's gaze was trained on him, the way his had been trained on Knox. Too self-conscious in comparison to Knox's body to even attempt to tease Knox, he quickly pulled on his sleep pants. He cocked his head to one side when a chuckle burst free from Knox.

Knox waved in his general direction. "Minions?"

Charlie froze before his gaze slowly panned down to look at his legs. "Oh, shit." Why had he not thought about what he was grabbing? Mind you, his drawers were full of sleep pants like this. "I, uh… they're comfy?"

"Are they?"

"Yes." Charlie slumped. "You might as well look in my drawers. They're full of ones as bad as this. I find them comfy, and they make me smile."

"I like them. They suit you and your personality."

"You don't think I'm a big kid wearing them?" Charlie struggled to even look at Knox. He heard movement and guessed it was Knox walking around the bed. His chin was gently lifted until he was forced to look into Knox's intense gaze.

"No, like I said, they're you, and I have yet to find a single aspect of who you are that doesn't enthrall me. I want to know more about the man who wears cartoon sleep pants, runs his own bookshop, loves his friends and extended family, oh… and wears unicorn slippers."

Charlie sighed. "They were a gag gift from Matt. I bought him witch's hats."

"I like them." Knox grabbed him by the hand and led him into his own en-suite bathroom before freezing in the doorway. "You have the Taristian shower?"

"I do, it was a treat to myself." Charlie took a leap of faith. "You want a shower?"

"In there? I could never say no to that. But, uh, will I be on my own, or…"

Charlie took a deep breath, quickly ordered the shower to his favorite settings, pushed his sleep pants and boxers down and stepped in. Turning back around to face a stunned Knox, he grinned. "Well, are you joining me?"

Knox sure could move fast when he wanted to. His boxers were off and he was in the shower within a couple of seconds. "Hey." He stalked towards Charlie, his gaze roaming Charlie's body, lust shining.

The smell of jasmine and sandalwood floated on the steam. At the moment, the water was set to a random cycle of colors. The water was a vibrant cobalt blue as it streaked over Knox's chest and on down to his rather impressive cock. His own cock twitched at the sight of it.

"You are stunning." Knox stepped forward as Charlie moved back, until he was leaning against the shower wall.

"Me?" Charlie shook his head, denials forming on his lips. "Your body is like a work of art."

Knox's hand gently trailed down Charlie's chest. "Can I wash you?"

Charlie could only nod.

"Creamy body wash," Knox commanded as he held out his hand. The pearlescent wash magically appeared in his hand. He quickly rubbed them together before he splayed them across Charlie's chest.

Charlie could have sworn his skin sizzled at the touch. Knox's hands glided over his skin, washing him gently, yet thoroughly. When his hands glided up to Charlie's shoulders, Knox stepped forward until they were almost touching.

"Do you know how much tension people carry in their shoulders?" His hands started to work on the kinks Charlie carried there. "Most don't realize it, but you carry a lot of stress there. When you factor in what you've been through today alone, it's no wonder these are as tense and full of knots as they are." Knox looked at his hands before washing away the body wash. Holding out his hands again, he commanded, "A mixture of frankincense and bergamot oil please."

"What are those for?" Charlie let his eyes slide shut, and his head tipped back until it rested against the wall.

"They help to ease stress and anxiety." Knox's voice was quiet, as if he was simply letting the oil work its own magic. "Soothing and relaxing music please," he ordered the shower.

"Why are you being so amazing?" Charlie couldn't help but ask.

"Because I want to look after you, want to protect you and help you in any way I can. Am I attracted to you? Yes, without a doubt I am. I want to kiss you so badly it hurts. But, it's also more than that. I want to help you, hold you, learn everything about you. I want to spend time, curled on the sofa like we were earlier, talking about our day, about the future. I want everything. I know we need to go slow and work towards that. I'm not expecting everything to happen overnight, I just wanted you to know how I was feeling. It feels right, to be honest with you. I hope you feel the same way, but if you don't—"

Charlie leaned forward and kissed him. When he pulled back, he grinned. "That's what I want as well."

"Good, then let me wash you and give you a massage." Knox held out his hands, waiting for an answer.

"Okay." Charlie slumped back against the wall and relaxed.

Knox stepped forward, so their bodies were brushing over each other as he moved. Knox's hands returned to Charlie's shoulders, gently turning Charlie around, guiding him so Charlie was braced against the shower wall. His hands took up a methodical pattern over his shoulders, down his shoulder blades, and onto his lower back. Between the steam, the scents, the warmth, the music, and Knox's touch, the tension and stress started to ebb from Charlie's body. He lost himself to the feeling, groaning when Knox's hands skated over the globes of his ass.

"So perfect," Knox leaned in and whispered in his ear.

Charlie couldn't get his mouth to form words, but was actually glad. He didn't want to spoil the moment by second-guessing Knox. For whatever reason, the man found him sexy. Who was he to argue? He lost track of the time Knox spent easing the tension in his body, only coming back into the moment when Knox's hands slid up the inside of his thighs. He shuddered as his sleeping nerve endings woke up with a start. The muscles in his ass twitched, and he pushed back into Knox's touch.

"So responsive, so beautiful." Knox placed a tender kiss on the crease between his thigh and his ass cheek. As his hands massaged up and over his ass, his thumbs trailed along the outer edge of his crease.

Charlie wanted so much in that moment, yet, at the same time, he was languid and relaxed. As much as he wanted to have some fun with Knox, the man was right. He needed a night of sleep and nothing else. His cock was rock hard, but he chose to ignore it, as painful as that was. He really didn't have the strength. As he tried to turn around, Knox placed a hand between his shoulder blades.

"Just wait. Let me wash up, and then I'll dry you off."

Charlie let his forehead rest against the wall and waited. A minute or two later, a warm towel wrapped around him. He hadn't even noticed the shower turn off. Knox gently rubbed him down, picking up their discarded clothes and walking back into the bedroom. He pushed Charlie down onto the bed, and carefully slid his sleep pants up his legs before starting to slip his own boxers back on.

Charlie reached out and stopped him. "Want a clean pair of boxers?"

The smile he got in response was blinding. "Thank you."

"Grab any pair out of the drawer."

Knox chuckled as soon as he opened it up. "I love these." He held up a couple of pairs. "Superheroes, minions, smurfs, cartoon aliens, anime, manga. You certainly like variety." Knox picked up a pair of Captain America ones. His shield rested over the bulge of his cock when he pulled them up. "Now scoot into position. I'll take whatever side you don't normally sleep on."

Charlie pulled back the covers, sliding into bed and shifting to make room for Knox. "I tend to sleep in the middle, so if I get in your way, just push me to one side." Charlie flushed at his confession.

"That's okay, I plan on holding you all night long anyway." Knox winked as he settled in beside Charlie. He immediately wrapped an arm around Charlie, bringing him close, guiding Charlie's head to his chest.

Charlie gulped at the move. Being so close to Knox was doing strange things to him. Yes, his cock was plumping up, but there was also a fluttering in his stomach. What he was beginning to feel for Knox was so much more than attraction on a purely physical level. He was attracted to every part of the man— mind, body, heart, and soul. Despite his outward appearance, all tiger, power, masculinity, alpha vibes and a stern expression, Knox Vaughn cared deeply for those he surrounded himself with. He would go out of his way to help someone, all his family would, as Charlie had seen that night. The strangest thing was, despite how difficult the evening had been, how scared and worried he was about and for Matt, being with Knox felt righter than anything had in his life before.

"What are you thinking about so hard?" Knox's hand threaded through his hair.

"That this feels incredibly right, no matter that it's really fast." It was strange, but being this honest with Knox didn't feel uncomfortable in the slightest. He didn't want to lie and pretend this was nothing to him. He was always one for honesty in every aspect of his life, and that wasn't about to change now.

"It does. Holding you like this is making me feel calm and relaxed. Like this is exactly where I'm meant to be." Knox leaned down and kissed the top of his head.

Charlie laid his hand over Knox's pec, feeling his heartbeat thrum underneath him. The beat soothed him, and he found his eyes sliding shut. Between the beat and the rhythmic strokes through his hair, he stood no chance of staying awake.

CHAPTER ELEVEN

All-encompassing heat. Whatever he was lying on was like a furnace. The only thing was, it didn't feel like his bed. Part of it was much too hard for that. Charlie racked his mind, trying to work out what had happened the night before. He didn't remember drinking with Matt and passing out in— Matt. He'd collapsed and been taken to hospital. The memories came flooding in thick and fast. Of Matt, Knox's family, and the man himself. That was what, or rather *who* he was lying on. Forcing his eyes open, he realized he was staring at the window, and a heavy weight was draped over him. Peering down, he realized it was Knox's arm, securely wrapped around his waist, holding him tight against his body. Parts of which were hard, harder than the rest. Charlie couldn't resist pushing back slightly.

"Behave," a sleepy voice whispered into his ear before it was nipped gently. Despite Knox's words, his hand drifted lazily over Charlie's stomach.

"It's still dark outside. Sorry, I fell asleep on you." Charlie pushed back a little more.

"I'm not. You needed to sleep." Knox was tracing a pattern around his nipple.

"I'm surprised I slept as well as I did. Sorry if I snored on you, or worse, drooled."

Knox's chuckling was making him bounce slightly, and he couldn't stop smiling. He quickly muttered the basic teeth cleaning spell and turned his head, searching out Knox's lips.

"You cheated."

Charlie could feel Knox's lips twitching against his. "I did. Morning breath is real."

"What about mine?"

"I just want to kiss you," Charlie confessed.

Knox pulled back enough to say the spell, and then immediately claimed Charlie's lips. When he tried to turn around, Knox stopped him, holding him in place. Languid and sensual, the kiss was sexual, but more about connecting than anything else. How long they kissed for, Charlie couldn't be sure, but the beginnings of dawn were peeking through the gaps in his curtains.

"It's a new day," Knox murmured against his neck.

"It is, in so many ways." Just then, Charlie's phone went off with a message. "Play text," he commanded.

Matt's good. He had a good night sleep and is eating breakfast. Don't rush here.

Charlie breathed a sigh of relief.

"That's good to hear." Knox squeezed him tight. "You have to be pleased."

"And relieved. I just wish we knew what was wrong with him."

"We'll help. None of you are alone in this." Knox was reassuring him as much as possible.

"I don't know how I would have done this without you."

"I do. You would have done everything you needed to do. You're stronger than you think, you know." Knox nuzzled into his neck. "Now kiss me again before we need to get up."

Charlie spun in Knox's arms so they were lying flush against each other. "Gladly."

The moment Matt's eyes opened, he was grinning. "Morning, Charlie Choo. Did you have a good night?"

"I thought it was me who was supposed to be asking you that." Charlie reached over and hugged Matt tightly. "How are you, Minx?"

"I had a good night's sleep, and my magic was stable." Matt's face fell. "I have more tests today though. I'm not looking forward to them."

"I would be with you for them if I could, but I'm guessing they won't let me."

"No, they won't. There's too much of a risk of my magic going bananas and hurting you. I would love to have you there for support, but I'll just have to think about you instead."

"You know I've been thinking of you." Charlie pulled the seat in close to the bed and took his friend's hand.

"I imagine I might have competition in your thoughts though." Matt looked around. "Where is Knox anyway? Did you leave together?"

"We did. He spent the night."

Matt sprayed out the sip of water he'd just taken. "How about you warn a guy next time."

"Where would the fun be in that?" Charlie chuckled.

"Are you telling me you slept with Knox last night?" Matt checked.

108

"Yes and no. We went to sleep, but we didn't do anything more than kiss. He was the perfect gentleman."

"I can see a little pouting going on there." Matt pointed to Charlie's face.

"I wanted to do more, but I also know it wouldn't have been right. I was, and still am, too upset about you. It would have been about seeking comfort, not about us. I loved being held in his arms all night long though. That was incredible enough."

He must have had a look on his face, because Matt was shaking his head at him. "Oh, you have it bad."

"I do. I admit it."

"I think you'll find he's quite taken with you as well." Matt winked. "I'll tell you what though, all the Knox brothers are good looking. At least, I'm guessing Tyler is, based on the others."

"He is. I met him and Cora last night." Before Charlie could say anything else, a nurse breezed in.

"Good morning, Matt. I'm Tomas. I'll be your day shift magical nurse. Now, we need to prep you for some tests, so I'm sorry to say your friend here is going to have to leave."

Charlie gave Matt one last hug, then stood. "I'll pop around as soon as I've shut the shop. Be good, and do as you're told, you hear me?"

Matt rolled his eyes. "Yes, Choo, I'll be good, but only if you dish up the gossip later."

"I will, I promise." Charlie waved and walked out the door, reassured by the visit.

The day had been busy enough, but not so busy he hadn't been able to finalize the plans for the party. He hated thinking of happy events when his friend was still suffering, but Matt would be the first to tell him off if he forgot about the event. He'd spent the day liaising with Casper at the blood bank to make sure they had enough synthetic blood. Sam's nephew, Forrik, a detective with the Corent police department, was designing the crime scene for him, and his partner, Josie, was going to place the blood as she was one of the forensic techs for the police. He'd ordered all the books, and the flyers, and invites had been delivered. There was nothing else to be done but wait. Unless Knox wanted other changes.

They'd texted a couple of times throughout the day, mostly with Knox checking up on Matt, but also random conversations. He wanted to see Knox again, yet was nervous to ask. He didn't want Knox to think that he only wanted him for the support. It was so much more than that.

A high-pitched giggle drew him to Danny. "What's up, Danny?"

Danny pointed to the window. Disbelief rocked through Charlie. Framed by the window, Knox was dancing about with Cora. Her long curls were flowing out behind her as Knox spun her around.

Oh, hot damn, he looked fucking sexy today. Knox was dressed in pale jeans that molded to his thighs, accentuating every curve, and cupping his bulge perfectly, at least as far as Charlie could tell from that distance. He wore a plaid shirt that was rolled up, exposing his forearms, revealing a smattering of hair and Charlie couldn't help but lick his lips. There was something about a man's forearms that Charlie found intensely irresistible.

"They're dancing, Danny." Charlie scooped up his nephew and, holding him against his hip, moved to the doorway. Leaning against the frame, he watched them dance about as music played out of the café's outdoor speakers. Sam and Alfie were clapping and cheering them on, and Tyler stood to one side, shaking his head. When he spotted Charlie in the doorway, he walked over.

"Who is this delightful bundle?"

Danny giggled.

"This is my nephew, Danny." Charlie tickled Danny.

"Ah, Lane's boy."

"That he is," Lane himself called from behind them. Leaning over Charlie's shoulder, he brushed a kiss on his son's head before he turned to Tyler. "How are you?" He pulled him into what Charlie called the classic guy clench. "Uh, what is your brother doing?" Lane was shaking his head.

"Dancing, I think." Tyler pursed his lips. "Damn idiot has been in a good mood since we got back." He stared at Charlie accusingly. "It's all his fault."

"What did I do?" Charlie spluttered.

Lane snorted, and Tyler shook his head. "He's happy because you went out on a date with him. Damn, I'd say you're almost as much of an idiot as he is."

"Hey!" Charlie protested. "Why do I get called an idiot?"

Lane lifted his son from Charlie's arms. "Maybe not an idiot, but I would definitely say you're currently a bit loved up. You have that secret smile. You're alternating between that and the frown when you think of Matt. Your poor emotions, and facial muscles for that matter, are suffering from whiplash."

Tyler snorted. "Nice one."

"We aim to please." Lane blew on his knuckles, then pretended to polish them on his sleeve.

"Would you stop teasing my poor brother," Evie scolded as she joined them. "What are we looking at— oh! Hot damn, the man can move." She shared a look with her brother.

"Hey!" Lane complained.

"What? He can move," she insisted. "He's much better than you are." She shrugged. "I love you anyway."

"You'd better," Lane grumbled, making Charlie laugh.

Just then, as Knox spun his sister, he caught sight of the group in the doorway, and his already smiling face deepened into one of absolute joy. Cora held her hand out to Tyler.

"Dance with me," she called out.

"M'Lady, it would be my honor." Tyler gave a dramatic bow and moving forward, grabbed his sister, and immediately dipped her, making her giggle.

Knox's gaze never left Charlie. "May I have the honor of this dance?"

Charlie's own smile reacted to the happiness on Knox's face. "You may." He held out his hand, trying not to sigh as Knox grabbed on. Knox pulled him close before spinning him back out and twirling him around. Dancing with Knox lifted Charlie's spirit. The stress of the day lifted from him. The worry of what was going on with Matt, the organizational issues of the party, everything disappeared, and just the fun of the moment remained. When the music finally stopped, he was breathless, and not only from the exertion of the moment.

"I was thinking we could go and see Matt, then I wondered if you wanted to go for a run?"

"A run?" Charlie stopped dancing.

"Yes, in tiger and unicorn form." Knox smiled down at him.

"Really?"

"Do you not want to?" Knox reached out and traced a path over Charlie's cheek.

"I would love to." Charlie cocked his head to one side for a moment. "Are you going to chase me?"

"My tiger would love to chase you. He loves the thrill of the chase. He's playful when he wants to be. He's eager to meet you and your unicorn."

Charlie stared into Knox's eyes, searching for something, anything. Years of worry about exposing his unicorn, about hunters, had him worried about ever showing his inner beast. But then, this was Knox, who had shown him nothing but compassion, friendship, and the chance for more. Knox didn't say anything, he just waited Charlie out. Knox waiting, his lack of attempts at persuading Charlie, and Charlie's instinctive trust in the man himself convinced him all would go well. "Okay." He breathed out a long sigh.

"Okay?" Knox's dimples appeared.

"Yes, I'll run with you. But only after we've checked on Matt. That has to come first."

"I planned on that. We can go there first and run in the forest afterward. That is, unless there is anything we need to stay at the hospital for. We will, of course, postpone it if we need to."

"Thank you." Charlie wrapped his arms around Knox, soaking up his warmth.

"We'll shut up the shop," Lane called from the doorway.

Charlie hid his head in Knox's chest. "I can't believe I forgot we have an audience."

"We both did. You probably don't want to look at the grins on their faces right now."

"You're right, I don't."

"Then let's go and visit Matt. Do you need anything from the shop?" Knox's voice was slightly muffled against his head.

"No, my keys and phone are in my pocket. Everything eise can wait."

"Then let's run." Knox gently wrapped his hand around Charlie's and nodded.

When Charlie returned the nod, Knox spun on his heel, and broke into a run, Charlie barely a heartbeat behind him.

"Hey!" Evie called, "You're chicken, you know that, Charlie?"

"Close the shop for me, sis! Love you!" Charlie yelled.

"No, you don't!" Evie bellowed right back. "Or you'd let me have my fun."

Charlie kept running.

Matt peered closely at Charlie. "Why do you look all sweaty?"

Orin, the evening shift nurse that Charlie had already met, was shaking in the corner with suppressed laughter.

"Eh, maybe you don't want to answer that." Matt grimaced.

Charlie snorted. "We ran away from both families."

"Huh, that will do it. Especially if the Vaughns are anything like Evie and Lane." Matt looked a little brighter.

"Is there any news?" Charlie looked from Matt to Orin.

"We're still waiting on test results, but Matt's vitals have been getting better. He's stable, and his magic hasn't so much as peeked out to say hello."

"That's good. How long do you think he'll need to stay here?" Knox moved over to talk to Orin.

Charlie watched as Matt's gaze bounced between him and Knox. "Have you spent any time apart yet?"

"Yes!" Charlie shook his head. "I've been at work all day, I'll have you know."

"Is everything ready for the release day party?" Matt looked crestfallen. "I'd better be out of here by then. If not, you're going to have to stage a jailbreak."

Charlie snuck a look to make sure no one was watching them. "I promise I'll get you out of here for it. Although, hopefully, you'll be out of your own accord and we don't need to resort to shady tactics to manage it."

"If he's good, behaves, and does as he's told, I'll make sure he gets out for your event," Orin called over.

"Shit, he heard us!" Matt hissed.

"How?" Charlie looked stunned.

"You weren't as quiet as you thought you were." Knox shook his head at them both, and Charlie was sure they look like a pair of kids trying to steal an extra cookie before dinner.

"Oops." Charlie tried to pull off as innocent an expression as possible, but from Knox's expression, he really wasn't buying it.

"Are they always like this together?" Orin asked.

"I haven't seen them together enough to be sure." Knox studied them carefully. "I can only imagine they are worse though."

"I'm insulted," Charlie insisted.

"No, you're not, because you know it's true." Knox winked, his dimples on full display.

"It's not fair. How can you be angry with dimples like that?" Charlie turned to Matt. "How will I ever win an argument against them?"

Matt sighed dramatically. "You're doomed. You might as well accept it now, and try and come up with your own secret weapon."

"Oh, I like that idea." Charlie sent Knox a smirk. "I'll have to see what I can do."

"Be afraid, man, be very afraid." Orin clapped Knox on the back.

"Be good, or we won't be going out to play." Knox tried to act stern.

"You're the one who suggested it!" Charlie protested.

"Suggested what?" Matt's head was going back and forth between the two men.

"He wants to go out for a run after we've visited with you."

"In animal form?" Matt's eyes widened. "You're going to show him your unicorn?"

"I am. My unicorn wants to meet him. He's not scared of being around his tiger at all." Charlie was surprised himself at that, and judging by the look on Matt's face, he was gobsmacked.

"Damn. That's big." Matt turned to pin Knox with his gaze. "I hope you realize how privileged you really are getting to see his beast. Charlie always has to be careful. You'd better damn well protect him. If I find out something happened and you didn't help him, you'll have me to deal with."

"And me," Mama Alice called from the doorway. "And I am far scarier than my son."

Mama Alice was right about that. She might be considered a diminutive woman, but she was feisty and incredibly powerful.

"I promise, I'll look after him. If you're that concerned, I can ask my brothers to run with us? They'll keep out of our way, yet still be on guard," Knox offered.

"Mama Alice, I'm capable of looking after myself. I know you're worried anytime I shift, but please, trust us." Charlie really didn't want any sort of chaperone.

"Fine, but so help you, Knox Vaughn, if anything happens to our boy here, you'll face my wrath."

"Yes, Ma'am."

"I like that boy. He has manners." Alice kissed Charlie on the head before leaning down and embracing her son. "You're looking better tonight."

"I'm feeling it. Bored, but I guess if I have the strength to feel bored, that's a good thing." Matt looked at Orin as if he wanted the reassurance.

"It is." Orin looked up from his machines.

Charlie lost track of how long they chatted, enjoying merely spending time with his friend. Matt, ever one to take advantage of a situation, took immense pleasure in talking about which nurses were hot, which were evil, and which were lovely.

It wasn't until a hand went to his back that he realized he'd been lost in the moment with Matt. He looked up to see Knox smiling down at him.

"You missed all that. Orin was just saying Matt's dinner will be here any minute. You want to get out of here for a bit?"

"Wow, I didn't realize so much time had passed. Sorry."

"Nothing to be sorry for. I wouldn't have bothered you, but we're being thrown out."

"Asked to leave, nicely..." Orin scoffed.

"Yeah, okay, nicely." Charlie shrugged. "End result is the same. We need to leave."

"You do. I promise we can come back whenever you want. I can come with you, or you can come by yourself. Whatever is best for the two of you." Knox wrapped his hand around the back of Charlie's neck, his thumb rubbing back and forth along the edge of his hairline.

Charlie's eyes fluttered slightly at the sensations. Matt was smirking at him, and he stuck his tongue out in reply. "I'll see you tomorrow, Matt. Get better, and sleep."

"Do as you're told, and I'll bring you something to read." Knox offered up the perfect bribe.

"How am I supposed to sleep now?" demanded Matt. "I have to go all night wondering what you're going to bring!"

Knox chuckled. "I'll be getting a report off Orin so you know what you have to do to get the goods."

"Oh, Charlie, your new man is evil."

"I'm starting to see that." Charlie grinned at his friend.

"No, no smiling. You're supposed to be on my side." Matt crossed his arms.

"I'm on the side where you do what you're told, so you get better soon." Charlie shrugged. "That's all I want, and I'll do anything to make sure I get it."

Matt slumped. "I'll be good, I promise. Trust me, I want this sorted as well. Being here by myself is boring. There's nothing to do."

"I'll tell you what…" Knox suggested. "I'll see if my brothers are free to come around and visit you tomorrow."

"Lane will come with them if they can." Charlie was already sending a text to Lane.

"Why would they bother coming to visit me? They don't know me." Matt looked puzzled.

"They were the ones who came racing to the house, no questions asked," Charlie told him.

"They'll come because you're a decent guy, you need some support, you're Charlie's best friend, and he's my… something."

Matt chuckled at the word something. Charlie turned to Knox, "I'm just something?"

"What do you want me to call you?"

"Oh, no, I asked first. What do you want me to be?" Charlie turned around to look directly into Knox's eyes. Behind him, Matt, Alice, and Orin were rapidly whispering.

Knox pursed his lips before he seemed to come to a decision. "If you're happy with it, I'd love to be your… shit, I don't know the

118

right word. Partner, boyfriend, lover, other half, mateling, mate… I mean there's so many words to use."

"It's a bit soon to be mate, or even mateling. We're not ready to pledge our lives together yet." Charlie cocked his head to one side. "How about… boyfriend?"

"That works." Knox brushed a kiss across his lips.

"And here I was hoping that I could start planning a mating ceremony." Alice pouted.

"There's plenty of time for that, Mama." Matt hugged her.

A rattle at the door brought Matt's dinner.

"I'll be around tomorrow. In the meantime, rest up," Charlie ordered, and gave Matt one last hug before he took Knox's outstretched hand and walked out the door.

CHAPTER TWELVE

Nervous energy thrummed through Charlie. It had been years since anyone other than Matt and his family had seen his unicorn. The only thing keeping him from backing out was Knox's steady presence by his side. The area was patrolled by the FDF, or Forestry Defense Force, and there were convenient lockers all around for clothes and gear to be stored. Each one was easily spelled to someone's DNA, so they couldn't be opened by anyone else. The FDF had been created partly in response to some of the rarer breeds being hunted, but Charlie was still exceptionally wary.

"I'll protect you, I promise. You're too precious to me already to risk losing." Knox lifted their joined hands and kissed Charlie's knuckles.

"Thank you." Charlie's smile was wobbly as they stopped beside a couple of lockers.

Knox quickly stripped. "I'll go first, that way I can protect you at all times. There doesn't seem to be anyone about, but even if there is, they won't be able to tell what you are until you start shifting. Use the bell on the locker to summon the FDF if you're worried at all."

Charlie bit his lip but nodded. His heart was hammering, yet he couldn't deny the yearning in him to run free. It had been so long since he'd done more than trot around either his or Lane's house under his sister's mate's watchful eyes. The chance to run free, to feel the wind in his mane, the leaves swirling around his hooves and the smells of the forest was something he couldn't deny he craved with all his soul.

He watched as Knox closed up the locker, and with a final wink, dropped into a crouch. He was captivated by the play of muscles as Knox's anatomy shifted from that of the man to the Siberian tiger. Legs elongated, hair receded, and fur appeared. It was a seamless shift and was over in a matter of seconds. It was obvious that Knox was more than used to shifting. He could only hope that his shift was as quick.

When Knox stood on all fours and shook out his coat, Charlie got his first real glimpse of the tiger. The classic orange coat, with black stripes, stood out brazenly against the green tableau of the forest. There was nothing shy or retiring about this tiger. The fur on his face was thick and a mix of white and orange, overlaid by the tell-tale black stripes. His eyes were yellow, with coal black irises, his nose a pale pink, and his whiskers were brilliant white. He yawned wide and deep, exposing his ferocious canines, before he shook himself again. Charlie got a glimpse of the backs of his round ears, seeing the prominent white spot on the back, surrounded by black. They were ocellus or eyespots. He'd forgotten tigers had them. He turned back around, and his real eyes focused on Charlie.

Charlie immediately dropped to his knees, not wanting to stand over the beast, and held out his hand, waiting for the tiger to approach him. He took a moment to realize he wasn't shaking. In fact, he wasn't even slightly nervous about meeting Knox's tiger. He should be. This was one of the most magnificent predators in their world, the intelligence of the beast shining out from his sharp gaze. With a huff, the tiger padded forward and nudged Charlie's hand with an extremely cold nose, making him chuckle. "Your nose is cold."

The tiger tipped his head to one side, merely looking at Charlie. The tiger took the last step forward and nuzzled the side of his cheek onto the palm of Charlie's hand. The soft fur there tickled slightly. The tiger's eyes were shut, and Charlie could have sworn it was smiling. There was definitely a rumbling purr echoing around them. Knox's tiger was pushing harder and harder against his hand, and Charlie took the hint and started to give him a good scratch. The rumbling got louder and louder, the tiger pushing more and more, until Charlie fell back.

Knox's tiger sprang forward, his large paws landing perfectly on either side of Charlie. He rubbed his face all over Charlie, from his hair to the very bottom of his toes. When he was satisfied, he shifted to one side and laid his head down on Charlie's stomach, his head turning to face Charlie. His purring vibrated Charlie's body, making him laugh. He used both hands to scratch Knox's tiger, and that seemed to finally appease him. Charlie was happy to just lay there and soak up the connection with Knox, in whatever form he was in. He could have lain there for hours.

Suddenly though, the tiger's head snapped up. He went from lazy and relaxed, to full on defense in seconds. He sprang in front of Charlie, pushing him so he had the lockers at his back. It was only when Charlie heard a distinctive rustle of leaves that he realized what was going on.

When he tried to peek around Knox, the tiger snapped his head around and growled. Charlie was in two minds for a moment, but the look on the tiger's face brooked no argument, so he caved and stepped back against the lockers. His gaze was continually moving, scanning the surrounding area, trying to find out what was making the rustling sound. It didn't seem loud enough to be a large predator, but you could never be sure if it was just a large predator playing smart.

The tiger was still, coiled, and ready to spring at a moment's notice. Charlie almost felt sorry for whoever was out there, especially if they were innocent. Having a tiger chase you would not be fun. Shit, even if it were a lion or panther, it would be a close match. Add in the fact that Knox was ex-PAF and his money was firmly on Knox's side.

Something suddenly caught his attention high up among the trees. "Knox, stand down."

There was no response.

"I mean it, stand down." When that didn't work, Charlie cautiously moved forward and gently ran his hand over Knox's back.

He cautiously took another step forward until he could lean into the tiger's ear. "It's not a threat."

The tiger cocked its head to one side and studied Charlie. His posture didn't lessen from his defensive position, but he was listening. "Follow my arm, okay?" Charlie crouched down beside the tiger's head.

The tiger drew back slightly, his surprise evident.

"It's a koala shifter." Charlie grinned and waved at the koala bear in the trees.

The shifter looked warily at the tiger but waved at Charlie. In his other hand, he had what Charlie was sure was eucalyptus. With his hand buried in the tiger's fur, it was easy to tell when he relaxed. "You ready for me to shift now?"

The tiger huffed, paced around a couple of times, and then nodded.

Charlie quickly stripped, throwing everything into his locker. It was bad enough that Knox was still watching him, but the thought of the koala watching unnerved him. He peeked out the corner of his eye to see the bear had turned so his back was to Charlie. Whoever it was, they were incredibly polite.

Charlie took a deep, cleansing breath and dropped to all fours. Concentrating, he called to his inner beast, bringing it forward, letting it take control. His legs lengthened and stretched. It was a strange sensation, almost like a cramp, yet not. His muscles rippled and flexed as they grew. His body stretched and expanded. He was always confused as to how he could become so much bigger in one form from the other. There was always an explanation, but if he was honest, he'd never really listened to those lessons at school. He'd been too interested in looking at the play of Reggie's back muscles. Of course, Reggie had been full of ego and loved having people looking at him. He was all muscles and nothing else.

Keeping most of his mind shut down, he checked on the shift. He'd never found it comfortable, so he'd learned to let his mind drift onto the most random of things. *Oh good, it's almost over.* He allowed his mind to refocus as the shift finished. Knowing he was

safe, he rolled over onto his back and gave a quick wriggle to ease
the itch along his back. As he rolled back over, he stuck his forelegs
out and pushed up with his hind legs until he was standing. Tossing
his mane from side to side, he shook out the hair and heard a huff.
Whipping his head around, he saw the tiger watching him intently.
Loose strands of his hair seemed to catch the moonlight shining
through the trees, and he knew what Knox was seeing. Both his
mane and tail were brilliant white, but they had a slightly iridescent
quality to them that meant, when the light hit them, they shone
slightly with the colors of the rainbow. Tossing his head back and
forth in the moonlight was giving Knox a full display. His mane, tail,
and horn were his pride and joy. It was the same for all unicorns.

He stood still as Knox padded softly around him, huffing out. He
blew out a snort when the tiger tried to sniff his rear, and swatted
him with his tail. He turned around and snapped his jaw in warning.
With a soft growl, the tiger came padding back around, but not
before he'd head-butted Charlie softly in the side.

Charlie cocked his head to one side and let out a soft snort, his
tail twitching lazily behind him. A quiet, sharply indrawn breath
drew his gaze back to the trees. The koala had turned around and
was staring at him wide-eyed and in wonder. A huff beside him told
him Knox's tiger wasn't too happy with the development, but tough.
As a unicorn, he rarely saw others outside his own family, so the
koala, whoever it was, was unlikely to have ever seen one before. He
tossed his head, hoping the koala would interpret the motion as he
meant— an invitation.

With more caution than even Charlie would have taken, the
koala carefully climbed down the tree and approached them. His
gaze darted between the two massive beasts in front of him, his awe
at Charlie overcoming his palpable fear of Knox. Charlie swatted
Knox's body again with his tail and sent him a warning look. With a
huff, Knox dipped his giant head and settled down onto the ground,
alert yet relaxed. The koala seemed to shake a little more with each
step he took, but overriding curiosity drove him on.

Slowly, so as not to spook the tiny bear, Charlie let his head
drop, allowing his mane to cascade freely down and around him. The
koala darted a glance at Knox one last time before he raced forward,

tiny paw outstretched, and brushed it over Charlie's mane. When he looked up, there was wonder in his eyes. The little paw clasped around some of his hair almost instinctively. The bellowing, grunting call of the koala, seemed at odds with such a small animal, but Charlie guessed he was saying hello. Charlie gave a soft whinny in reply.

There was a long sigh from the koala, followed by a darting glance at Knox, before he brushed his paws through Charlie's mane one last time and ran back to the trees. Clambering up the same tree Charlie had seen him in, he gave one final wave and disappeared.

The moment he was gone, Knox was back on his feet, paddling softly around Charlie as he inspected him. He held perfectly still. No matter how much he knew Knox cared for him, this was still a predator and nature controlled much of a shifter's behavior when in animal form. He wasn't worried though, and it was barely a minute later when a cold nose pressed against his own. He slowly let his tongue unfurl, watching as Knox's tiger narrowed his gaze. He swiped his tongue over Knox's face, amusement dancing in his eyes at the put-upon look the tiger was wearing as a response.

Knox retaliated by swiping him gently on his flank and motioning for him to get moving. Tossing his head, stomping his hoof, he gestured for Knox to go first, but huffed when Knox narrowed his eyes and waited him out. Fine. It looked like he was going first. He broke into an immediate trot, his hooves finding his position quickly, even on the slightly uneven ground. As soon as he was comfortable with his surroundings, his unicorn wanted to move, and his gait shifted into a canter. The breeze ghosted along his coat and ruffled his mane and tail. Beside him, Knox kept up with his speed, loping along, ever alert and scanning their surroundings.

Charlie lost himself in the freedom of being able to run properly, to experience the thrill of new surroundings, knowing he was completely safe with Knox running beside him. With a quick glance up, checking the way was clear, he focused on the tiger beside him. They must make an unusual sight. They weren't exactly a common pairing, even considering how few unicorns there were in existence. Knox's tiger somehow managed to quirk a brow at him and challenge him with that look. Charlie huffed and broke into a gallop.

They raced through the trees, down an embankment, and ran along the edge of the river. Knox took the opportunity to splash about in the water as Charlie raced along the edge. He lost track of time, simply enjoying the exhilaration of the moment, the peace, beauty, and tranquility of the moment. Being able to run, completely free, was a joy he hadn't experienced in a long time.

Slowing down, he panted slightly, his breath fogging in the frigid air. As soon as he stopped, he took a long drink of water, enjoying the coolness as it slid down his throat. Beside him, Knox greedily drank before frolicking in the water for a moment. The river, deep enough to dive under the surface, was a massive draw to the big cat and he swam deep. When he surfaced, his face was one of joy. Knox's eyes were shut and his mouth tipped up into a wide grin. He was chuffing away at Charlie. The chuff was a tiger's greeting, one of their ways of communicating, and was a reassuring sound. They were the most vocal of cats in the wild and possessed a variety of sounds they used for assorted reasons. He couldn't remember much more about tigers, other than they were the only cats to adore water. He guessed he should research them some more.

Still chuffing, Knox padded out the water and sent Charlie an evil grin. Charlie tried to back up a little bit, the wicked gleam in his eyes warning him that Knox was up to something. Every time he tried to take a step back, a warning snarl slipped from Knox's throat as he advanced. Charlie froze, not worried or nervous, but wary, wanting to know what his tiger was up to. He tried to be sneaky and back away, but how could he hope to out-sneak the cat? He couldn't, so he merely waited Knox out.

Suddenly Knox jumped, pushing up from his back legs, front paws outstretched, and he pushed them against Charlie's side before dropping them to the ground. There was almost a smug look on Knox's face, and he couldn't work out why. What had been the point of leaping and touching him? It made no sense to either Charlie or his unicorn. In fact, the tiger was shaking with what he could only guess was laughter.

His eyes narrowed. Damn tiger was up to something. He cautiously moved forward, but the tiger was happily lying on the grass watching him... really watching him, especially his side. Why was he staring at his side? With a huff, he walked to the water, looking at his reflection. When he turned so he could see his side, he whined at Knox.

The tiger threw back his head and roared, sending birds flying from the trees. He was chuffing and looking very pleased with himself. There on his flank were two perfect and incredibly muddy paw prints. Turning, he walked towards Knox, who was happily laughing to himself. Sadly, he couldn't come close to Knox on the intimidation stakes, but he'd give it a good try. Knox wasn't bothered in the slightest. He stayed exactly where he was— the only thing moving was his eyes, which tracked Charlie as he moved.

Rather than bite Knox, although that was incredibly tempting, Charlie stalked right up to him, and then promptly flopped down beside him. He was dirty already, so it wasn't as if he should worry about his coat. As soon as he was down, Knox shimmied closer, and a huge tiger paw draped over him, the paw settling over the mark he'd made on Charlie's flank. There was something remarkably possessive about the move. Charlie found himself wondering if the tiger was loving having his mark on him. He tried not to let his mind drift to what it would be like to wear Knox's mark— the mating mark. He slumped against the tiger as best he could in this current form and let his mind drift, enjoying the moonlight dancing along the river and the occasional splash from fish and other, smaller animals. No one else came close; whether they were intimidated by the tiger, or there just weren't people around, Charlie wasn't sure.

Eventually, though, they had to move, no matter how much he didn't want to. Clambering back up, he went to nudge the tiger, thinking he might have fallen asleep, to see him watching him intently. Before he could do anything, a green Crowned Hairstreak butterfly landed on the tip of his nose. Both he and Knox froze. He cocked his head slightly and crossed his eyes, so he could see it. It was one of the green variations, and was one of the rarest butterflies there was. He had no idea if it was a shifter or not, but it was stunning to look at. The tips of upper part of the wings were a deep midnight blue, which graduated to a vibrant cobalt, and then onto a rich turquoise. He couldn't see the body, but he guessed it was a variation of blue. The tips of the bottom part of its wings were a slash of dynamic red, with longer black, stem-like appendages. The moon, by accident or some cosmic design, was bathing both Charlie and the butterfly in a moonbeam. The little antenna twitched as if saying hello, yet Charlie didn't dare move for fear of scaring it off.

Knox's grin surprised Charlie. He'd never have taken the tiger for someone who liked anything as small as a butterfly. The tiger carefully moved forward, being as slow and gentle as he knew how to be, until his nose brushed up against Charlie's. It was the closest they could get to a kiss in animal form, and there they were, bathed in moonlight, tenderly rubbing noses, with a butterfly watching over them. It was a moment that would be forever etched into Charlie's memory. There was a peace, a gentleness in that moment that restored some of his soul.

Charlie swore he could feel the butterfly dancing on the tip of his nose, but he doubted he could genuinely feel it moving. After all, the butterfly was tiny, and his skin was thick. They stayed that way for a few minutes before, with a twitch of wings, the butterfly took off. Knox let it get a certain distance away, then pretended to chase it, with soft attempts at swats and jumps. The butterfly, seemingly catching on to Knox's game, darted back and danced in front of the tiger before speeding off again. The grin on the tiger's face was massive. After the butterfly flew off, he did what could only be described as some weird tiger shuffle.

Charlie locked eyes with the tiger, let his nostrils flare slightly, took a few lengths of trotting, and broke into a gallop, racing back to the lockers. He wanted to spend more time with Knox, out enjoying the moonlit night, but it was better not to push their luck. Besides, he was sure Evie, Lane, Matt, and Alice were all wanting to know that it went okay, protective bunch that they were.

Pulling up to the lockers, he waited for the tiger's orders. While a part of him balked at that, he knew it was the smart thing. Rather than nudging him towards the lockers, Knox moved right up against him. He was rubbing himself all over Charlie's fur, back and forth, up, and down, covering every part of his skin. He tried swatting Knox with his tail, but the damn tiger grabbed the hair with a paw and rubbed it over his face. Oh, they were going to be having words once they were back in human form. If that damn man thought he could get away with scent marking him every damn minute, he had another thing coming.

Finally, Knox let him move towards the lockers and tossed his head at them. With a huff, he began the process of shifting back. Thankfully, for whatever reason, it was quicker for him in the reverse shift, although he had no idea why. It wasn't long before he was standing there, Charlie once again. Knox's tiger was pacing around him and pushing him almost into the lockers. He tapped him on the nose and tried to push him back slightly, so he could open the locker door. The tiger was having none of it.

"Damn it, Knox, what are you trying to do, get inside me?" Charlie's voice was slightly husky from lack of use, and as the words registered in his mind, he froze, wide-eyed. "Uh, I didn't mean that quite how it sounded."

Knox was shaking beside him, little chuffs streaming constantly, and it was obvious the tiger was laughing at him. As soon as Charlie was dressed, he turned and swatted at the tiger, not at all intimidated. "You are a pest."

The tiger pouted.

"No, don't you dare try and sweeten me up. You keep putting marks on me." Charlie tried to scowl, he really did, but the damn tiger was stupidly adorable as he tried to pout his way out of trouble. "Just get shifted and dressed while I check in with people." Charlie picked up his phone and grimaced at the collection of texts there. Quickly typing, not wanting to spoil the peace of the forest by dictating, he sent out a group message.

Everything went fine. I've shifted back. Knox shifting now. Stop worrying, and I'll talk soon.

Knox's shift was even faster returning to human form than it had been shifting to the tiger. What Charlie was sure was only seconds later, Knox was standing there in all his naked glory, grinning at him.

129

"I'm in a bad mood with you." Charlie crossed his arms and waited.

"No, you're not." Knox's grin deepened.

"I am." Charlie scowled. "You keep trying to mark me. With your paws, with your scent…"

"Oh, beautiful, there was no trying about it. I succeeded." Knox pulled up his jeans, but left them undone, instead choosing to stalk towards Charlie.

"What are you doing?"

"Claiming my prize for marking you." Knox's eyes still glittered with traces of his tiger. They were still predatory.

"There's no prize for that," Charlie huffed out, trying to tear his gaze away from the trail of hair running from Knox's belly button down into his jeans. Without realizing he was doing it, he licked his lips.

"You like what you see. I think you want me to claim my prize." Knox took a couple more steps towards Charlie.

"No," Charlie protested, but the breathy quality to his words gave him away.

"Liar." Knox shook his head. One more step and he pulled Charlie into his arms, claiming his lips in one swift move.

CHAPTER THIRTEEN

The PAF Para-Tone's sing "Another day, another battle, but I feel good…"

Charlie's alarm blared. He really should change the damn song, yet he couldn't deny that things were looking up in his life. He was feeling good, well, unless you included muscles that were aching. It had been so long since he'd run as much as he had last night as a unicorn. He was definitely feeling that this morning. Stretching to work out the kinks, he rolled over and sighed at the empty space in the bed beside him. Knox had only stayed one night, yet he was already missing him.

After they'd got home from their run, Knox had kissed him breathless and left. Charlie hated that he'd felt so lonely afterward. All the feelings he'd been putting off dealing with had come crashing down, and he'd sat in his overly large armchair and stared into the fire trying to process everything. Realistically, it was the smart thing to have done. He couldn't ignore everything forever, no matter how much he wanted to. He didn't want to be one of those people who gave up their friends because he'd found someone he connected with. He spent hours, curled in that chair, trying to process everything that had happened over the last week. So many conflicting emotions were playing havoc with him. Worry for Matt permeated everything, and he still hadn't really processed the fact he and Knox were becoming a thing. Despite the hours of letting his mind wander the night before, he was no closer to sorting anything out. Time. He needed to give himself time and not worry about everything until he needed to. When his snooze played on his alarm, he groaned and hauled his ass out of bed.

Taking a slightly more extended lunch break than usual, he took the chance to visit with Matt, smiling when Matt's eyes lit up.

"You'll never guess?" Matt's words were rushed the moment Charlie walked in the door.

"Nope, considering I've just walked in." Charlie moved around the bed, taking a seat, and grinning at the amount of flowers around the room. Spying the massive box of chocolates to one side, he grabbed a strawberry whip and white chocolate combo, popping it in his mouth with a groan.

"You always did love white chocolate." Matt shook his head, but picked up a cherry bomb from the box.

"What's not to love? Now, enough about chocolate and tell me what I'll never guess?"

"I had a visitor this morning." Matt looked smug.

"You've always got visitors. I'd be more surprised if you didn't have one," Charlie drawled.

"Yes, but this one was extra special."

"Oh? Some hot man?"

"Yes. Your hot man."

Charlie choked on his chocolate. "What do you mean, my hot man?"

A TALE OF TWO HORNS - HANNAH WALKER

"Knox came around." Matt's eyes twinkled with amusement at the look on Charlie's face. "Calm your bloomers, idiot. I'm teasing you." Matt was tsking at him. "He brought me a present. I made sure to grill him about his intentions towards you first though."

Charlie hid his face in his hands. "Please, tell me you didn't."

"Oh, I did. You're my best friend, no way was he getting away without being interviewed."

Charlie sighed and peeked through his fingers. "Well, did he pass your approval?"

"He did. I even decided he did before he gave me a present, so there can be no accusations of me being bribed either."

"What did he bring yo—" Memories of the promise Knox had made filtered into Charlie's mind. "He didn't."

Matt danced as best as he could, still attached to various pieces of medical equipment. "Oh, he did." He nodded to a bound file on the bedside table. "It's a novella that he's been keeping a secret. It comes out between *A Date with Death* and the next book. But this one… oh. Charlie, it's full-on romance."

"What?" Charlie's eyes went wide. "Are you telling me that Detective Callohan and the hottie Teaks…"

"Oh, yes." Matt's head was bobbing up and down.

"Gimmie." Charlie made a gesture with his hands.

"Nope. I promised him I wouldn't show it to anyone."

"But I'm not just anyone! I'm his… whatever… and you're my best friend!" Charlie spluttered.

"I don't know what to tell you. I made a promise."

Charlie already had his phone in his hand and was dialing Knox. As soon as the man answered, he was laughing.

"I wondered how long it would take for you to call me. How long have you been with Matt?" Knox could barely get the words out for laughing.

133

"Three minutes," Charlie snarled, his voice rivaling Knox's tiger's from the night before.

"Huh, that actually took longer than I expected."

Charlie had put Knox on speakerphone, and Matt chimed out, "He got distracted by chocolate!"

"That will do it." Knox chuckled.

"Enough about the bloody chocolate!" Charlie's voice rose, a slight whinny escaping on the end. His unicorn was a calm beast, most of the time, but it did react when Charlie got angry, filling his mind with mental pictures of skewering people with its horn.

"Charlie, sweetheart, your copy is waiting at home for you." Knox was still chuckling.

"What?" Charlie snapped.

"You really think I would give one to Matt and not you?" Knox sounded offended even as he was still laughing.

"I… I wasn't sure." Charlie huffed out a breath.

"Well, then, you're being stupid. Of course, I'd give you one." There was a pause. "I mean give one to you."

Matt sent his water everywhere at Knox's comment.

"Shut up, Matt," Knox growled. "Hey, Charlie, Matt was in on the teasing."

"Traitor!" Matt cried out.

"I'm not going to be the only one in trouble over this," Knox retaliated. "No way, no how. We share the blame on this."

"You concocted this up between you?" Charlie's head snapped between the phone and Matt, who at least had the good grace to blush.

"We thought it would be funny and cheer Matt up."

Charlie could pick up the contrite apology in Knox's voice, but wasn't sure if he wanted to forgive him. Oh, hell. Who was he fooling? If he got the damn novella as well, of course, he would forgive Knox. "Fine." The word came out long and drawn out as he sighed. "You're both forgiven. As long as my copy is waiting for me."

"It is."

"Wait a minute… how can my copy be at home? You have no key." Charlie's forehead wrinkled.

"Uh, Mama gave him her spare key." Matt had the grace to look slightly sheepish.

"She did? Huh, I guess she must trust you, Knox. She doesn't do things like that normally."

"I am trustworthy!" Knox roared.

"But you're messing about with one of her boys," Matt teased.

"I'm not messing about!" Knox roared even louder.

Charlie and Matt shared a look, and both burst out laughing.

"What?" Knox demanded.

"No need to get defensive. Mama Alice just likes to be protective, that's all," Charlie teased. "So, if she gave you a key, does that mean you're going to be there waiting for me to get home?"

"I was," Knox grumped, "I might just have to change my mind now."

"Oh no, don't try pouting at me, you're the one that started this teasing. Don't dish it out if you can't take it," Charlie retaliated.

There was muttering down the line, and Charlie could only imagine the curses that Knox was repeating to himself.

"I'll be here. If you're nice, I might even have some food ready for you." Knox still sounded slightly put out, but Charlie would make it up to him. "I'll see you when you get home." He cut the link.

Charlie flopped back in his seat.

"He's going to keep you on your toes that one." Matt sipped at his water. "It's going to be fun to watch."

135

"You know what they say about things like that?" Charlie glared at his friend.

"No, what?"

"Be careful, revenge is at its sweetest when it's served cold."

Matt scrunched up his face. "I'm not sure that's exactly how the saying goes."

Charlie threw up his hands in exasperation. "You know what I meant."

Matt stuck his tongue out.

"Novellas aside, how are you doing? Do they have any ideas yet?"

Matt shook his head. "They keep telling me not finding anything is good. But I just can't get my head around that."

Charlie crossed one leg over the other, leaning back in his chair. "It is good. They're working on anything it could be and eliminating them. Not having those conditions is what we want."

"It is, but what if they can't work out what's wrong with me?" Matt's question tore at Charlie.

"We won't stop until we get some answers, I promise. Let's just concentrate on them eliminating what it isn't. That's something. Each thing they cross off the list is one less thing it can be. Take heart in that."

"I suppose." Matt scowled at nothing.

"I want to know you're going to put everything into getting better, Matt." The look Charlie sent his friend was one that brooked no argument. "I mean it. I need to go back to the shop, but I want you to promise me, or... I'll have to cancel the event, get Evie to take over everything, and stay here with you. And you know that Lane has only just got back."

"You are evil, Charlie Choo. You know that will get me to behave."

"Why do you think I did it? I'm not above using any means necessary, and it's best you remember that." Charlie lifted an eyebrow and waited Matt out.

"You should listen too, Matt." Orin, the nurse, was leaning against the doorframe. "He is wise for one so young."

"You're not that much older than me!" Charlie protested.

Orin shrugged as he walked in. "It sounded good. Now, Matt, if you don't do as you're told, I'm under orders from a certain man—" he sent a wink to Charlie— "to kidnap that folder right there and hide it from you. It's your choice, be good, don't complain, and let us work on the tests, or misbehave and you don't get to read that. Knox assured me it was extra spicy as well." He moved about the head of Matt's bed, checking the equipment.

"You're all ganging up on me!" Matt threw up his arms.

"Next thing you know, your—" Orin's words were silenced by Matt's hand.

"Do not say her name. She's like the bogey monster. Say it, and she will appear." Matt warily stared at the door, breathing out a sigh of relief when his mama didn't appear. "Phew, we got away with that one."

"I'm sure she doesn't just appear when you say her name," Orin teased when Matt released him.

"Oh, trust me, she does," Charlie smirked. "I don't know if she has magic tracking us or what, but she always managed to find us when we tried to hide. If we mentioned her name, she just appeared."

"Wouldn't you like to know my secrets, young man." Alice strode into the room.

Charlie had to laugh at the shocked look on Orin's face.

"I think I believe you now." He darted a glance at Alice and away again. "That's scary."

"I know, right?" Matt shook his head. "I could never get up to anything as a kiddo."

"On that note, I'm out of here." Charlie reached over and hugged Matt, brushed a kiss across Alice's head, waved at Orin, and walked out the door.

The afternoon had been long and busy. So many people had popped in, phoned, or sent messages, checking about the event. It was five days away now, and if things were picking up this much, he had high hopes for how well the event was going to go. It was almost closing time, and the shop was finally, blessedly quiet. Yet, there was a whispered frantic conversation going on. He spun around, looking into the office to see Lane and Evie arguing furiously. He didn't want to intrude, but their voices were rising rapidly.

"You only just got back!" Evie yelled.

"What would you have me do, Evie?" Lane looked exasperated.

"Stay! Be here, with the babies and me." There were tears in her eyes and Charlie really wanted to comfort her, but it wasn't his place to interfere, no matter how much he might want to.

"You think I don't want to? They're calling everyone in. There won't be a team that isn't out there looking. If something happens here, in Corent, if anything else happens, they're going to have to call in the reserves, for fuck's sake! Would you want them not to look for me? If that was me missing, if there was the potential that ferals were holding me captive, wouldn't you want them to come and look for me? How can you expect me to be any different when it's anyone else in the PAF missing?"

Lane ran his fingers through his hair. "I really wish I didn't have to go now, but I can't abandon them. I just can't. This is who I am, Evie. This is who you married. Please, don't ask this of me."

Evie broke down in tears. "I'm scared of losing you."

"I know." Lane drew her into his arms. "I know, and I wish I could fix this, make it easier for you, but I have to go."

As Charlie pulled away to give them privacy, he heard her sobbing words. "You'd better come back to me in one piece, Lane Dellon, or you'd better watch your ass. I'll be keeping hold of it for years to come."

"There's my girl."

Charlie quietly shut the door on them.

It was slightly early, but he flipped the sign to closed and shut everything down. Evie was in no fit state for anything, and he would need to be there to help her if she needed it. When the door opened and they walked out, he saw the slightly red eyes, but her brave face. He smiled softly at her, his eyes full of sympathy.

"I take it you heard some of that," Lane checked.

"Sorry, I couldn't help overhear."

"No, it's fine. I need you to—"

Charlie cut Lane off. "You know I will. I'll be here for whatever she needs. You don't need to worry about her, or the babies. I'll look after them and protect them."

Lane strode forward and wrapped Charlie into a giant hug. "Thank you. The fact you're here for her, for all of them, means everything to me. It means I can focus on the mission without worrying about everything here, knowing they are safe with you protecting them."

"Worry about coming back to them, let me keep an eye on everything here." Charlie's voice was muffled in the hug.

Lane ruffled his hair, making him scowl, before turning back to his mate. "Do you want me to take you home?"

"You need to go, I know you do. It will be just as hard if you come home. What's the point in prolonging the agony? I'll be alright."

Charlie could see his sister forcing a smile. It was tremulous, but it was there. She was a brave woman, she just needed to remember it. She needed to find her core of strength, and embrace it. He would make sure she clung to that as much as possible. He turned his back on their last embrace and closed his eyes, his own heart aching for what his sister was going through.

Looking up when the door closed, he saw Evie holding it together, just. Wrapping her in his arms, he let her cry. He knew her. She would do this and then pull herself together. It was what she did.

Wearily opening the door to his house an hour later, he'd forgotten about meeting Knox there. What he hadn't expected to see was Knox dressed in full PAF uniform. "Knox? What's going on?"

"You know." Knox walked forward, pulling Charlie into his arms. "Lane was called in."

"Yes, but's Lane's active PAF."

"They need me."

"You're going as well?" Charlie pulled back, stunned.

"I am. We need to keep an extraction route clear. I shouldn't be in direct danger, but it's better if the current members don't need to waste resources securing their return." Knox cupped his face.

Charlie's heart was hammering. If this was even a fraction of what his sister went through every time Lane went away, she had to be the strongest woman Charlie knew. He wanted to throw up, the worry curdling his stomach. Instead, what he did was summon what little strength he had, and forced himself to man up. "Promise me you'll be as safe as you can?"

"I will," Knox vowed. "After all, I have so much to come back to."

"Do you have any idea how long you'll be gone?" Charlie refused to look away from Knox, taking the opportunity to memorize every part of Knox's face.

"We hope it won't be more than forty-eight hours. I should be back in plenty of time for your party."

Charlie waved him off. "I can cancel that."

"Don't. Not until you really have to. If we can't get them back that quickly, then all hope is probably lost. Just hold off as long as you can. I want to do this for you. It will help give me something to fight for, something to make sure I come back, just to see the smile on your face."

"Come back to me, okay?"

"I promise I'll do everything in my power to walk back through this door." Knox claimed his lips in a punishing kiss. When he pulled away, he cupped Charlie's face one last time and searched his gaze. "I…" His eyes slid shut briefly, before opening, but hiding his emotions. "Stay safe."

And with those words, Knox grabbed a bag Charlie had missed by the door and walked out the house, leaving Charlie stunned and rooted to the spot, staring after him. What had just happened? How had a day that started out as if it was the start of something new and amazing, with Matt stable and a potential future with Knox, turn out to be as emotional as it was? All of a sudden, he was dealing with a distraught sister and his own fears over Knox.

Without conscious thought, he staggered into the kitchen, working by rote to make himself a cup of honeysuckle tea. Staring out the window, he pictured Knox, Lane, and all the other members of the PAF, out there, fighting. He hissed in a breath at the prospect of some of them not making it home. He never heard of the ferals taking hostages, and he wondered if this was the start of something so much bigger? As citizens, not just of Corent, but the para world, there was so much they didn't know, that was hidden from them. Was it a good thing? Who knew. If the citizens of Corent knew just how active the ferals were, there would be a lot more panic. Yet, if they did, they would surely be able to defend themselves easier, to be prepared. He didn't envy those who had to make the decisions about what to tell the general population, that was for sure.

His heart ached for his sister, knowing she went through this every time Lane went away. As if he'd summoned her, his phone rang with her distinctive ringtone. "Sis, are you doing alright, do you need me?" No matter how much he was worried about Knox, his sister needed him to be the strong one.

"It breaks my damn heart every time he goes, Charlie. How can I keep doing this?"

"Because you love him. That's how you keep doing this. Because you need him, and you can't imagine life without him in it."

"But it hurts."

"I know."

"I never know, if when I say goodbye, it's the last time I'll ever speak to him." Her voice was on the edge of breaking.

"The sad thing is, truthfully, we never know if any goodbye, if any conversation will be the last one we ever have with someone. You need to love him with all your heart, show him how much you love him. If you can't be strong for him, you need to pretend. It breaks his heart to leave you, that's obvious, but this is who he is. The only alternative is to walk away, Sis."

"What are you suggesting?" Her voice was lethal, but Charlie ignored it.

"If you're struggling to cope with him going away, then you need to walk away from your mating, set you both free, no matter how much you love each other."

"No! I'll do no such damn thing. I love Lane with all my heart." Her vehemence poured through the line.

"Then you know what you need to do, Sis. You need to pull up your big girl panties and deal with this. You need to show him you can cope. Show him that you're strong enough to deal with this. He doesn't need to be worrying about you while he's out there, and I'm sorry to say it, but while he's out there potentially fighting for his life. He needs to have his focus fully on that. Not worrying about how things are at home."

Evie was silent for a moment. When her voice came back through the line, it was ragged. "You're right."

"I know."

"Don't be an ass."

"You love me anyway," he teased.

"I really do, you know that?"

"I know, Sis. And I know it's hard on you. But you're stronger, so much stronger than you think you are. Hang onto that. Don't ever give up on that strength. That being said, I won't think you're weak if you need me to come over and help."

"No, besides, I know from Matt's text that Knox was going to meet you there. You need time to yourself, time with him."

"He was here." Charlie sighed.

"Was?" Evie picked up on his choice of words immediately.

"He's been called in."

"What do you mean, he's been called in?"

"I mean, he's ex-PAF. He and several others have been called in to help guard the extraction route. They want to make sure there is no chance of ambush by the ferals and want to get everyone back as quickly as possible."

"Holy shit, Charlie!" Evie's voice came out as a squeak. "Were you even going to bother telling me?"

"No. I didn't want you to worry about why so many were being called in, but then I realized that you would prefer to know that so many people were there to make sure that your mate got back okay. That they all come home."

"This is… I honestly don't know what to say."

"What can any of us say?" Charlie pursed his lips as he watched an owl fly through the night in the darkness of his backyard.

"I'm so torn. Don't get me wrong, I'm thrilled they're making sure there's a safe route out, but the fact they think it's needed…"

Her words trailed off, and Charlie got it. He'd never heard of them doing such a thing before.

"Then there's the fact they've called in some reserves. I know Knox has this bad-ass rep from when he was in the PAF, but come on, Charlie, this is seriously fucked up. He's been out a while, and yet they've still called him in. I'm scared. Scared for Lane, scared for Knox, his brothers, and everyone else out with them."

"Oh, shit." Charlie's eyes went wide.

"What is it?"

"Cora, Knox's sister. She's going to be on her own. If Knox has been called in, you can bet all the brothers are there as well."

"Call her. Ask if she wants to stay with you, or me, for that matter. She shouldn't be on her own. Do it now and call me back."

"Will do." Charlie cut the call off and immediately dialed Cora's number.

"Hello?" The voice that answered was both wary and slightly shaky.

"Cora? It's Charlie."

"He's not here."

"No, I know. I'm guessing they were all called in. Are you by yourself?"

"Yes." He could hear so many emotions in her voice he struggled to pinpoint just one.

"Lane's gone too. I wondered if you wanted to either stay with me, or my sister has offered you a place at hers. There are the babies to consider if you go there, but both offers are open."

"Really?" Cora's breath whooshed down the line. "I'm used to them going, but Knox is always here when the others are away. This is... I've never dealt with them all being gone at the same time, you know? I've always thought I was independent, but the minute they are all gone, I realize how much I need them."

"Cora, you're an amazing young woman, feeling like this doesn't make you weak. It doesn't mean you can't look after yourself. Those brothers of yours would never leave you alone if they didn't think you could cope, no matter what their bosses ordered. Knox, even wanting to protect your brothers' backs, would still have refused to go if he thought one of them needed to be here for you. Your brothers trust you, have faith in you, Cora. Never forget that."

"Are you sure I can stay with one of you? This house is so big and quiet without them."

"Now that is something I can easily see. They are a larger than life, noisy bunch."

Cora giggled. "You don't know the half of it."

"So where would you rather stay? If it's with my sister, I promise I won't be offended. Girl time might be good for you after being surrounded by all your brothers. Besides, I know she'd be more than happy to have the company."

"Are you sure she wouldn't mind?"

"I'm sure. She's waiting on me calling her back to tell her what's going on. Frankly, if you'd have said no, I think she would have enlisted me to come and get you. She's pushy when she wants to be." Charlie scowled, even though no one could see him.

"I'd love to stay with her. Thank you." Cora already sounded happier.

"Do you want me to come and get you, take you over there?"

"You don't mind?"

145

"Not in the slightest. I'll see you in a few minutes."

As soon as Charlie hung up, he called his sister as he locked up. This was something he could do for Knox and his brothers. Not knowing if Knox would have his phone on him still, he sent a quick text.

Picking up your sister. She's going to stay with Evie while you're all away. Stay safe. C XO

You are incredible. See you soon. Think of me. XO

When do I never? As much as Charlie wanted to reply, he knew it wasn't fair to keep Knox talking. The last thing he needed was for Charlie to distract him.

Understandably, Cora was quiet on the tram ride over to his sister's house. It was hard enough worrying about one family member, but to have to worry about your entire family? He'd meant what he'd said earlier, Cora was incredible and strong.

As soon as they walked up the path, Evie opened her arms wide and pulled Cora into them. "We can help each other through this."

Cora clung onto Evie, soaking up the maternal support. It would be good for her to have that; in a family dominated by big and strong men, having that female support would help Cora to no end.

"Charlie, you're dead on your feet," Evie chided.

Charlie hadn't realized he was swaying.

"Get home and sleep. Are you sure you're okay to open up in the morning?" Evie looked him over with a combination of maternal worry and critical assessment.

"I'll be fine. Besides, you have the babies to look after. Just promise me, the minute you hear anything, anything at all, then let me know," Charlie pleaded.

"We will," Evie assured him.

Cora spun around and grabbed hold of Charlie, holding him tight. "Thank you. I'm thrilled Knox is so taken with you. I can see why he is. You're perfect for him."

Charlie flushed but stayed silent. He gave both women a gentle kiss on the forehead and walked back down the path. Now the ladies were safe and together, he needed to process everything he was going through. That was not going to be easy.

CHAPTER FOURTEEN

Lying in his recliner on his balcony, comforter wrapped around him, hands holding onto a soothing mug of tea, Charlie stared out into the early morning sky. The stars were still out, and he found himself wondering if Knox was staring up at the same stars, thinking of him. Was he safe? Injured? D… no, he couldn't even think that word. What about Lane, Knox's brothers, all the other PAF members? The last few days had been hell, but he'd made sure to keep himself busy. The hardest times were now, when the world was quiet, and it was just him, a lack of sleep, and his thoughts. Part of him was scared at the depth of his feelings for Knox, but as Mama Alice always said, sometimes mates just knew, even if their human counterparts didn't always accept it. Could that really be what he was feeling? He blew out a breath, watching it fog in the frigid air. Who knew? The only thing on his mind was getting Knox back. Getting them all back safe and sound. With a sigh, he put his mug down, gave up trying to get to sleep, and got up. He might as well start his day early.

Three and a half days of silence. Eighty-odd hours of hearing nothing. A day and a half past the time Knox thought they'd be home. His temper was frayed, his nerves ragged, but he stayed strong for Cora, Evie, and the kittlings. They all needed him far more than he needed to allow himself to break down in worry. He'd forced Evie to stay at home with Cora and the babies. Danny, Faith, and Jasper were all missing their daddy, and concentrating on them would be good for all five of them as they waited. Sure, it left him with too much time to think. Yet, he needed to steel himself for whatever news would come their way. Goddess forbid it were sad news, he would need to be the rock the women could cling to through the confusion. He could only hope that anything forthcoming was good.

He looked around the shop, just as Casper, the vampire, walked through the door. Casper had come from the blood bank with a cooler full of bags of synthetic blood. The vampire hadn't been what Charlie had expected after their phone calls. For a guy who had been stoic on the phone, he was incredibly smiley when he got there.

"I heard you 'Vant to dwink my bwood!'" Casper's words were highly exaggerated, and he was waggling his eyebrows.

Charlie burst out laughing. "Casper?"

"In the flesh, my dear. My, my, aren't you a delicious and tasty morsel. I could just imagine snacking on you…" His eyebrow twitched as if he was waiting to see how Charlie would react.

"Are we talking my blood, my lips, or…"

"Oh, I like you!" Casper dropped the cooler on the counter and held out his hand. "Casper Vickaris at your service."

"Charlie Taylor." Charlie found himself smiling for the first time in days. "You're not what I expected."

Casper held a hand to his chest. "It's the name, isn't it? That and my pale skin. I see your mind ticking. Go on, say it… I've heard it before."

Charlie's nose wrinkled. "I'm not following you."

"With my name and my skin—" he gestured to his incredibly pale flesh— "I should be a ghost. I know, I'm cursed."

Charlie chuckled. "Is it wrong that it hadn't even entered my mind?"

"If it didn't, then I think I may love you," Casper teased. "So, what did you mean, that I'm not what you expected?"

"You just seemed a lot more serious on the phone, that's all."

"Ah, well, the boss man was looking over my shoulder when that happened. You know what bosses can be like… 'you have to maintain a corporate image.'" Casper rolled his eyes. "Here, though, I'm just me. Besides, I'm hoping if I win you over with my amazing charm you might dish up the dirt and the goods."

"Dirt and goods?"

"Firstly, I want a copy of the book. I can't wait any longer to see what happens! You have to put me out of my misery." Casper's face was pleading. "Secondly, I need to know who Davidson is. It's killing me not knowing."

"Uh, I hate to be the one to tell you this…" Charlie drawled and leaned forward conspiratorially, "But you're already dead."

Casper clasped his hands to his chest and let out a mock wail. "Oh! Woe is me! I'm a thing of nightmares! Someone save me from the damnation of Hell!"

"Always the same, Casper, you never change." A man in a suit stood in the doorway.

"Forrick." Casper's eyes sparkled. "Good to see you again." Casper's eyes raked over what Charlie realized had to be Forrick, the Corent police detective, and Sam's nephew.

"And you." Forrick strode forward and offered Casper his hand, but the vampire pulled him in for a hug.

Charlie took in Casper's hand hovering just over Forrick's ass, as if he wanted to touch it. He shrugged. Whatever was going on, he was staying well out of it. He had enough on his plate.

"I'm Josie, one of this lug's partners." A beautiful, blue-haired fae stepped forward.

"One of his partners? How many does he have?" Charlie always thought cops came in twos.

"There's me, his forensic partner, Ollie, his shifter partner for when they are after criminals, and then there's Jake, his witch partner for when he's investigating. Really, we're a unit of four, but we still call each other partners. It's just the way the force works." Josie shrugged.

"I never knew there were units like that." Charlie shook her hand.

"We're one of two units being trialed in Corent to see if it works out. They're trying to see if it helps speed up the process, from investigating, right through to a trial. They think it will help if each unit knows the case inside out. Mostly, it's designed to keep the forensic techs from getting lost in a sea of reports and not always knowing what case they are meant to be at a trial for."

"That's a clever idea, to be fair. Is it working?"

"We think so." Josie looked back at her partner, who was talking quietly to Casper. "Of course, the teammates leave a lot to be desired…"

"I heard that!" Forrick's voice carried over to them.

"You were meant to!" she called back.

Sam and Alfie joined them, Sam pulling his nephew into a hug and messing up his hair.

"Uncle!" Forrick groaned. "Will you stop doing that, I'm not five anymore, for fuck's sake!"

Sam just shrugged and did it again.

Charlie's head was bouncing back and forth, watching all the interactions. He had a feeling his day was about to get crazy. He still hadn't heard from Knox, and was guessing that he wasn't going to make it to the event, but he'd agreed with Evie that it needed to go ahead. He would face the angry customers when it came to it. He just hoped they understood.

Looking around the room, Charlie was stunned at the transformation that had occurred. Sam and Alfie had called in some friends. Witches and wizards had been stopping by all day to get things ready. They'd transformed the outside of the shop to look like a processing center in a police station. There were areas to have your photograph taken against the window. The traditional mugshot, but with a difference. The board that normally held the booking information, would hold their name, the book release date, and the booking officer's name would be listed as Detective Callohan. Each 'crime' would be listed as 'Hitting on an officer of the law' rather than hitting an officer.

The next booth along the window was where each 'suspect' could get their fingerprints magically taken and placed on a card, with the same details as the mugshot.

The last booth outside was where the visitors could pretend to be in jail, behind bars, and could again have their picture taken. The card and photographs were then given to each visitor for free, but any donations for the families of police lost in the line of duty were gratefully received. He didn't doubt that the good people of Corent would be donating lots to the fund. There were tables set up in the courtyard which had been decorated with various twinkling red, blue and white lights. The witches and wizards had gone above and beyond in their help. He owed Sam and Alfie big time for all their support.

Walking around the shop, he marveled at the crime scene Josie, Forrick, and Casper had created. The synthetic blood made all the difference. It honestly looked like someone had been killed there. Josie had assured him it would easily clean up with a simple spell, but frankly, even if he had to spend hours scrubbing it in the morning, it would have been worth it. They hadn't told him what details they had decided on for the crime. It was for the best, he didn't want to be accused of giving anyone clues.

He'd spoken to Illy at Whisps and Whirls that morning, and everything was ready for both the refreshments and the serving staff. The uniforms were also ready. That was one beautiful thing about being surrounded by paranormal beings. The uniforms could be altered by a simple spell, then changed back to their original state.

The theme of a police station carried on inside the shop, but every now and then there were flashes of the serial killer Detective Callohan was hunting, and of course the evening would not be complete without small reminders of Teaks the fireman.

Standing in the center of the room, he couldn't believe how amazing it looked. Reporters from across Corent had got wind of what was happening, and several were planning on turning up. It would be a good night, but it wouldn't be the same without Knox. Part of him struggled to think of him as the enigmatic author he'd always adored. He just missed Knox, pure and simple. Since that first text, he'd heard nothing. None of them had. He was putting on a brave face for everyone, but inside he was crumbling.

"He'll be okay, I promise." An arm went around his shoulders.

Charlie turned to look at Matt. "I'm so glad you're here." He pulled his friend into a hug. "I was so scared they weren't going to let you out."

"They have, I just have to wear this." Matt held out his arm, where a small medical device was wrapped around his wrist. "It will set alarms off if it detects my magic starting to build. Then, they'll come and transport me back to the hospital, but they insist it will help them work out what is actually wrong."

Charlie was getting fed up with the fact the hospital had ruled pretty much everything out. Nothing was making any sense as far as they were concerned. Matt was apparently a medical marvel in the worst conceivable way. "They need to be doing something soon. If Knox comes back, he'll probably put out some feelers into the PAF community. See if anyone knows what is going on."

"What do you mean *if*?" Matt demanded. "Knox is coming back. It's a when and not an if."

"It's been days, Matt."

"And? We don't know where they went, what's happening. You need to have more faith in your man, Charlie."

"I know. I do have faith in him, I just miss him, you know?"

"Good, because I missed you too."

That voice… Charlie froze, too scared to turn around. He sensed more than saw Matt step away, and a shadow move in front of him.

"Not going to say hello?" Knox was in front of him.

Knox was there! Uncaring who was around to witness anything, Charlie almost threw himself into Knox's arms, pulling his head down, and kissing him senseless. Nothing registered other than the feel of Knox kissing him. His soul soared, his heart hammered, and his mind spun. Knox was back.

The need for air finally drew them apart. It was only then that Charlie registered the whoops and catcalls. He blushed, but couldn't bring himself to care, not when his man was back. His eyes widened. "Lane, your brothers, everyone…"

"Made it safely home, with no serious injuries." Knox traced a pattern over his lower back, where his arm still rested.

Charlie narrowed his eyes. "No *serious* injuries? That means there were some."

Rather than answer, Knox held up his left arm. A left arm that was cast up to the elbow.

Charlie's eyes widened. "What happened?"

"Not here, I'll tell you later." Knox's eyes darted around, guiding Charlie, reminding him there were lots of people about.

"How serious?" Charlie ran a finger over the cast.

"I can't write." Knox looked heart-broken, and whispered into Charlie's ear, "I'm good enough with my right hand that I can sign autographs tonight, that and my signature is messy enough anyway, but I will struggle to do much else."

"We can still cancel all of tonight, or just parts of it if you want." Charlie caressed Knox's cheek, taking a moment to marvel at his presence.

"I don't want to cancel. This event and seeing you again are what kept me going. I want to do this for you."

"When did you get back?" Charlie couldn't stop touching Knox.

"Three hours ago. I got cleaned up, had a debrief, was cleared by medical, and came straight here. I needed to see you."

Charlie's heart leaped at the words. "I missed you so damn much." His gaze tracked over Knox's face. "Lane, your brothers?"

"Are all well. My brothers went with Lane to his place, to collect everyone, get cleaned up and bring them here. None of us wanted to miss this."

"You've got to all be so damn tired, though. Do you want me to postpone this for a day? It isn't a problem, I'm just glad to have you all back and safe."

"I want to be here for this. I've been looking forward to it. You have no idea how much this event is being talked about, do you? I keep overhearing snatches of conversations between the PAF guys, in the complex's hallways, on the streets, everywhere. I don't think either of us realized how big this was going to be."

"The draw is seeing you," Charlie muttered softly.

"Some of it will be to see Davidson, but a lot is the amazing event you've got planned. People have seen your flyers. Guys I know have never really read books are interested in stopping by because of what you have planned. People have this perception that books are for geeks. I think, hearing about the event you've put on has helped pique their interest and they want to come and see what it's all about. Besides, I get the impression a lot of mates are dragging their other halves here." Knox's grin made his dimples appear. His eyes flared with lust as he caught Charlie staring at him.

Charlie jumped when he was suddenly dragged across the room and into the office. As soon as he walked in, Knox slammed the door behind him and pushed him up against the frame. "I missed holding you in my arms, missed seeing your smile, running my fingers through your hair, kissing you...."

"Then why aren't you kissing me now?" Charlie's words were breathless.

"Challenge accepted," Knox muttered seconds before he claimed Charlie's lips.

The kiss was intense and devouring, and Charlie gave himself up to the sensations. Sliding a hand around Knox's waist, he hauled him tight against his body, needing as much of them touching as possible. The other hand played with the buttons on Knox's jeans, popping them one by one. His fingertips teased the exposed skin just above the line of Knox's boxer briefs. When he tried to push them down, a hand stopped him. He drew back from the kiss struggling to breathe. "Why did you stop me?"

Knox dropped his forehead to rest against Charlie's. "Trust me, there's nothing I want more, but listen."

"To what?" Charlie struggled to get his mind to work.

"To what's happening beyond the door."

Charlie forced himself to focus, to listen. "That's insane." Voices, a whole lot of voices were there. He flicked a look at his watch. "We still have an hour to go."

"That will be mostly the staff and friends who are helping out, but there was already a large group of people milling around outside when I got here. The booths you set up outside are incredibly busy. They're amazing. I could see people laughing and having fun. All the other shop owners are out there, talking to people, explaining what they sell. You've made this little section of Corent very popular. I think you might be a hero to the other shops." Knox was chuckling.

"I'm glad they're getting some benefit out of it. They're all good people." Charlie's fingers were still determinedly tracing a path along the edge of Knox's boxers.

"You need to stop, sweetheart, or I won't be able to stop pinning you to this damn door," Knox chided.

"And if that's exactly what I want?" Charlie licked his lips.

"The first time we're together is not going to be a damn quickie up against a door with hundreds of people, potentially our families, listening in on the other side. You deserve something much better than that. I respect you too much to do that."

"I want to hate you for not taking this further, right this minute," Charlie grumbled.

"But you don't, and if you're honest, you want our first time together to be in a bed as well. Just think, I can take my time kissing every inch of your body, loving it, worshiping it. Taking my time to take you to the very edge of orgasm, holding you there, deciding when I let you go over."

Charlie shuddered as Knox's words slithered other him, igniting a fire deep within him. Knowing he couldn't do anything was one thing, but he damn well had to kiss his man right then. Pushing up on his tiptoes, he pulled Knox's head back down and claimed his lips once again.

Banging on the door broke them apart. "It's time to get out here!" Nate's voice was full of laughter. "Your public awaits!"

Knox dropped his head back to stare at the ceiling as Charlie struggled to regulate his breathing. "Damn, I was enjoying that." Charlie managed a grin as Knox struggled to tuck his bulging erection properly back into his jeans and do them up. He narrowed his eyes at Charlie when he smirked. "Like you're in a much better predicament." He nodded at Charlie's own bulge.

Charlie looked down and winced as he adjusted himself. Neither of them needed to be sporting hard-ons when they left the office.

Knox tenderly stroked a hand over his face. "Come on, gorgeous, let's go and have some fun." He held his hand out to Charlie.

Laying his smaller hand in Knox's open palm, Charlie looked up and smiled. "It's going to be fun now you're here." And with that, he opened the door.

CHAPTER FIFTEEN

The shop was packed. Charlie had hoped for a decent crowd, but this certainly exceeded his expectations. The servers from Whisps and Whirls were doing a fantastic job keeping everyone's glasses topped up and the food coming. The mini cakes were incredible. Charlie was currently munching on one with a pair of handcuffs.

"You and handcuffs…" Knox whispered in his ear. "Is there something you're trying to hint to me there?"

Charlie coughed as he attempted to swallow. "That was evil."

"But funny." Knox chuckled.

"It was funny." Lane joined them.

It was the first chance that Charlie had found to see his sister's mate, and he wrapped his arms around him. "It's good to see you back safely." He looked up into Lane's eyes, seeing the creases around the corners, the bags under them. "She was okay, after you left, you know. She always is, it's just hard for her to watch you go."

"I know, it's hard for me too. I wish I could give it up, take a different job for her, but this is who I am."

"You have to know that's not really what she wants."

"What do you mean?" Lane checked.

"She doesn't want you to quit, not really. She just wishes she didn't have to say goodbye to you so much, but she does understand why you do what you do. We all do. It takes a particular type of man to put their lives on the line for others, day after day. You wouldn't be who you were if you gave it up to appease her, and she knows that. It's just harder because of the kiddos. Give her time to adjust to everything, because she will adapt. She's never going to stop worrying about you, but it will become easier for her to deal with. I promise. My sister is a force to be reckoned with."

"That she is." Lane's whole face lit up as they discussed his mate.

"Go find her and give her a kiss." Charlie winked.

"Now that's something I'm happy to do." Lane strode off with a wave.

"You ready to out yourself?" Charlie searched Knox's face for any sign of wanting to back out. "This is your last chance."

"No, I'm good." Knox reached out and threaded his fingers through Charlie's. "Let's do this."

Charlie led the way to the small platform one of the mages had added to the shop. He climbed up and left Knox to one side. Letting out a shrill whistle, he watched as the crowd fell silent. "Thank you everyone for coming to our event tonight. It's fantastic to see so many fellow sufferers who are as desperate as I am to know if Detective Delicious ever gets it together with Teaks!"

Chuckles rang out throughout the room. "They'd better, the sexual tension is killing me!" someone called from the back of the room.

"Trust me," Charlie drawled, "You aren't the only one who is frustrated. Our mysterious author might find he has a rebellion on his hands if those two don't get it on soon."

"That means the author's a guy then?" a random voice demanded, picking up on the gender Charlie used.

"Yes, it's a man." Charlie's smile was wide. "I know you're all here to get your hands on *A Date with Death*, but it's truly amazing to see so many of you here and supporting both a local, independent bookshop and a local author. I never for one moment believed our mysterious author would be a para, but I was thrilled when he responded to my pmail, and definitely stunned when he agreed to be here today for his first ever signing. I know speculation has been rife as to who is the man behind Callum Davidson, so I'm not going to make you wait any longer. May I present to you Mr. Callum Davidson, otherwise known as our very own Knox Vaughn!"

Stunned silence and open-mouthed stares greeted Charlie's proclamation as Knox joined him on the small stage. "Good evening everyone! It's great to be here, and I want to thank Charlie and Evie, the co-owners of A Tale of Two Horns, for inviting me to be here with you tonight. I can see from your faces that I've stunned you all. Yes, I truly am Callum Davidson. I'll be here signing books, but please bear with me as I'll need to write with my right hand, so will be a little slower." He held up his cast to the crowd.

Finally, Casper shouted, "Are you serious?"

"That I'm Davidson?" Knox looked over to Casper, who nodded. "I am. I know, I'm the last person you'd expect, right?"

There was a smattering of agreement from several areas of the crowd.

"Is it the fact I'm ex-PAF?"

"It's more the fact that you're Knox bloody Vaughn!" a cultured British accent called from the front.

Knox's smile was wide enough for his dimples to make an appearance and Charlie caught sight of several people within the crowd blinking as they looked at him. More than a couple had open lust in their eyes and Charlie's unicorn was sending him visions of skewering all of them with his horn. The beast was rarely violent, but was extremely protective of anything it considered his, and he definitely considered Knox Vaughn as his. Charlie dug his nails into the palms of his hands. It wasn't the done thing to attack your customers, after all. He ruthlessly forced the unicorn to the back of his mind, promising the beast they could have Knox in their arms by the end of the night. It was the only thing that worked in persuading it to stay calm.

"Why did you start writing?" a woman asked.

Knox threaded a hand through his hair and seemed to take a moment to himself before answering. "Most of you know my story, my family's story, so I don't really need to go into that. What I will say is that sleep deprivation does strange things to a mind. When I suddenly found myself in a situation where I had to look after my family, it was a living hell. I don't think I managed more than two or three hours sleep a night for months. I used to sit, holding one of my siblings as they tried to sleep and tell them stories. Only, we're the Vaughns, and my brothers in particular, didn't want your traditional stories." Knox grinned at his family gathered to one side, all there to support him. He looked back at the crowd and deliberately rolled his eyes. "Demanding bunch that they are." Chuckles rippled through the crowd. "My sleep deprived mind started to tell this story of a police detective who was chasing criminals. After what my family went through, I thought it might be reassuring for them to have this fictional character who was incredible. That, combined with the amazing men and women of the PAF who gathered around us, helped my siblings. From those early stories, Detective Callohan was born."

Knox looked at his sister, shaking his head, but smiling away. "For those of you who love the romance, the 'will they, won't they' between Callohan and Teaks... you have my sister to thank for that. She was grumbling that it was all action and nothing else. Our brothers were not too impressed when I added a potential love interest into my stories. But, at the end of the day, those early stories are what made me start to write. It helped me to keep my sanity. Ask any writer— the voices in your head, the characters, they can be very determined when they want to be. There was no one more surprised than me when the books started to become successful. All these years later, here we are with the series where it is."

Knox looked out over the crowd. "I want to thank you. *All* of you. While my family may have been the key to me starting to write, it is you, the readers, who keep me writing. It's the messages I get, the ones that tell me my books have helped someone escape from the harshness of life for a few hours. The ones that tell me that my books have kept them company while they watch over a relative in the hospital, or while they are in the hospital themselves. I've had messages from humans, cops, who have told me they love reading a story about a gay policeman. It gives them hope that they will be accepted when they finally come out to their colleagues. Hearing your stories… I will never tire of that. If there is one thing I've learned over my writing career, it's always chase your dreams and be true to yourself. Now, go and have some fun, enter the contests, especially the crime scene one. I've seen some amazing things, but this event is incredible. Charlie and Evie have gone above and beyond with this event. Take the time to do everything, look around, find new books, not just mine, talk to each other and enjoy! I'll see you all at the signing table." Knox stepped down from the small stage and turned to Charlie.

Charlie could see the relief in his eyes that the speech part was over. Exhaustion lingered in Knox's eyes, and Charlie wanted nothing more than to take him home, put him to bed, and look after him. He also wanted to look him over, see what other injuries Knox had that he was trying to hide. He wanted to hear about the rescue, check that everyone had made it home. Those questions would have to wait though. For the moment, they all needed to put that to one side and smile through this event. There would be time enough to hold Knox in his arms later.

Charlie wanted to hover, to make sure Knox was coping with the influx of people around the signing desk, but he left him to it. Although, the sheer volume of people stunned him. They weren't just selling the new book, people were buying every book in the series to get them all signed. Even people who already owned the books were buying them again.

"You already own them all," Charlie teased Tannic, a fae warrior.

Tannic stroked the cover of one of the books. "I do, but I read those, these are going on my shelf and won't be read. I had no idea Knox, a fellow PAF member, was Davidson. I'm still stunned about that. I don't know how he managed to write and look after that family of his. Those brothers must have been a nightmare. Hey!" Tannic grumbled when he was cuffed around the head.

"Why is it us that put Knox through hell? What about Cora?" Nate grumbled from beside Charlie.

"Why would that little beauty be anything other than innocent?" Charlie struggled to hold back the laugh at the look of disgust on Nate's face.

"You have no idea how she is." Nate looked serious.

Tannic smirked. "I've seen the way she has you all wrapped around her little finger."

Nate prodded Tannic in the shoulder. "Don't you start, I know your superior officer."

Tannic swallowed loudly.

"Talking of Cora… who is that she's talking to?" Tannic nodded in her direction.

Nate's eyes went comically wide and his jaw locked. "Oh, fuck no, he is not getting his claws into my sister."

"I thought Dorian was a hippo?" Tannic cocked his head to one side. "They don't have claws."

If looks could kill, there wouldn't be anything left of Tannic. Nate stomped off, his gaze never leaving the hand Dorian rested on Cora's forearm.

"Don't you think someone should warn Dorian?" Charlie looked at Tannic and Carter, who had overheard the last bit of their conversation.

"Nah." Tannic chuckled. "Fucker stole all my chips at poker the last time we played."

"I thought he flushed you?" Carter stole a cupcake from the tray of a passing waiter, biting it in half in one swift move.

"Like I said, he stole my chips," Tannic grumbled. "Oh, excuse me, I'm next."

Charlie and Carter moved to one side, out of the way of those queuing for Knox's autograph. Charlie kept his gaze pinned to Nate who was now looking contrite as Cora whisper-yelled at him. "She really does have you guys wrapped around her finger, doesn't she?"

"Like you wouldn't believe," Carter shook his head sadly. "She gets away with anything, that girl."

"I think that's only fair with so many overprotective big brothers." Charlie nudged Carter with his shoulder.

"Just wait, you'll have to deal with her soon enough." Carter waved to a waiter, grabbing one of the magical traffic light drinks. The red was berry and sparkling, the amber, freshly squeezed orange juice, the green was peppermint crushed ice. He shuddered slightly as he sipped the green layer.

"Why would I have to deal with your sister?" Charlie lifted an eyebrow.

Carter was looking at him like he was completely stupid. "Because you're dating Knox."

"And?" Charlie looked over, seeing Nate leading Cora to the makeshift drinks bar, a protective hand on her back, guiding her. He had a brief thought that it must be a family trait, as Knox's hand always rested on his back.

"Anddddd…" Carter drawled. "He always is her first port of call for anything. Considering he's going to be spending as much time with you as he can… that means you get to deal with Cora and take her off my hands."

Charlie's mouth opened and shut. "I already have a sister."

"Well, now you have two." Carter looked entirely too pleased with that fact.

"We'll see." Charlie couldn't be happier when Evie called him over, needing him to talk to reporters from The Sentinel. "I'll talk to you later, but it's good to see you back here and safe."

Charlie joined his sister, smiling at the reporter. "I'm Charlie Taylor."

"Mike Glasson. Thanks for inviting me tonight. I was just saying to your sister, this is an incredible event. You two have done an amazing job on this. I was a little wary about coming, thinking it was just going to be people in a line waiting for their books to be signed and maybe a reading. I was only coming because my editor wanted to know who the man behind the writer was. But, honestly, if this is the way you do events, then please, keep me informed of any coming up. This is simply remarkable."

"Thank you. We've tried to make it fun and based all around the series."

"The ideas outside are inspired. No one will be forgetting this for quite a while. I love how all the shops in the square have stayed open as well. They must be loving this."

"We're a close-knit group here. I wouldn't survive without my morning stop at the café." Charlie blushed slightly.

"Not a morning person?" Mike was scrawling in a notepad.

"No, he can be." Evie nudged her brother. "But he tends to stay up to late reading and loses track of time."

"I guess that's an occupational hazard then." Mike looked up from his notepad.

"It is, but I've always loved reading."

Evie scoffed beside him. "He always had his nose buried in a book as a kid."

"What can I say, I love escaping to another world. Whether it's one set in space, with aliens, in the past with epic battles, in the present with hot cops…" The three of them chuckled. "Or even non-fiction. I love the written word, the way it expands your mind. You can learn something from any book, whatever genre it is. For example, I was reading a romance series based around the homeless.

I know, you wouldn't think they were a group that could easily find love, but the author did an amazing job of educating the reader, without preaching. We don't get homeless here in the para world, but I keep hoping that it will make humans think a little more."

Charlie caught the eye of two waiters as they neared them. One was dressed as a serial killer, his cupcakes either drizzled with fake blood, or tiny weapons on them. The other was dressed as Teaks, in turnout gear. He was carrying a tray of drinks in mini hydrants, the yellow hydrants contrasting well with the blue raspberry drink inside with white ice stylized as fire extinguishing foam floating on top.

"The attention to detail is incredible." Mike stared in wonder at the drinks.

"Thank you. Whisps and Whirls have been amazing at helping me get the food and drinks right, and their servers are perfect." Charlie smiled at the two waiters. "Have you had a go at the crime scene?"

"That's my next stop. In fact, if you don't mind me checking in randomly throughout the evening, I'll have a wander around." Mike's gaze was darting everywhere.

"Of course, feel free to find us at any time." Charlie gestured to the crime scene, where lots of people were gathered, trying to make their guesses. "Don't forget to have a guess."

"This is where I wish I'd done a beat as a crime reporter." Mike chuckled as he wandered off.

As soon as he was gone, Charlie leaned into Evie.

"Tired?"

"Emotionally wrung out," Charlie admitted.

"It's hard to keep that smile on your face all the time, isn't it?" Evie sympathized.

"More than I ever realized. You do an amazing job, Evie, I know I've told you that before, but perhaps I haven't told you enough."

"You have, but it's always nice to hear." Evie kissed the top of his head. "You holding up, seeing him injured, and not knowing what's going on?"

"Barely. I've seen him wince a couple of times, and it scares me that he's hiding a lot of other injuries." Charlie watched Knox, smiling and joking away with his fans, but there was a tightness around his eyes that worried Charlie.

"You're in deep already." Evie scanned his face.

"What? No, I'm not," Charlie protested.

"The fact you were so quick to answer, and knew exactly what I meant by that says everything, oh brother of mine."

"How can I be? I haven't known him that long? I can't possibly be in love with him." Charlie's breathing started to pick up speed.

"I didn't say you were. But you have to consider the possibility that you might be forming a mate bond. You said your unicorn accepted him completely."

"He did. We ran, we played, everything. His tiger marked me." Charlie's eyes unfocused slightly as the memory played out in his mind. A sudden flare of pain in his arm pulled him back to the here and now. Evie was dragging him off to one side.

"What the fuck do you mean, he marked you?" She hissed, her nails breaking through the skin on his arm.

"Woah, calm down, Sis. He slammed his muddy paws onto my side, leaving the impression of his pawprints. That's what I meant. He didn't *mark me*." Charlie gently pried her fingers from his arm.

"Shit." Evie braced herself against the wall beside the office. "Don't bloody do that to me. I wanted to throttle him for doing that to you without doing things properly."

"Sis, I love you, but I am capable of making sure he courts me properly. If he does decide, if we decide that mating is something we want to do, it will be done properly." Charlie leaned against the wall beside her. "It's too soon to know whether it's something I'll consider."

"I knew with Lane straight away." Evie rolled her head to look at him.

"Maybe you did, but you had the benefit of both of you being unicorns. We're mixed species, Sis. You know that isn't always easy to work out, mating wise."

"Would you want to?"

"I don't know." Charlie looked inside himself. If he was honest, at least with himself, then yes, he really could see himself with Knox, long-term, mated, the works, and that scared him more than anything else had in a long time.

CHAPTER SIXTEEN

Charlie pushed everything else from his mind and focused on the event— that was what was important right now. Walking over to the crime scene area, he listened in on the various conversations around him. People were still talking about the fact Knox was the author. He was getting the distinct impression that would be a source of gossip for a long time to come. Not just because it was Knox, but because Davidson had finally been unmasked as a para.

"How's it going?" He leaned in to whisper to Josie, so he didn't disturb those concentrating on the staged scene in front of them.

"No one's guessed correctly yet," she whispered back. "There are several who have come close, though."

"Do you know, I'm not actually sure what you went with in the end."

"Because that way you can't give anyone any clues by accident, or be accused of doing it." While she talked, she was watching someone studying the scene. "Huh."

"What?" Charlie followed her line of sight.

"He's the only one who has done that."

Charlie studied the man squatting on the floor. "Done what, you've lost me."

"He's crouched down, looked at eye level, been up on tiptoes, looked at it from all angles and heights. See the thing about blood spatter is that it can be incredibly complicated. Yes, you can follow the trail of drops, but drops can drop on other drops. The victim can be moving as they are struck… there are lots of factors that complicate an analysis. The way he's studying it he looks like he has a good eye for detail. I can't wait to see what he comes up with."

"Want me to go spy and see what I can find out?" Charlie offered.

Josie's eyes lit up. "Would you?"

"Back in a few." Charlie walked over to join the man. "Hey, having fun?" He squatted beside him.

"Oh! Hello. Sorry, I was in a world of my own there." The grin directed at Charlie was sheepish.

"Intent on winning the signed box set and dinner with the author?" Charlie teased. He still wasn't happy at the thought of Knox going out for dinner with a fan, but that was the jealous part of him talking. Adding it as a prize had certainly attracted a lot of attention. More so now people knew it would be with Knox.

"I would love talking to him about books, but I love solving puzzles as well and this is nothing more than a giant puzzle."

"I'm Charlie by the way." Charlie winked.

"Seth." He shook Charlie's hand.

"So, what do you do, Seth?" Charlie stood up, Seth following a moment later.

"I work at the lone shifter sanctuary. I'm one of the housemasters there. I take care of the small shifter house. So, butterflies, house cats, ducks, those sorts of shifters."

"If you don't mind me asking, are you a shifter yourself?"

"I am, and I have a confession." Seth's cheeks heated.

"Oh?"

"I saw you in your shifted form." Seth pitched his voice as low as possible.

"You did? When?" Charlie's heart picked up speed.

"Don't panic. Would it help if I told you I was a koala shifter?"

171

"Oh! That was you?"

"It was, and you are stunning. I don't think I've ever seen a shifter as beautiful as you were," Seth confessed.

"Not trying to muscle in on my man, are you?" Knox appeared behind Charlie, wrapping his arms around his waist.

"Hey, you on a break?" Charlie leaned back and kissed Knox's neck.

"There's only so much signing I can do right handed." Knox looked over at Seth. "Well, are you trying to get my man?"

"Behave," Charlie chastised. "Seth here saw us on our run."

"He did?" Knox raised a brow.

"Remember the koala?"

"Ah." Knox grinned. "I hope my tiger didn't scare you."

Seth shook his head. "I was just saying how beautiful he was."

"That he is. Now, have you any ideas on the crime scene here?" Knox nodded towards the closest spatter pattern.

"I think so." Seth squatted back down.

Charlie beckoned Josie over.

"There's a fair amount of blood, which makes me think there were cuts, so I'm thinking because we're paranormal, it's a shifter. There's quite a bit of what I think might be cast off patterns on the walls, and there's some smeared marks on the wall by the door that look like they could have been done by fur as someone moved. There's a pattern to the drips on the floor— most of them are circular and I'm thinking that is a drip stain path from claws hanging down."

Charlie cast a quick glance at Josie to see her eyes shining. He wondered if that meant Seth was getting it right.

"There's a tiny print I can see hiding just under the chair over there, and a couple of drips leading up to it."

"Which tells you what?" Josie leaned in, obviously eager to hear the answer.

Seth looked around for a moment, letting out a startled 'eep' when Josie dragged him off to one side.

"Tell me what you think." Josie's look was intense.

"Like I said, the volume of blood made me think of cutting wounds, and because of where we live, I think we're looking at a shifter. I think they made repeated strikes on the victim because there are cast off patterns where the claws must have already been coated in blood. There's a gap in the spray pattern on the wall."

"Which means?" Josie prodded.

"I think the victim had his back to the wall for at least some of the fight. There are bloody smears made by fur, a small paw print, lots of drips and drip stain patterns, cast off patterns..." Seth trailed off.

"So, who do you think did it?" Josie pushed.

"I think the victim might have been an adult shifter, looking by the void pattern on the wall. But, looking at the height of the cast off patterns, the bloody smear, and the size of the print... I believe the attacker was a small shifter. I'm guessing they attacked our victim on the legs in particular. We should be looking for a small shifter with claws. I'm thinking something like a fox that has retractable claws as the paw print doesn't have claw marks. It's the only thing that makes sense given the height of the blood spatters."

Judging by Josie's smile, Seth was very close, if not exactly right. "I can't say for definite, but right now, you are most definitely in the running to win."

Seth did a large fist pump before blushing again.

"Now, how about you find me after the winner is declared. I have a feeling I want to chat with you a little more."

"Oh?" Seth looked to Josie in confusion.

Josie patted Seth gently on the cheek. "I like the way your mind works." She nodded to someone in the distance. "I'll see you all later. Someone wants to record their entry. Seth, I've recorded yours." With that, she was gone.

Seth was standing there looking confused and lost.

"Are you okay?" Charlie steered him to a quieter side of the room.

"I, yes, I think so? What was all that about?" Seth watched Josie's retreating form.

"I think Josie was impressed with you."

"Oh, does that mean I got the scene right?"

"I have no idea, I don't know the answer, but I'd say you did, or close to it." Charlie watched Seth take off his glasses and wipe them on his sweater. He huffed out a breath when they slipped down his nose slightly the moment he put them on.

"Are you signing again?" Seth's gaze darted to Knox before he looked away again.

"I am, but if you want to wait until the end, I don't mind. From the way Josie reacted, you might be winning a set." Knox grinned.

"Would that be okay?"

"Of course."

"In that case, I think I might go and wander around and get a drink. They do look delicious." Seth looked longingly in the direction of one of the waiters.

"I'll see you soon, if I don't see you later." Charlie dug a card out of his wallet, passing it over. "If you want a place to hang out, just give me a call."

"Really?" Seth seemed surprised.

"Really, my unicorn likes you, so whichever form you'd rather, I'd be happy for that."

Seth clutched the card to his chest. "Thank you!" With a small wave, he went off in search of a drink.

"Found a friend?" Knox asked as he nuzzled into Charlie's neck.

"I think so." Charlie grinned, laughing when he felt Knox's deep exhale over his skin.

"I'd better get back to it. Come and rescue me soon?"

"I promise." Charlie turned and gave Knox a quick kiss before watching him walk away, his gaze fixed to Knox's ass.

Concern radiated from Charlie. Knox looked exhausted. The evening had gone well, but he was glad, for Knox's sake, that it was almost over. They'd drawn most of the contest winners; it was just the crime scene left. He focused on Josie up on the small stage.

Josie's gaze searched the crowd as if she was checking that the winner was there. "When we got word about this event, we weren't sure how this would play out. Solving crime scenes isn't as easy as some people think. Although, I will say Knox here does an amazing job of describing them in his books. What I've been impressed about is how everyone took the time to really look at what they were seeing, taking time to study it. Having spoken to Charlie, Evie, and Knox, we've decided to add a couple of extra prizes for some honorable mentions. There are a couple of people who, while they didn't win, they were close and noticed things I thought would be missed. Daniel S., Sally Q., and Shan V., you've all won a signed copy of *A Date with Death*. If you've already purchased one, please see Charlie and he'll refund you."

Charlie watched as Josie's gaze landed on Seth.

"Now, the winner. What I want to say is he noticed things that even some professionals may have missed. He made sure to look high and low, under things, on things, everywhere, not just where our body outline was. Yes, he missed a couple of things, but they were minor. You never know, I might actually try to recruit him!" Laughter followed her statement. "Without further ado, Seth T., congratulations on winning the boxset and an evening with Knox here!"

The crowd turned to look at Seth, and he flushed so red Charlie thought he would go up in flames. "T-thank y-you," he stammered out.

Charlie stepped up to join Josie. "I want to thank all of you for coming by tonight. It's been amazing seeing you all here. I'd like to think I can persuade Knox to do another event for his next release. I guess time will tell."

"Kiss him! I bet that works!" Matt yelled from the back of the room.

"You just had to say something, didn't you?" Charlie groaned, hiding his face in his hands, making everyone laugh.

"Don't knock his suggestion. It probably would work." Knox smiled as he joined them.

"We're going to finish up everything that's been officially planned for the evening, but we'll be here for another hour. Feel free to finish off the fantastic treats from Whisps and Whirls and I'm about if anyone needs any book recommendations. Most of all, I want to thank everyone for coming. It's you who make these events special. It's the readers, the fans, that I do these for. I hope you've all had fun."

There were a series of whoops and hollers which Charlie took as a yes. "I'd like to thank everyone who helped out with tonight. From Whisps and Whirls, to Casper and the blood bank, Sam and Alfie, the Corent Police Department, my sister, all the mages who helped with the effects, and the volunteers who manned the booths outside. But, most of all, I want to thank Knox, or rather Callum Davidson. Without him, none of this would have been possible." Charlie turned and trying to be respectable, he held out a hand to shake.

Knox, however, had other ideas and pulled him in for a kiss, much to the delight of the crowd.

CHAPTER SEVENTEEN

Being a member of the PAF family certainly had its advantages, that was for sure. He was lucky most of the members would do anything for Knox, especially as he'd stepped up when needed, donning the PAF uniform the moment he'd been asked. Ford, one of the mages, had happily transported them to Knox's house. It was strange, Charlie hadn't actually been there yet, and was nervous at being inside Knox's room and facing all the siblings again.

Waving goodbye to Ford, he raised his hand to knock on the door. Knox was draped over him and half asleep, and the man weighed a damn ton. Before his knuckles landed against the wooden door, it opened, and Tyler rushed out, taking Knox from him. As soon as he cleared the door frame, Nate was there supporting his other side.

"We'll get him upstairs if you want to follow us," Nate called out to him, already helping to maneuver Knox up the stairs.

"Here, carry this." Carter shoved a box into his hands as he ran up the stairs after his brothers.

Charlie looked at the box in his hand, completely bewildered for a moment. Max wrapped an arm around his shoulders and pulled him along. "What's going on?" he mumbled.

"Carter wants to fully check Knox over. He shouldn't have done the event tonight, but my fool of a big brother insists he knows what he can handle and what he can't."

"Oh shit. He's a lot worse than he's been letting on, isn't he?" Charlie's arm shot out, grabbing for purchase on the wall.

"Hey, calm down!" Max steadied him. "Yes, he's worse than he told you, but he isn't that bad. Knox gets away with a lot as big brother, but if he'd been that bad, we wouldn't have let him do it, even if the doctors had discharged him. He's exhausted and suffering. He hasn't had any sleep in over forty-eight hours. That's going to be affecting his mind and we can't be sure he doesn't have any hidden injuries. Now, stay calm, and let's help Carter check him out. I promise you can help keep watch over him all night. If you want to, that is."

Charlie's head snapped around to stare at Max, anger clouding his vision. "Of course, I want to look after him." His unicorn was snorting inside his head.

"Woah, take it easy. I didn't mean anything by it." Max held his hands up, palms out, trying to placate him. "Not everyone wants to look after someone who is sick or injured."

"Yeah, well, I'm not one of those people." Charlie's face looked thunderous, his eyes flashing with anger at the implication in Max's words. "I don't abandon my friends and I damn well don't abandon anyone I'm seeing."

Max grabbed hold of Charlie's arm, stopping him going anywhere. "I get that. I should have known that because of Matt. I am sorry, Charlie. I honestly didn't mean to imply anything. He's my big brother, you know? He's this rock in all our worlds. He's been the one stabilizing force since we lost our parents. He gave up his active PAF status for us so we wouldn't worry. Seeing him hurt, on the first time he's been called in for as long as I can remember, has shaken us all to the core. He's like a father-figure to us, even though he's just our brother. It's not right to see him hurting. I'm scared stiff it's something a lot more serious than he's letting on."

"You told me not two minutes ago that he wasn't that bad?" Charlie was confused, emotionally raw and at the end of his tether.

"And he isn't that bad." Max pinched the bridge of his nose. "I know that intellectually."

"But emotionally it's another matter?" Charlie guessed.

"Exactly." Max looked up the stairs. "Cora is worried sick. I know we all looked like we were having fun at the event, but the Vaughns have an incredible game face. We can hide shit like you wouldn't believe. People have this perception of what we're like and we prefer to maintain that. It stops people messing with us. We may all be PAF now, but back then, I was this weedy little cub, and the bullies thought I'd be an easy target. No parents, tiny guy, well, you can guess. The only thing was, I may have been small, but we'd been taught from an early age how to defend ourselves. I may have ended up with a broken nose—" Max touched a small scar in the middle of his nose— "but the bullies came off a lot worse. I know you're probably wondering why I'm telling you this."

"A little." Charlie winced apologetically.

"It's because you need to know, Knox has learned to hide things. Not just from those in the PAF, the community, but from us as well. It was a tough time when we lost our parents, and us younger cubs were paranoid we were going to lose him as well. He hid anything even remotely wrong with him, so he didn't scare us. Whatever you do, look at him, listen to what he doesn't say, rather than what he does say. He won't tell you if he's struggling. He never has, never will. But promise me, you'll look after him? He needs to know he has someone he can turn to, even if he never does it."

Max's genuine concern for his brother warmed Charlie's heart. "I swear I'll look after him. I don't know where exactly all this is going between us, but I promise I want to work with you guys where it comes to him, not against you."

"I know where it's going." Max smirked, ignoring Charlie's questioning look. "Come on, let's go and see what's going on." He didn't wait for Charlie to say anything else, just jogged up the stairs.

Charlie walked into Knox's bedroom for the first time, but saw nothing but the man in bed. His face was set into a deep scowl, and he was staring Carter down.

"I'm fine!" The roar held tinges of his tiger and shook the windows.

"You are not fine, for fuck's sake," Carter snarled right back. "Let me get a good look at you."

"No. I've told you, there's no need." Knox was not backing down.

"Hey," Charlie called from the doorway before it could degenerate into a full-scale argument.

"Charlie!" Knox's entire expression relaxed, and he beckoned him over.

Charlie perched on the edge of Knox's bed and ran a fingertip down his face. "Knox, can you do me a favor?"

"Anything," Knox quickly vowed.

"I know you're alright, that the doctors checked you out and everything. But this is me, and I'm still worried because I didn't get to hear it from them. Can you possibly let Carter look you over, let him tell me you're okay? I need to hear the words from someone I trust." He held up a hand, stopping Knox from talking. "Of course I trust you to tell me if you're injured, but Carter is a medic and I know it's strange, but I just need to hear a medic say the words. Can you do that for me? Can you help me settle my mind? I'm worried that you doing the event for me has made you worse. I need to know it didn't do anything to aggravate your arm. I'm sorry to ask this of both of you, but it's what I need to hear." Charlie stared into Knox's eyes. He wasn't lying, he did need to hear the words, but he hoped, appealing to Knox in the way he had, it would give Knox an out and let him allow his brother to check him over.

It seemed like everyone in the room held their breaths as they waited for Knox's reply.

"Fine. I'll do it for you. But you stay right here with me." Knox used his good hand to haul Charlie further onto the bed.

Charlie settled in, letting his head drop onto Knox's shoulder and lacing their fingers together. "I wouldn't want to be anywhere else." From the corner of his eye, and out of Knox's line of sight, he saw Max mouth 'well played' to him. He pulled off a quick wink before focusing his attention on Carter.

"Remove your top please, Knox." Carter didn't look away.

Knox grumbled, but went to do as he was told. Suddenly he froze, his arms crossed over his chest as he tried to pull his tee shirt up. The hiss of breath that escaped him wasn't missed by anyone in the room.

Charlie shifted quickly and helped Knox out of his top. "I have to say, when I woke up this morning, I never thought I'd be undressing you in front of your family," he quipped.

There was a beat of silence before chuckles broke out.

"Just don't go getting any ideas," Carter warned. "Some of us have seen more of our brother than we ever want to see."

"Damn it, I'd only just got the whole twink and daddy tiger memory out of my head. You just had to remind me of it, didn't you?" Nate grumbled from the corner of the room where he was sitting on a sofa, Cora cuddled into his side.

Charlie didn't know who was blushing the deepest, Knox or Nate.

"I don't think any of us need the reminder of that night again." Tyler's face contorted like he was going to be sick.

Charlie didn't respond, his gaze was locked onto Knox's chest. His hand flew to cover his mouth. Knox's chest was mottled with heavy bruising. There were blacks, browns, greens, yellows, and a whole lot of red there. The whole of his left side was completely covered, and it spread up over his left pec, down his arm, and halfway across the center of his chest. "What, how?" Charlie's heart picked up speed.

"For fuck's sake, Knox. You could have told someone it was that bad." Carter's nostrils flared as he struggled to keep his temper in check.

"It's not that bad," Knox protested, yet his voice sounded slightly unsure.

"Not that bad!" Charlie winced at the screech in his own voice. "I can't even tell what color your skin is there. I call bullshit. You knew it was bad. You shouldn't have done the event. You shouldn't even be out of the medical unit."

"It's not that bad," Knox continued to argue.

"With all due respect, big brother, it is that fucking bad." Max peered over, wincing at the sight of Knox's injuries.

"I need to know exactly what happened, how you got these." Carter didn't look up from one of the many medical devices he was using. "Just as I thought, there's absolutely no mention of anything other than some bruising above the cast on your PAF medical records. You didn't tell anyone, did you?"

Knox didn't answer.

"Just as I thought." Carter dropped the medical note interface on the bed and ran a hand through his hair. "We need a fae healer here to scan for broken ribs."

"No," Knox refused.

"It's that, or you're going back to headquarters and through the scanner there. Your choice."

"I choose neither. My ribs aren't broken."

Charlie could see the two brothers gearing up to argue again. "Please, for me? Can you do it to put my mind at rest? I trust your judgment if you say they aren't broken, but I need to know." He cupped Knox's cheek, turning his face, so they locked gazes. "I don't want to worry about you hurting, and no one knows about it. I want you to have whatever meds you need. I just…" Charlie blew out a frustrated breath. "Please, Knox, for me?"

Knox closed his eyes briefly. When he opened them, Charlie could see annoyance, frustration, and something he couldn't, or wouldn't, name yet. "Alright, call a healer. I'm not going back to headquarters. If I do and bump into Ignatio, you have to know I'll go for him."

"You wouldn't be the only one," Tyler spat out.

"Uh," Charlie hoped he wasn't about to get his head bitten off. "Who's Ignatio?"

"Sub Commander of the Vamp unit. He sent in two newbie vamps as back up. One of them was overcome with the smell of blood. It wasn't his fault, there was a lot of blood as the injured were carried out. The vamp's name was Tirion, it was his first damn mission. He went into bloodlust."

Charlie bolted upright. "Bloodlust?" It was when a vamp reverted to their most base form and were dominated by the need to drink blood, any blood, they didn't discriminate. The problem with that is that some shifters were poisonous to vamps. It could have resulted in the death of several people. Throughout time, more than enough vamps had killed their victims in bloodlust and then died themselves from ingesting poisonous blood.

Knox dipped his head. "Revin was there."

"Who is Revin?" Charlie asked.

"Revin is a shifter. He's an *Ophiophagus hannah*."

"I don't know the term."

"He's a King Cobra, the second most poisonous animal in the world. His poison would kill an adult human in fifteen minutes, another shifter in between thirty minutes to an hour, depending on their classification. For a vamp? They'd be dead three minutes after drinking their blood. The blood of a King Cobra is the most poisonous substance to a vamp," Max explained.

"Oh shit." Charlie stared at everyone, horrified.

"Exactly." Knox shook his head. "When the bloodlust hit Tirion, it hit him hard. He's so young his control just snapped. He reached out for the closest person. That was Revin in his human form. I saw what was happening and managed to slam Revin out of the way, just before Tirion's fangs punctured his skin. We all fell to the ground, and it was a battle trying to keep Tirion from biting either of us. That and Revin was pissed that I was there protecting him. He wanted to prove he could take the vamp on."

"None of us could get in the middle of them. It was too much of a blur of limbs. The speed at which the three of them were fighting made it impossible." Tyler seemed slightly lost in the memory.

"How did you take him out?" Charlie looked between them all.

Knox smiled. "Carter called my name. I didn't even look. I knew he had a plan, my trust in my brothers is absolute. I managed to free an arm, stuck it in the air, and Carter threw something at me. The second it was in my hand, I slammed it into Tirion's neck. It seemed… poetic to do it there. Plus, it's the fastest way to get it into his system."

"What was it?"

"It was maspetaline, one of the tranquilizers designed by vampires for any vamp going through bloodlust. I don't know exactly what is in it, but that shit works in ten seconds. Tirion dropped like a stone. Sadly, he dropped onto a rock, my arm trapped between the two." Knox lifted the arm in the cast.

Charlie reflexively rubbed his own arm. "Shit. So your bone, or bones are broken. Were Tirion and Revin okay?"

"Tirion is still in seclusion. We had to go to Porter, the Commander of the Vamps, to stop Ignatio booting him out of the vamp unit. It was Ignatio's fucking fault," Knox hissed. "Anyway… while Tirion is in seclusion, he is still a member of the vamp division. Revin has a couple of bruises, but that's it."

"Apart from you." Charlie looked pointedly at Knox's chest.

"Yes, apart from me." Knox kissed Charlie on the forehead quickly. "I promise I'll be okay."

"Let me be the judge of that," a voice called from the far side of the room.

Charlie blinked in astonishment. A fae had appeared, looking incredibly angelic with a glow about him and cherubic features. He blushed when the fae winked.

"Ignore him, he's a damn flirt." Knox pulled Charlie in tighter to his right side.

The fae studied Knox. "Knox Vaughn, I'm here to check out the not quite as damn fine as normal chest of yours, rather than flirt with your man."

"Nylian Lukalyn at your service." The fae performed a bow in front of Charlie.

"What did you mean, his not quite as damn fine as normal chest?" Charlie's jaw tensed.

Nylian froze. "I, uh…" He looked to Knox who groaned.

"Thanks, Ny."

"Sorry." The fae winced.

Charlie's gaze was bouncing between the two men. "Wait a minute, you two used to…"

"Date?" Nate supplied helpfully.

"You dated?" Charlie's heart stuttered. How could he compete against a man who looked like that?

There was a loud cracking sound as the wooden bed frame cracked under the force of Knox squeezing his injured hand tight on the side of the bed. "You just had to tell him that, didn't you?"

"Would you stop using that hand!" Carter roared.

Charlie's mind spun and the voices all blurred into one. He was face to face with one of Knox's exes. He wasn't stupid enough to think Knox hadn't been serious with anyone before, but that didn't mean he wanted to be face to face with them. Especially when he looked like that and was about to… to put his hands all over Knox. It was Charlie's turn to grasp the edge of the bed tightly.

"Oh no, you don't. One hand to check over is enough, thank you very much." Carter had grabbed hold of his hand.

Charlie snarled at him, his unicorn snorting in his head. He tried to soothe it, but the damn beast was pissed.

"Charlie…"

Charlie ignored Knox's voice. He couldn't even look at him. How could he compare to Nylian?

"Charlie?" The next voice belonged to Nylian, who was now crouched in front of Charlie at the side of the bed. "Can you look at me a second?"

Charlie forced himself to look up from where he'd been staring at his hands in his lap.

"Yes, I dated Knox, for a while. It was years ago." Both ignored Knox's request to 'shut the fuck up.' "Like I said," he carried on, "it was years ago. We didn't work out. We weren't right together. I was too forceful, too set in my ways. I refused to compromise on anything. I had a chip on my shoulder about being the son of Fae Councilor Lukalyn. I was a bastard if I'm honest. Knox is the same now as he was then, a wonderful guy, but not for me. You have nothing to fear from me. I wasn't and never will be the right man for him. Please, accept my apologies for you finding out that way and from me being stupid, and not from Knox. It was not my intention to hurt you."

Charlie looked at Nylian, seeing the sincerity in his gaze. He took a steadying breath and nodded. "Thank you for telling me that. I'm sorry, my beast can get the better of me at times."

"You're a shifter?" Nylian's eyebrows shot up. At Charlie's questioning look, he continued, "There aren't many beasts that can get on with Knox's tiger."

Charlie nibbled on his lip. He didn't often tell people who he was, what shifter he was. It was a self-preservation thing, but if Knox dated this guy, he must be trustworthy. Besides, no one was making any attempt to stop him talking. "I'm a unicorn."

"Seriously?" Nylian's eyes lit up. "I would love to see you in your beast form. I've never seen one. Oh, I bet you are just stunning to look at." His eyes raked over Charlie, assessing. "I can see it now, all that sleek grace."

"Stop hitting on my man!" Knox roared.

Charlie turned to look at Knox. He was beyond agitated. He took pity on the man, reaching out and grabbing ahold of Knox's good hand. "I'm not angry, it took me by surprise that's all. It's not something I was expecting, and well, looking at Nylian, it's hard not to feel inadequate. I mean, look at him."

"I don't need to look at Nylian. You're all I need and want to see, Charlie." Knox searched his gaze. "Are we good?"

"We are." To prove it, Charlie darted forward and placed a chaste kiss on his lips.

"Now that is adorable," Nylian called from beside him.

"Ny, shut up." Knox slumped back on the bed. He looked even more exhausted now than he had a few minutes earlier.

"Knox, be good and let Ny check your chest out while I check to make sure you haven't fucked up your arm all over again." Carter was scowling as he took out a small device, slicing through the cast on Knox's arm. He took a few minutes to check the bone placement before sighing in relief. "You're lucky."

Charlie watched as Carter pulled out what looked like a long thin glove. He slipped it up his brother's arm, making sure it lay flat, and that Knox's arm was in the right position. Taking a blue and white medical stone from his bag, he laid it in the outline on the top of the glove. Turning the stone three times, he sat back and waited as the stone glowed and the glove grew and morphed into a cast. When the stone dimmed again, he picked it up and dropped it into his bag.

"That will hold as long as you don't do anything stupid again. You need to keep it on for three, maybe four weeks." Carter refused to look away, his gaze intent and serious.

"Can he not just shift and have it heal?" Charlie was slightly confused. Most of the time, shifting healed the bones.

"Not with the type of break he has. The way the tiger shifts, the bone would buckle under the stress and fracture further. Of all the breaks he could have had, this is the worst one." Carter moved to give Ny more room to work.

"Can I write, or type?" Knox demanded.

"No. You need to give it time." Carter insisted. "And I know the doctors at headquarters told you that."

"But…"

"I said no, Knox. You'll just have to take time off." When Knox went to argue, Carter growled. "Look, we can argue about it later. Let's just get your chest checked over, okay?"

"Fine," Knox grunted, but laid back down and waited.

Nylian kneeled on the bed on the other side of Knox. Charlie watched as he closed his eyes and ran his hands barely a centimeter over Knox's body. He lingered in several places, as if he were assessing those areas to a deeper level. There was silence in the room as everyone watched him, waiting on his prognosis. A bead of sweat formed on Ny's forehead, and it slowly dribbled down the side of his temple. He ignored it as he worked. Charlie was captivated as he watched.

Beside him, Nate leaned in to whisper, "He's literally seeing inside Knox right now, looking at either his bones, muscles, or organs. He'll do each one in turn, checking everything out to make sure there isn't any damage. I guess in some senses it's almost like x-ray vision, or an MRI, but it's magical. It's unique to the fae, and even then, there are few who are strong enough and with the right amount of training to be able to do it. Frankly, Knox should have worked out it was likely to be Ny who turned up."

"How long does it take?" Charlie made sure to keep his voice low, not wanting to disturb the fae as he worked.

"It depends on how much damage there is, the type of shifter, so many factors really. Not too long though."

Charlie nodded, but didn't take his eyes off Knox. Time seemed to take forever, but it couldn't have been long before Ny pulled back and slumped, Tyler stepping forward to catch him. Carter immediately handed over a replenishment drink. Tyler took it from his hands, bending the tube in half, until he heard the thin inner barrier snap, and shook it to activate the spelled liquid. He quickly pulled the straw up at the end and held it to Ny's lips.

Charlie turned to Knox, pulling the covers back up over his chest before he pushed a stray strand of hair out of Knox's eye. "How are you feeling?"

"I'm…" Knox appeared to take in Charlie's expression and changed his words. "Sore, uncomfortable, pissed off, and worried."

"You're worried about the results?"

"No, not even slightly. I'm worried about how you're taking Ny's appearance." Knox reached out with his good hand and wrapped it around Charlie's neck, hauling him close.

"I overreacted, and I'm sorry for that. I'm just worried about you, and it took me by surprise. Sorry." Charlie could feel his cheeks heating up.

"Then we can be sorry together." Knox gave him a quick kiss and turned to look at Ny, while keeping his good arm around Charlie. "What's the verdict then?"

"You'll live." Ny's lips twitched. "Seriously, you've got a broken rib, a small splenic laceration, probably from the rib, and some serious bruising, including to your kidneys. I would advise, if Carter here agrees, two weeks bed rest."

"What?" Knox spluttered. "I can't stay in bed two weeks."

"You can, and you will." Carter stared his brother down for a moment before turning to Ny. "What did you see, how bad are the ribs and how deep is the splenic lac?"

"It's only a small laceration, but I don't want to risk it. He needs to move as little as possible. Up for showers and the bathroom only. After a week he can move a little more, say about the house, but that's it, and not too often. And in terms of the rib, I've channeled some healing around the rib as much as I can, but it will be painful until its properly healed. There's nothing else that anyone can do. Knox just needs rest from this point on."

"You're serious, aren't you?" Knox looked completely crestfallen.

"I'm sorry, Knox, but I am." Nylian managed to sit up, but still looked weak. "I've looked at the PAF file Carter gave me, but all that's there is the damage to your arm. Seeing your chest, you took some bad knocks there. Do your family a favor, stay in bed and let them, and Charlie, look after you."

Knox's eyes slid shut, but his face was wracked with pain. Charlie couldn't be sure if it were physical pain from his injuries, or from the emotional effect. "If it's what you think is best, and Carter agrees, I'll stay on bed rest. But, I need to know, truthfully, what about writing?"

Charlie didn't need anyone to answer, the looks on their faces said it all. Knox must have come to the same conclusion.

"I can't write, can I?"

"I'm sorry, Knox." Carter reached out, but let his hand fall before he did anything. "We'll find a way so your story doesn't suffer."

"Like what?" Knox scoffed. "There's no decent software out there, even the magical programs. You have to say every bit of punctuation. That's incredibly frustrating, and it can ruin your flow. Plus, I write on total instinct. I don't plot, I don't think about it, I simply let the words flow out of me. I won't be able to do that if I keep having to add in all the grammar."

"I can do it," Charlie offered.

"What?" Knox turned to stare at him.

"I'll work out some shifts with Evie, see if I can arrange to do the morning shift, then come over here at lunchtime every day, then you can dictate to me. I'll write it for you. I know enough about books to get most of the grammar right. You can then edit it when you're up to it."

"You'd seriously do that for me?" Knox's gaze was intent and filled with wonder.

"Of course, I would." Charlie scoffed. "You really don't understand just how much I love your work. Even if I didn't, I'd still do it for you. Please, let me do this for you. Let me feel like I can actually do something useful for you. I can't help you medically. I can't heal you. Let me do this for you. I want to do this for you."

"I warn you, I can go for hours without stopping." Knox grasped at Charlie's neck, pulling him forward until their foreheads touched. "You really want to do this for me?"

"I really do," Charlie promised before he closed the small distance between their lips and gave Knox a kiss.

"Is it wrong to say how adorable they are together?" That was Ny's voice.

"They really are, aren't they?" Cora muttered.

"Knox, don't gut me for this…" Ny hesitated.

"For the love of all things celestial, what now." Sheer exasperation tinged Knox's tone.

"You're not going to be able to go at it for hours…" Ny fought a smirk. "Without a break. At least not to start with. Your body needs rest, and it will make sure you get it, whether you agree or not. You may not be able to pull off your epic writing sessions."

"I'll be here to help anytime you need it," Charlie promised.

Knox slumped back against the pillows. It was obvious he wanted to argue, but that he was fighting exhaustion. Charlie knew he had to be tired, but it seemed surprising just how quickly Knox was starting to fall asleep.

With a snort, Carter held up a syringe. "That will help him sleep."

"Bastard." Knox's voice was slurred. "Never forget I know where… you… sleep."

Charlie chuckled and placed a soft kiss on Knox's forehead.

CHAPTER EIGHTEEN

Charlie snuggled deeper into the pillow. He couldn't remember his bed being this comfy before. He really didn't want to have to get up and work. Maybe Evie would take pity on him and… a deep chuckle permeated the thick fog of his mind. That was Knox. Memories flooded into his mind thick and fast.

"Morning, gorgeous."

Charlie forced his eyes open and looked straight into Knox's vivid green eyes. "I fell asleep?"

"Guessing so. I woke up a few minutes ago to the sight of you in my bed. I could handle waking up to that every day." Knox ran a finger down Charlie's face. "The last thing I remember is arguing with Ny about epic writing sessions and not being allowed to do anything."

The smile emanating from Knox's face at the mention of his ex was pained. "I am sorry about Ny. I don't feel anything—"

Charlie reached up and covered Knox's mouth. "I'm not upset. Yeah, I reacted last night, but I was worried about you and it took me by surprise. Ny is stunning, there is little doubt about that. But, if you wanted to be with him, you would."

Knox's eyes sparkled with happiness, and he gently pulled Charlie's hand away from his mouth, kissing the palm. "I would like to still be friends with Ny. He's a good man, but if it's going to upset you…"

Charlie shook his head. "No, I trust you. There are going to be times when we both bump into exes. We both have pasts, but the way I see it, they are exes for a reason. If either of us wanted a different man, we would be with them. I have no problem with having Ny in our lives. Are you still happy with dictating to me?"

"As long as you're happy to do it. As much as it pains me, dictating will be the only way I can write. But I don't want to put you out. If you can't do it, if you need to be at the shop, I'll understand. I always have some leeway in my schedule anyway."

Charlie traced a finger over Knox's bruises, being careful not to press hard. "Oh, trust me, I want to do this. Not only do I want to help you, but I get the added bonus of being able to see the story take shape, see your words come to life in a way no one else ever could. I consider it a privilege that you would let me do this for you. Besides, I like the thought of helping to look after you. We'll be able to get to know each other a little better."

Knox groaned. "You know something?"

"What?"

"It's going to be hell to spend all this time with you, in bed, and not be able to do anything about it."

Charlie frowned. "We'll have to find out what we can do and when we can do it."

"If you think I'm about to ask my brother whether I can have sex, you have another think coming."

Charlie's lips twitched. "Put it this way, what will be less embarrassing, asking your brother, or asking your ex? Because if you want to do anything, we need to ask one of them."

"Oh, for the love of the shifter goddess, it isn't bad enough that I can't write, that I'm injured, oh no, you subject me to talking about my sex life with people who will never let me forget it."

"Who's having sex?" Max breezed into the room.

"Someone's having sex?" Nate called out from somewhere else in the house. "It's too early for that!"

"You shouldn't be doing anything in your state. Stop it!" Carter's voice joined the others.

"Will you guys shut up? I'm trying to sleep, not imagine my brother getting his freak on!" Tyler grumbled.

There was a beat of silence. Charlie opened his mouth, but Knox stopped him. "Wait for it."

"I'm scarred for life, I don't need to be hearing this. I'm a sweet and innocent freaking lady!" Cora's voice was the loudest of all.

"Um, wow?" Charlie blinked a couple of times, completely unsure what to say.

"Lady, my ass!" Max leaned out the door to yell.

Charlie pulled the pillow over his head and hid. Seconds later, Knox's head appeared next to his.

"I'm afraid if you stay here for any length of time then you're going to have to get used to this. Most mornings are about the same." Knox turned his head and nuzzled his nose against Charlie's.

"How do you survive the mornings?" Charlie wondered.

"Like this…" Knox pulled the pillow away and shouted. "If you don't leave now, you're going to see things you can't recover from. Lips, sucking and…"

The door slammed shut.

"That's how you get peace." Knox chuckled.

"You think so?" The door opened again, and Carter breezed in. "There will be no monkey business between you guys. Not until I give the okay."

"I guess that answers the question about who we talk to about this," Knox grumbled.

Charlie was of the principle, if you can't beat them, join them. "Carter…"

"Charlie…" Carter lifted an eyebrow and waited.

"When you say no monkey business, do you mean fast and furious fucking? Slow and sensual making love? Blowjobs, rim jobs, rutting, making out, what?"

Knox started to cough, groaning as he wrapped his arms around his waist. When he got himself under control, he stared at Charlie, completely flabbergasted.

"Oh, you fit perfectly into this crazy ass family." Carter smirked. "To answer your question… you can make out, and I'll be nice and say the occasional blowjob, but only if you do all the work and my brother does nothing."

"Sounds about normal for him anyway!" Max teased as he strolled back in the door. "He always was a lazy bastard."

"Hey! I spent years running around after you, I'll have you know." Knox tried to sit up, but Carter moved around the bed and with a gentle hand on his shoulder, stopped him. "Stop. What part of 'you need to take it easy' do you not understand?"

"But I need to kick Max's ass," Knox whined.

"It's going to have to wait, I'm afraid."

"I'll do it for you!" Nate's voice bellowed down the hallway.

"You and what army!" Max yelled back.

"My little army, which comprises of me, my fists, my arms, legs, feet, my tiger, you get the picture." Nate was quick off the mark, running into the room and slamming into Max. They both went tumbling to the ground, rolling around, dummy fighting.

Charlie looked at Knox who was pinching the bridge of his nose with his good hand. "If Charlie decides being with me is too much because of my crazy ass family, I'm going to throttle all of you when I'm better."

"Is it wrong to say that I like it?" Charlie shrugged when both Knox and Carter looked at him like he was crazy. "What? I love how close you all are. Yes, there's fighting, but I bet the moment anyone needs the others they would be there in a heartbeat. The fact you all came running that night with Matt said everything. The fact you are all here now, when Knox is bedridden, tells me everything I need to know about how close-knit you all are. So, if you're all going to stand there and try to tell me that you hate each other, then I'm sorry, but I'm not buying it. Not even slightly."

Knox looked exasperated. "If you think I'm going to confess to even liking them, you have another thing coming."

"Goddess forbid you do that," Charlie drawled.

"Now shut up so I can finish checking out your ribs and abdomen," Carter ordered.

"Damn bossy brothers," Knox muttered under his breath. When Carter glared at him, Knox used his good hand to mime zipping his lips closed.

Charlie grinned when Cora came in carrying a tray.

"Now, I'm not going to be doing this every damn morning, but I thought you two might like some breakfast, especially as you have work, Charlie." Cora's smile was sweet.

"Thank you."

"Listen…" Cora was fidgeting with her hands and looked anywhere but at Charlie. "I was thinking, you're here looking after my brother, but that means leaving Evie alone in the shop."

"It does." Charlie had an inkling where this was going, but let Cora get there on her own.

"What about if I help her out in the shop? I've only just finished school, I'm not working yet, and it would be nice to feel helpful and to spend some more time with her and the babies. I had a wonderful time staying with her considering everything that was going on."

"Are you sure?" Charlie reached out and gently lifted her chin, so he could look into her eyes. "It will mean getting there early in the morning? Evie would do most of the back-room work, which would leave you out front with the customers all the time. You don't have to. Between Evie and I, we can make it work."

"I want to do this. You're helping my brother, and I want to help you. Plus, Evie was wonderful with me when these guys were all on their mission. I want to be able to return the favor."

"Neither of us invited you to get a favor back."

"No, I know, but I really appreciated it," Cora insisted. "It made the whole thing a lot more bearable."

"You have no idea how much better it made us all feel when Knox told us he'd got that text from you." Carter joined the conversation. "It was one less thing we had to worry about. We, and Lane, knew that everyone back home would be fine, and we could focus on the mission. It made a world of difference not to have that constant worry in the back of your mind. We could devote ourselves fully to the task at hand, knowing the girls were together and that you would be keeping an eye on them."

"What actually happened?" Charlie looked between the brothers. "Knox fell asleep last night, so I didn't get to ask."

Tyler came in and sat on the end of Knox's extra-large bed. "The ferals somehow managed to kidnap one of the PAF units. Right now, we still don't know how they managed it. They were being held in a cave system outside of Corent limits. Of course, that means we need to be a lot more careful about what we use, when we shift and so on. The last thing we need is for the humans to find out about us. We had to take a lot of our strongest mages with us to create a protective shield that would effectively replicate the barrier that's around Corent. The problem is those mages have little in the way of an offensive arsenal, and all their magic would be taken up with keeping the shield going. We needed all the extra manpower to protect them. Knox and the others who were called in were on duty protecting them and keeping that route home intact."

"I'm presuming by the fact you are all home that the rescue succeeded?" Charlie bit his lip.

Tyler's eyes looked pained from the memories of the experience. "It was, but only after two days of constant fighting. To say those caves were heavily guarded is the understatement of the decade. It was torturously slow going getting inside of them. They were heavily fortified. It's the first time we've seen the ferals band together as much as they did. Normally they operate in small groups only. This was more like a damn army."

Nate took over, having finished play fighting with Max. "We were lucky. The unit was still alive, although another day and two of them would have had injuries they couldn't recover from. Carter and some of the other medics had to operate in the middle of one of those damn caves on one of the shifters."

Carter shook his head. "That is something I never want to be a part of again. We had three doctors with us and eight medics. It took all of us to keep them alive." He cast a quick look at Cora, then back again. "Let's just say the ferals had a lot of fun and leave it at that."

Bile rose in Charlie's throat. He could only imagine how bad it must have been. "You've said they survived. Will they still be able to be part of the PAF?"

Carter gave his first real smile. "They will. It's going to be a long recovery for them, mentally and physically, but they will make it back. Their places will be held for them for as long as needed."

"That's good to hear." Charlie blew out a relieved breath. "You say the ferals were more organized. How much more? I mean, how much of a threat do they pose to Corent and the para world as a whole?"

"Hard to say," Tyler answered. "Yes, we've never seen them that organized, but recently, we haven't been picking up any other unusual activity. There will always be ferals. We all know that. The key is to keep their numbers down until our doctors and medics can work something out that will stop the progression into madness or the corruption of a para mind when they turn criminal."

"That's a conversation for another day." Knox looked pointedly at Cora who merely rolled her eyes.

"Cora, are you sure about working at the bookshop? There could be a lot of work and clean up after last night." Charlie really didn't want to impose on her, but any help would be fantastic.

"I'm sure." Her tone of voice said everything.

"We're off today. We have two days off all duties after the mission." Nate looked at his brothers who nodded. "Carter can stay here if he wants to keep an eye on our invalid, but the rest of us can go and help with the clean-up."

"Are you serious?" Charlie stared in astonishment at the men.

"Completely," Tyler assured him.

"Then yes, thank you. With you all working, it will get cleaned up in no time."

Cora bounced off the bed. "I'll leave you to breakfast and go and call Evie."

One by one, the brothers left. Carter stopped in the doorway. "I'll be back to check on you later. If you need, me just shout."

"Hi," Charlie said lamely, making Knox grin after everyone had gone.

"Hi, gorgeous."

Charlie couldn't have stopped his snort if he tried. "Yeah, right, I know what I look like in the mornings. My hair is probably everywhere, I'll have pillow marks on my face, and I'll—"

"Look totally adorable," Knox interrupted him. "The perfect sight to see when I first open my eyes."

"Whoever said the Vaughn brothers weren't charming totally lied." Charlie chuckled. "You, Knox Vaughn, have a way with words."

"I just tell it like I see it, nothing more, nothing less." Knox shrugged.

Charlie sighed. "That's what makes it so special. I know you don't say things to try and get me into bed, you say them because you mean them."

"Oh, make no mistake, Charlie, I want you in my bed, but I'm not going to lie to get you there." Knox's eyes flared with heat. "But, sadly, anything we do will have to wait. As much as it pains me to admit, Carter was right. I'm in no fit state right now."

"There's plenty of time." Charlie leaned over and gave Knox a quick, chaste kiss. "I'm not going anywhere. Unless you want me to go, that is."

"And if I never want you to go?" Knox stared at him, his gaze intent and suddenly severe.

Charlie's heart thundered loudly. "Careful, Knox, I might just take you up on that offer."

"I'd be happy if you did." Knox refused to break their connection.

"What are you saying?" Charlie wanted him to spell it out.

"I'm saying I feel a connection to you. My tiger feels a connection to both you and your beast. I'm saying…." Knox took a deep breath, obviously painful, but like he was preparing himself. "I'm saying that I can feel a bond forming between us."

"A mate bond?" Charlie clarified. Now was not the time to be ambiguous.

"Yes, a mate bond. The pull is there. My tiger would be happy to be your mate, to be your unicorn's mate." Knox went silent, waiting Charlie out.

There was little doubt in Charlie's mind that he was feeling the same pull. The question was, did he have the guts and the honesty to be as truthful as Knox was? Did he really have a choice? To deny it would be an injustice to both Knox and the bond forming between them. Besides, to deny it would be the cowardly thing to do. Swallowing, he didn't look away from Knox as he spoke. "Yes, I feel it. Yes, my unicorn feels it. There is a bond forming between us, a mate bond."

Knox caressed his face, his thumb stroking over Charlie's cheek. "You stun me. Everything about you intrigues me. My tiger wants to show you his box."

Charlie was stunned to see Knox's cheeks flush red. "His box?"

"I may be a tiger, but I'm still a feline, and as you know, felines like boxes. My tiger has a box in the closet. It's got cushions and playthings in it. He goes there sometimes to just simply be."

"And he wants to show it to me?"

"He wants to cuddle with you in there." Knox actually looked bashful, an unusual look on an alpha, but it made Charlie grin.

"I would love to cuddle with him in your box, although I guess that's something else that is going to have to wait until you've recovered."

"I fucking hate this." Knox bit into his sausage with extra force, taking his frustration out on his breakfast.

"I know. I do too, but here's the thing. You're here, you're alive, and to me, that's the only thing that matters. Things could have been a lot worse. I'm thankful they weren't. Look at it this way, we'll have time to truly get to know each other. Now, be good and eat your sausage." Charlie narrowed his eyes when Knox's body shook slightly, but the man wisely stayed silent.

CHAPTER NINETEEN

Teaks struggled to breathe. The air in his breathing apparatus had run out a few minutes ago. His mind was going foggy, even as his lungs burned. Fighting against the smoke in front of him and the flames at his back, he crawled towards where he thought the exit was. He was dying, and he knew it. With every second that passed, his chance of surviving this clusterfuck diminished rapidly. There were so many things he wished he'd done differently, most of all, he wished he'd never trusted his damn partner. Noah had sold him out, sold the entire unit out. How long had he been working with the local crime lord, taking out his competitors, firebombing their meth labs? Teaks could barely get his head around it. His partner was a damn arsonist, responsible for the loss of five firefighters already. The way things were going, Teaks would be the sixth.

His radio was shot, leaving him with no chance of calling for help. Noah had seen to that. He'd smashed the device when they'd fought, Teaks having caught Noah planting evidence as they attempted to search the property for survivors. A loud cracking sound reverberated around him, and Teaks knew it was time, his time to die. The beam collapsed on top of him, pinning him to the ground. As flames licked at his feet and his breathing faltered, Teaks' last thought was of the detective he wished he'd kissed, just once, even if he'd earned a punch to the face for the privilege.

Charlie's fingers virtually flew over the keyboard, trying to keep up with the speed of Knox talking. He was desperate to ask questions but refused to interrupt Knox's flow. Someone needed to rescue Teaks, and do it now. Where was Detective Delicious when you needed him? As Knox went silent, Charlie took the opportunity to save the document and shake out his fingers. When it looked like he was thinking things through, he grabbed a quick sip of his juice before sticking a mint in his mouth, and waited.

"The question is… is Callohan brave enough, determined enough to go into the fire without protection to rescue Teaks?" Knox mused.

Charlie wanted to answer, to argue on behalf of Teaks, but he didn't know if he could, if that's what Knox wanted him to do.

"Well? What do you think?" Knox waved a hand in front of his face.

"Oh, sorry, I didn't know if you were actually asking me, or just talking out loud. I didn't want to interrupt your flow."

Knox dipped his head, stole a quick kiss, and tapped the screen. "I'm asking you what you think."

"Then yes, Callohan definitely needs to go and rescue his man."

"Does one of them end up in the hospital?"

"Well, Teaks at least is going to need checking out. He's going to have lungs full of smoke, and there's the fight with Noah to think of. Then, of course, there's that damn beam that fell on him. That was evil, Knox, truly evil. You couldn't have let him escape?"

"It's not me that makes up the story, Charlie. It's the characters. I may write it, but it truly is them who control the story. It always has been, always will be. I think of it more like I'm a conduit for them."

"If that's the case, aren't they telling you what to do?" Charlie wondered.

"No, they're kind of busy right now."

"How can they be busy?" Charlie wasn't sure he understood what Knox was getting at.

Knox clutched his hand to his stomach as he laughed. "Put it this way, right now, they are getting far more action than I am!"

"They're doing it, in your *head*?" Charlie was incredulous.

"They are." Knox grinned. "In fact, leave a couple of blank lines, type 'add in more,' another couple of blank lines and then get ready to type again.

"What are we writing?" Charlie did as Knox asked.

"A sex scene." Knox's grin was wicked.

"No…" Charlie whimpered.

"Oh yes. You ready?"

Sam traced the spine of the man standing in front of him in the shower. His fingers danced over the pattern of the phoenix, rising from ashes. It was broad, spanning the width of the man's back. The wings expanded from the edge of one shoulder to the other. The head rested at the base of the man's neck, the tail feathers trailing down into the crack of his ass. When his fingers danced over the edge of the most delectable, biteable ass he'd ever seen, the skin pebbled under his touch.

"This is incredible, so much detail." Sam dropped to his knees so he could get a better look. When the temptation became too much, he dropped a gentle kiss right between the cheeks.

"Sam…" The man's voice was husky. "Please."

"Your wish is my command, Teaks."

Charlie gasped before biting his lip, trying to keep quiet.

Knox grinned at him before he carried on with the story.

Sam gently eased apart those sexy ass cheeks and licked a stripe from top to bottom, making Teaks shudder. The man was edible, there was no doubt about it. Pushing the ass cheeks wider, Sam stiffened his tongue and flicked it over Teaks' hole before probing it gently. One hand grasped Teaks' hip, as the other moved around in front of his body, to grasp his stiff cock in his hand. Giving it a firm pump, he grinned as best he could in his position as Teaks let out a ragged groan and thrust forward, before thrusting back, hard.

"Damn you, shove your finger inside me," Teaks snarled. "I need it."

"What if I want to take my time?" Sam pulled back just enough to answer him.

"We can go slower later. I need you to fuck me, right the fuck now!" Teaks' voice ended on a roar.

"So demanding," Sam drawled before he soaked his finger with his saliva and gently eased it into Teaks' ass.

Charlie's cock was rock solid. He wanted nothing more than to take his cock in hand, or better yet, have Knox take him in hand.

"You alright there, Charlie?" Knox whispered.

"What? Oh, yes." Charlie didn't look up from the screen.

"If you say so. Personally, you look a little flushed to me. Do you need me to get Carter in here to check you out?"

"No, no, I'm fine," he insisted.

"I'll carry on then."

"O-okay."

Soaking wet, Sam lifted Teaks into his arms, carrying him out the shower and straight into the bed.

"The bed," Teaks muttered.

"Like I give a fuck about the bed," Sam snarled. "I'm having your ass, right now."

"Yes, Sam."

"No, you use my other name. I've always wanted to hear it in your husky voice, screaming, begging for more."

"Yes, Callohan."

"Fuck!" Sam dropped his fireman on the bed and crawled over him, taking his lips in a bruising, punishing kiss. "You're mine, you know that?" He snarled when he managed to tear his lips away.

"I know it." Teaks spread his legs wide, letting Sam fall into the gap between them. "But show me."

Sam's restraint snapped and two fingers plunged into Teaks' ass, the fun in the shower already having prepared him.

"I'm ready, just fuck me."

Without another word, Sam grabbed a condom, groaning at the touch of his own hand as he slid it on. Lining up his cock with Teaks' hole, they locked gazes and he thrust forward.

Charlie was struggling to type. His cock was leaking and his ass flexing, imagining the feel of Knox taking him the way Detective Callohan was taking Teaks.

"Fuck this." Using his good hand, Knox lifted the laptop from Charlie's lap.

"Stop that." Charlie grabbed the laptop back and placed it on the table beside the bed.

The moment he was done, Knox beckoned him closer. "Kiss me."

Charlie was only too happy to comply with the demand. Leaning over Knox, being careful not to lean on any part of his chest, Charlie licked Knox's lips, pushing against them with his tongue, probing for entrance. When Knox's mouth opened, he pushed in, taking the opportunity to dominate the man beneath him while he could. Any other time and there was no way Knox would sit back and let him control the pace like this. A thrill raced through him at having an alpha, his alpha, under his spell, his command.

"Don't get too used to this. As soon as I'm well enough, you're going to be under me. I have plans to ravish you the way Callohan ravished Teaks." Knox nipped at Charlie's skin.

Charlie had to fight against the urge to thrust forward. He wanted to rub his cock up against Knox's until they both came. He couldn't though, anything like that would have to wait. All they could do was kiss.

Time lost all meaning. The connection between the two men was intense and all-consuming. Something deep inside Charlie flared to life. There was no easy explanation as to what it was— there was a sensation, a knowing, that not only was this right, but something that was meant to be. That it was something that he was destined for. His unicorn settled, no longer as restless as it had been when Knox had left for the mission. Now they were with Knox, it was calm, content, happy.

A sudden groan from Knox broke through his lust-fogged mind. That wasn't a groan of desire, that was one of pain. Charlie quickly pulled back, only to discover he'd started to lean down more on Knox. "Oh, shit, I'm sorry." Charlie's hands fluttered uselessly around Knox's chest.

Knox took a moment to regulate his breathing before he answered. "It's okay, honestly. It wasn't you. I shifted position, and it pulled on one of the muscles. Don't think for one moment that I wasn't enjoying it, or that we won't be doing it again, because we will, and plenty of it."

"But Carter said—" Charlie began.

"I don't give a flying fuck what my brother said. If I want to kiss my mate, I'm damn well going to do it."

Charlie struggled to breathe. "Your mate?"

"What? I didn't say that."

"Uh, you did." Charlie was too shocked to grin or tease Knox. "Did you… did you mean it? Or was it just the heat of the moment?"

Knox's hand clenched and unclenched rapidly. "Shit. I so wasn't intending to have this conversation this soon."

Charlie felt like hyperventilating to get out of the conversation. He had no idea where Knox's mind was going, not really. He knew Knox cared, but mates? That was a whole different ballgame. They may have been skirting around the possibility earlier, but talking in vague terms about the future was completely different to saying the word out loud, right then. He fiddled with a loose thread on the edge of the pillow, too scared to say anything.

"Okay. I said it. I said the word mate. I mentioned earlier that I was thinking along those lines, right?" Knox looked directly at him.

Charlie didn't lift his head, but nodded.

"When we spoke about it earlier, well, I wasn't quite as truthful as I could have been." Knox was silent for a moment. "Charlie, will you look at me, please?"

Charlie wanted to say no, but instead, he summoned up his courage and lifted his head.

Knox looked deep into his eyes. "I wasn't honest because I didn't want to scare you. You see, my tiger has already made up his mind. He wants you and your unicorn as his mate. For now, and forever. As far as he's concerned, it's a done deal. The only way it doesn't happen is if you don't want it to."

Letting his mind process the words, Charlie stayed silent for a few minutes. Was this something he and his unicorn truly wanted? Was he ready to commit to a future with Knox and his tiger? His mind was spinning out with all the possibilities. Confusion, desire, elation, fear, no one thing occupied center stage for long.

"Charlie?" Knox sounded pained.

Charlie wondered just how long he'd been silent.

"You don't want that, do you?"

Charlie finally looked up to see the anguish in Knox's eyes. "You took me by surprise."

"It's the same for me, but, here's the thing, out on that mission, there was no chance to sleep. All we could do was to keep guard over the passageway, that small section of retreat. With nothing happening, it gave us all a whole lot of time to think. It wasn't as if we could spend a lot of time talking to each other. Sure, the protection was in place, but there was no point tempting fate and making ourselves a bigger target than we already were. I spent the time thinking. About the past, the present and the future. I looked back on all the relationships I've had in the past. Yes, with Ny, among others. But, here's the thing… none of them, no matter how long I'd been with them, came even slightly close to the depth of feelings I have for you after so short a time."

Knox looked off into the distance, while absentmindedly rubbing the skin above his cast. "I hate to say this, but Ny was probably the closest of them all. He understood me more than anyone else outside of my family. But even *he* didn't understand me fully, not really. He couldn't see the real me. The me that cares deeply for his family, that frankly would rather stay at home, writing, having a family meal, than be out socializing with the top society in Corent, or any other para city. That was a life he was accustomed to and one I didn't want in any shape or form. We fought over it bitterly. He grew up in a life like that— being seen. That was one reason, among many, that we weren't right for each other."

Holding his palm out, Knox waited. Charlie laid his hand on top and linked their fingers together.

"Do you, *did* you, love him?"

"At the time, if you had asked me, I would have said yes. In truth, with the benefit of hindsight, no. I'll admit I had deep feelings for Ny, but it wasn't love. I know that now. See, we've only known each other a short while, yet what I feel for you has already surpassed what I felt for him. I'm not saying that I love you, but I know I *will*, given time. What I *do* feel is the mate connection, a bond forming that is so strong it takes my breath away. That I am completely confident about." Knox started to trace a pattern on Charlie's hand. "I'm not saying we make it official and become matelings, just that it is something I want for the future. I want time with you first, time to get to know each other properly, to make sure we really are compatible. Having a bond between our animals is one thing, but making sure we get on as men is just as important. I guess that's what I'm really asking for. A commitment to give it time, a promise that you'll at least consider it."

Charlie searched his own feelings, his mind, and deep into his heart. Knox was right, his unicorn was already feeling the pull of a mate bond. But, like Knox said, as much as their beasts ruled a part of them, it wasn't the only aspect of who they were. They were men as much as they were beasts. Neither part held greater control or dominance over the other. There were times he ceded control to his unicorn, and times his unicorn gave it to him. Like any relationship, it was about balance and compromise. His unicorn wanted Knox's tiger, but even it understood that the two men needed to get along as well.

"I know it seems like I don't want this, don't want to consider a future with you, but that's not what this is about. I want to be sure. I don't want to commit if I'm not ready, if neither of us are truly ready. All that would do is hurt all of us. I already care deeply for you, Knox, and this is as much about making sure you don't get hurt as it is anything else."

"Which means what?" Knox asked.

"Which means that yes, I can see us being mates in the future, and I want to give that reassurance to both our beasts, but I also want to make sure we are compatible as men first. There is no rush to do this, we have all the time in the world, but yes, in the future, I can see myself mated to you. So how about this… we agree that it's likely to happen, reassure our beasts that it will happen, and spend time with each other first."

The smile lighting up Knox's face was blinding, his dimples deeper than Charlie had ever seen. "You don't know how happy you have made us both."

"Oh, I think I do, because it makes both of us happy as well. I don't think my unicorn has ever been this content. I'm sorry if I made you worry, taking my time to answer, but it's not something either of us should be agreeing to lightly."

"Trust me, I'm taking this anything but lightly." Knox lifted their joined palms and kissed the back of Charlie's hand. "Now, how about we seal this discussion with a kiss."

"As long as I don't hurt you again." Charlie rubbed the back of his hand over Knox's cheek.

"You didn't hurt me the first time," Knox promised.

Charlie leaned forward and took possession of Knox's lips.

CHAPTER TWENTY

There was little doubt in Charlie's mind now that he loved Knox, but after a week of Knox being on total bed rest, he was ready to throttle the man. The saying that alphas made lousy bed patients was so true. He was currently hiding out in the kitchen, chatting to Matt, who had come over to visit.

"He can't be that bad, surely?" Matt stared in astonishment at Charlie after he'd been recounting some of what could only be described as epic tantrums from Knox.

"Oh, trust me, it's so much worse." Tyler walked into the room and stared at Matt. "You're Matt. I've seen you at the hospital, but we've not had a chance to meet properly yet."

Charlie watched as Tyler took Matt's hand, both of them seemingly lingering over the connection for a moment.

"It's, uh, great to meet you." Matt stared at Tyler.

Charlie's head bounced back and forth between the two men, wondering what he was watching happen. Both of them seemed uncharacteristically quiet.

"Where's my coffee!" Knox's yell broke the trance the two men had been in.

Tyler dropped his head and groaned. "Seriously, Charlie, he's my brother, and I suppose I have to care about him, but how the fuck have you not throttled him already?"

212

"What, you think I haven't considered it?" Charlie drawled as he walked over to the industrial coffee machine the Vaughn siblings had. The first time he'd used it, he'd scalded his hand, needed Carter to patch him up, and received a lecture from Knox. He'd been so tempted to hit the man.

"Thank the gods for that. I was beginning to think you were some sort of weird saint." Tyler looked disgusted at the prospect.

"Oh, trust me, Charlie is no saint. Oh, the stories I could tell." Matt's wicked grin lit up his face.

"But you won't be telling them, will you, Minx?" Charlie locked gazes with his best friend. Neither of them looked away. If Charlie was right, he'd seen a flash of something between Tyler and Matt. Therefore, the last thing Matt would want is for Charlie to start dishing up the gossip on him. It was one of their epic stare down contests and Charlie was vaguely aware of Tyler's head bouncing between the two of them.

Matt caved first. "You're right, I won't be telling them."

"Well shit, that was an epic, silent contest there. It's a wonder one of you two didn't burn up on the spot," Tyler teased.

"Where the fuck is my coffee!" Knox's roar had shades of his tiger present.

"Tyler, can you entertain Matt while I go and take Mr. Grumpy Ass his coffee?"

"It would be my pleasure." Tyler never looked away from Matt.

Charlie grabbed Knox's coffee and beat a hasty retreat. Upstairs, he bumped into Carter coming out of Knox's room.

"Praise the gods for coffee." Carter grimaced. "I wish I could have given him the full all clear, just to shut him up, but he's not fully healed yet. However, he is cleared for light activity."

"Light activity? What like getting to and from the sofa, that sort of thing?" Charlie checked.

"Well, yes, that, but what I meant was sexual activity. I'm clearing him for sex." Carter looked pained to be discussing it. "The only thing is, you need to do all the work. I mean it, Charlie. If he tries to take control, you'll have to stop him. You need to be on top, putting no pressure on his chest. If I check on him later, and things have gotten worse, I'll confine him to bed for another two weeks. That's something none of us want, so do me a favor and take it easy on him? Although I can't help but think that a good orgasm will do him a world of good."

Charlie was flushing beet red from his ears to his toes. He so didn't want to be having this conversation with Knox's brother.

"Trust me, it pains me just as much to be talking about it." Carter looked back at Knox's doorway. "Just, cheer him up. Please!" He stalked off down the stairs.

Charlie grinned as he walked through the door. It was about damn time they could get up to something.

"What's the smile for? I can't think of a single thing worth smiling about." Knox was definitely grumpy.

"The smile is because Carter has given you the all clear for light activity."

"So?" Knox was pouting. His big, bad alpha was definitely brooding.

"That means I can straddle you, make love to you as long as we're careful." Charlie leaned against the doorframe, grinning.

"Then what the fuck are you doing all the way over there. Get your butt in here, naked and on my bed," Knox ordered.

"My, my, you are demanding today."

"Charlie!"

"Knox…"

"Now is not the time for teasing. I'm on a knife's edge. Please."

Charlie took pity on them both. Stripping as he walked, he focused on Knox, propped up in the bed. "You want me."

"Yes."

"You need me."

"Yes."

"You've just got to have me?"

"Fuck, yes."

"We need to work on your language."

"Fuck my language."

"I think I'll fuck you instead," Charlie teased.

"No."

"No?"

"You can make love to me instead," Knox insisted.

"Now that I can do." Having spent a week rarely leaving the room, Charlie had given up caring about bed head and being self-conscious. They'd seen each other at their worst— tired, grumpy, sleepy, and they'd seen each other happy. They'd spent hours talking, nights merely holding on to each other, content to experience that connection when they couldn't do anything else. He knew Knox now. Truly knew him. His hopes and dreams, his desires, and fears. They'd spoken about the death of their parents, the devastation, loss, heartbreak, and confusion that had followed. The last week had cemented their burgeoning bond, and it was past time for them to focus on the physical side of their relationship.

Climbing onto the bed, he crawled towards Knox, letting his man see the lust and so much more shining from his eyes. He was ready to say the words, but would wait. He didn't want there to be any doubt in either of their minds that he meant them. Too much was said in the stupor of desire.

Knox ran hotter than Charlie, and had taken to sleeping in just a pair of boxer-briefs. Charlie slowly pulled the covers down, exposing them. Knox was already hard, his cock straining the seams of his boxers. Shifting so he lay between Knox's legs, Charlie pulled the boxers down, freeing Knox's hardness. Licking his lips, he took in the sight of Knox in all his glory. Unable to deny himself any longer, he gently kissed the tip, surprised when Knox bucked. "Stop," he commanded. "You know the rules. You have to let me do the work."

"Charlie…"

"No, if you don't behave, we stop. As much as I want this, I refuse to hurt you."

Knox's good hand curled into a fist, but he didn't say anything.

Charlie cautiously licked the tip, ready to hold Knox down if needed, but for once, Knox did precisely as he was asked. The taste of Knox burst onto his tongue. It reminded him of a snow-covered forest and fresh pine needles. Crisp, clean, and vibrant, he wanted more. Sliding his lips slowly down Knox's shaft, he sucked, desperate to taste more of him. With the fingers of one hand, he gently caressed the skin around the root of his cock, while the other hand drifted lower to cradle Knox's balls, giving a gentle squeeze.

A guttural moan rippled through the room, and Charlie looked up to see Knox's gaze trained on him. Keeping his eyes locked onto Knox, he sucked, licked, and tasted. Letting everything he felt shine from his eyes, he wondered exactly what Knox saw in them, when his own widened and then heated even more. With his good hand, Knox reached out and cupped his cheek. No doubt he could feel his own cock under the skin he touched. His thumb traced the edges of Charlie's lips, and he could feel the tremble in it. Knox may be silent, but his body was telling Charlie just how affected he was.

Taking his time, Charlie curled his tongue in on itself and sucked, creating a vacuum as he dragged it up Knox's cock. Underneath his hand, he could tell Knox was having a tough time not moving, his muscles tensing and releasing, again and again. He chuckled around Knox's cock, and a burst of precum flooded his mouth.

"Charlie…" Knox's ragged voice reached his ears. "Please…"

Charlie hummed and was rewarded with more precum. When he pulled off, he grinned at the look of disbelief on Knox's face.

"Why did you stop?" Knox's eyes were pleading.

"I'm not stopping." Charlie crawled up the bed, lying next to Knox. Grabbing some lube from beside the bed, he coated his fingers and dropped the tube on the bed. He slid his fingers between his own ass cheeks and pushed one into his hole.

216

"What are you doing?" Knox grabbed the lube with his good hand, coating his fingers and grabbing hold of Charlie's cock.

"What does it look like?" Charlie moaned as he brushed up against his prostate. "I'm getting myself ready to ride your cock."

"You're going to…"

"Ride you. I'm going to straddle you, and I'm going to slowly sink down, driving your cock deep into my ass. I'm going to take you all in, keep you there, feel you deep inside me. You know we need to make a decision."

"You want me to what?" Knox maintained a steady stroke on Charlie's cock.

"We need to decide. Condoms or not."

The hand on Charlie's cock froze. "Do you want to use them?"

"No," Charlie answered honestly. "I want to feel you come deep inside me."

"Yes, I want that."

"Then no condoms. I'm safe. I have no doubt you are." Charlie maintained the gentle pumping in his own ass.

"I'm clean. It's not as if shifters can get most diseases, since we burn them off. But there are some." Knox resumed his stroke over Charlie's cock until Charlie reached out a hand and stopped him.

"Lube yourself up."

Knox squirted some lube over his shaft and stroked.

"Oh, fuck me, that's hot." Charlie nibbled on his lips, his fingers picking up speed in his ass. "I could come like this, watching you do that, but I want you inside me more." He pulled his fingers free and moved so he was straddling Knox, reaching underneath his own ass to take Knox in hand. He gave Knox's cock a few lazy pumps, twisting as he went, before he guided him to his hole. Nudging Knox's cock inside him, he slowly sank down, whimpering as his mate's cock filled him.

"You feel good."

Charlie was past the point of being able to talk. When he finally had Knox buried inside him to the root, he hung his head, simply breathing, becoming accustomed to the feel of having him inside him. What he hadn't told Knox was that it had been a while since he'd last been with anyone.

"Charlie?"

"Give me a second to get used to you."

"I'm that big, huh?" Knox grinned up at him.

A surprised laugh burst free from Charlie. "Only you could take that from what I said."

"What?" Knox asked innocently.

"Nothing. Now, lay still and let me have my wicked way with you." Charlie grinned as he lifted up and then slowly sank back down onto Knox's cock. Up and down, rolling his hips, Charlie kept a momentum going. Slow and steady, full of sensuality.

"Fuck, you feel good." Knox's voice broke at the end.

"You feel incredible." Charlie tipped his head back, bracing his arms on the bed, refusing to put any weight on Knox. Even as he lost himself to the sensations, he wouldn't do anything to set Knox's recovery back. "When you're better, the next time I ride you, I'm going to be teasing those nipples of yours. Squeezing them, biting them." As he spoke, he squeezed Knox's cock inside him. "I'm going to stand in the shower, braced against the wall, the same way Teaks was when you dictated that scene. I'm going to stand there, with my legs wide, my ass pushed back, and give you free rein to do as you want."

"Oh, fuck." Knox thrust forward.

"We may be going slow now, out of necessity, but soon enough I want you to take me hard and fast. I want to be on all fours as you ram your cock into me. I want you to make me scream your name. I want you to bite me, mark me. You know, I was thinking, maybe I should get a copy of your paw, get it tattooed on my skin, so it's always visible on my shoulder."

"Fuck!" Knox jerked beneath him and warmth flooded his ass. The shock of it set his own orgasm off, and he jerked forward, only just managing to brace his hands on either side of Knox before he collapsed onto his bruised chest.

Charlie trembled as aftershocks raced through him. His cock spurted a little, adding more cum to the pooling mess on Knox's stomach. Climbing off Knox, he staggered to the bathroom, wetting a cloth, and moving back to the bed. Quickly cleaning up Knox, then himself, he clambered back into bed beside his man, smiling when Knox lifted his arm. He oh-so-gently laid his head down on Knox's good shoulder, rolled his neck and kissed the skin he could reach. Before he could say a word about how good it had been, he fell asleep.

When he woke up, he realized someone must have been in the room. The curtains were drawn and there was a fresh bottle of water by the side of the bed with some pills and a note.

Make sure he takes these when he wakes up. You'd better not have killed my brother with your wicked ways. Carter.

At the bottom of the note, he'd drawn a stupid face sticking its tongue out at him. Charlie quietly chuckled to himself, not sure if it was because it was funny or out of sheer embarrassment of Carter having been in the room, and no doubt having seen the mess they'd made of the bed.

"What's funny?" Knox mumbled as he pulled Charlie back against him, giving him a kiss.

"Your brother."

"Which one?"

Instead of answering, Charlie handed over the note.

"Oh, fuck me, he's as bad as the rest of them."

"Take your pills." Charlie held them out.

Taking them from his palm, Knox grumbled, "Yes, dear."

"Hush, you know they're for your own good."

"I know, it doesn't make it any easier though, having to rely on them, or having you all order me about. It's a good thing I love you."

Charlie froze, staring at Knox as he swallowed his pills with a large gulp of water.

"Uh, why do you look like you've seen a ghost or something?"

"Or something, that's for sure." Staring at Knox, Charlie realized the man had no idea what he'd just said.

"What?" Knox focused on him. "You're being weird."

"You, uh, just said you loved me."

Eyes sliding shut, Knox swore. "Oh, fuck me, things just keep slipping out."

Charlie coughed out a laugh. "Are you saying you didn't mean it?"

Knox gingerly rolled onto his side so he was facing Charlie. "I meant it. I just planned to tell you properly, take you out to dinner, pamper you properly, show you how much I adore you, how much I appreciate everything you've done for me, then tell you that I love you."

"Knox, I don't need flashy declarations, I don't need your thanks, as much as they are appreciated. I've done what I have because of how I feel about you. If you didn't realize it already, I am completely and irrevocably in love with you, Knox Vaughn."

Charlie couldn't say anything else. Knox surged forward, wrapping his good hand around the back of Charlie's neck and kissing him senseless.

"Am I going to have to keep walking in with my eyes closed now, so I don't see something else that's going to scar me for life?" Nate drawled, forcing the two men to draw slightly apart.

"I'm busy," Knox grumbled against Charlie's lips.

"Well, I'm trying to be nice and give you a heads up. Evie and Mama Alice are on their way. I thought you might want to get dressed… and air out the room." Nate walked to the window and opened it wide. "It smells like someone had far too good a time in here for being injured."

Charlie fought the rising blush, but refused to apologize. He'd made love to his man; there was nothing wrong with that.

"I love how easily you blush. It's going to be a failsafe way of knowing if you're guilty of something." Nate cackled as he walked into Knox's closet and grabbed sweats for him. "You'd better grab your own clothes, Charlie. I don't think my brother would appreciate me helping you get dressed, although the offer is there…" Nate waggled his eyebrows before leering at Charlie.

"Do I need to get one of the others in here to beat you up?"

"Oh, hush, big brother, you know I'm teasing you both." Nate shook out the sweats and threw two pairs of boxers at them both. "Charlie, help him into those, and I'll help him into his sweats."

Charlie dived under the covers, sliding the boxers up Knox's legs and under his ass. Being cheeky, he placed a quick kiss to the top of Knox's cock, smirking to himself when Knox's hand fisted in his hair. As soon as he was done, he came up for air, his expression deliberately blank, valiantly trying to ignore the evil look that promised retribution on Knox's face.

Nate looked at them as if trying to work out what was going on, shrugged, and gestured for Charlie to hurry up.

Sliding his own boxers on, Charlie jumped out of bed, grabbed his cartoon unicorn lounge pants and a plain green tee, and blitzed around tidying up the room, making sure the lube was safely back in the drawer. Five minutes later, he and Knox were both propped up on the bed, Knox under the covers, him on top. It wasn't a moment too soon as Mama Alice and Evie came in, followed by Lane and Cora carrying the babies.

"My poor, sweet boy." Mama Alice didn't go directly to Charlie. Instead, she went to Knox's side of the bed, leaned down, and kissed him on the forehead before smoothing back his hair.

"Uh…" Knox looked around wildly, as if begging someone to save him. No such luck. There was no being saved from Mama Alice if she wanted to dote on you.

"Are they feeding you properly? I brought stews, casseroles, and my secret chocolate pudding, just in case."

"Mama Alice!" Charlie protested. "I can cook, you know."

"Yes, dear." She carefully leaned over Knox and patted his hand.

"I put everything in the kitchen." Matt breezed in as well. "Looks like the gang is all here."

Jasper was making gimmie hands at Charlie, so he held out his arms, only just catching him as he took a leap from Lane's arms.

"I missed you too, buddy." Charlie looked at the other kiddos. "I missed all of you."

"Hot choc man!" Danny cried as he raced to stand beside Mama Alice.

"Hey, Danny. I don't have any hot chocolate here. Sorry." Knox ruffled his hair.

"Coz hot choc man poorly." Danny nodded sagely.

"Yes, he is, but remember Carter?" Lane gestured to his PAF teammate. Danny nodded. "That's his brother, and he and Charlie are helping to look after him and make him better."

"Good. Bed boring. Hot choc man will want to play," Danny announced to the room.

Charlie hid his face in his hands, smirking at the muffled laughter coming from various parts of the room.

"That's right, Danny." Mama Alice lifted Danny onto her lap as she perched on the edge of the chair by Knox's bed.

"I tell you what, Danny, when I'm all better, I can come and visit, and we can play something together then. How about that." Knox looked around, grabbing a pen off the bedside table. "How about until then, you draw me a picture so I have something to smile about?" He gestured to the blank cast on his arm.

Charlie's heart melted. Knox must have been an incredible big brother/father figure when his siblings were growing up. Who knew, maybe one day they would be able to adopt some shifters who needed a home? When Charlie looked up, he saw Mama Alice looking at him, a knowing grin on her face. He merely smiled sweetly and said nothing, simply enjoying the time surrounded by family and friends.

CHAPTER TWENTY-ONE

Charlie saved the document, turning to grin at Knox. "How does it feel?"

"Amazing. I didn't think I was going to be able to get it done. Seriously, I appreciate everything you've done for me, but I can't wait to get this damn cast off." Knox tapped the cast still wrapped around his wrist.

"Tomorrow." Charlie tipped his head to one side and Knox took advantage, kissing a trail along his skin.

As much as he wanted to stay and enjoy the experience, Charlie had something else arranged. "Come on, we're going out."

"You mean my jailor has given the okay?" Knox pumped his fist.

"Yes, as long as you take it easy, he's letting me take you out. Your rib has healed and the splenic laceration is well on its way to repairing itself. You might struggle to walk great distances until all the bruising has gone, but a short walk will do you some good."

"You have something planned?" Knox was no doubt picking up on the excitement emanating from Charlie.

"I do."

"Do I get to know what?"

"Nope."

"Why?"

Charlie rolled his eyes. "Because if I told you, it wouldn't be a surprise now, would it? Now get ready, and I'll meet you downstairs, I need to get something from Max."

"What's my brother got to do with this?"

"You'll find out later. Be patient." Charlie shook his head, exasperated. Honestly, Knox was worse than the kiddos. He left his man to it, and joined Max in the kitchen. "Did you find it?"

"Yes. I always knew there had to be a reason Knox kept everything as we were growing up." Max slid a piece of paper across the table, already in a protective sleeve.

"Thank you. Without it, I couldn't get this done today."

"He's going to freak, you know that?"

"I hope you mean in a nice way?" Charlie toyed with a coaster on the kitchen table.

"I mean in the best way. Relax." Max patted his hand.

"Stop trying to move in on my territory," Knox called from the door.

Charlie grabbed the paper and slipped it into a bag at his feet.

"What was that?"

Knox tried to peer over Charlie's shoulder, but Charlie hunched over, stopping him seeing. "Later," Charlie insisted.

Knox's growl had no effect on Charlie; he was too accustomed to it now. "You should be scared of my tiger. He's a lean, mean, fighting machine."

"He's a pussycat that wants to cuddle," Charlie retaliated.

Max sprayed juice everywhere as he choked.

"You, clean that up and shut up," Knox ordered.

Max wheezed, his hands fluttering around his throat.

"Carter! Knox has killed Max!" Charlie roared, now entirely used to the way things were done in the Vaughn household.

The thunder of running feet echoed around them as Carter, Nate, and Tyler all raced into the room. "What happened?" Carter demanded as he whacked Max on the back, forcing him to take a massive gulp of air.

Knox stayed stubbornly silent.

"He…" Max wheezed, "Called… Knox's tiger…. a pussycat… who loves to cuddle."

There was a beat of silence before roars of laughter filled the kitchen. Charlie turned to Knox and shrugged apologetically. "Sorry," he mouthed. "I'll make it up to you."

"Oh, man…" Carter fought to gain his own breath. "That's fantastic. Nice one, Charlie!"

"I hate you all." Knox crossed his arms and glared at everyone.

"Come on, let's go and sort out your surprise." Charlie grabbed Knox by the hand and started to walk out.

"Clean that shit up before we get back," Knox demanded.

"Yes, Dad!" Max was laughing as they left.

Charlie was pleased to get out the house, even if they were traveling by tram. Typically, he walked everywhere, but he didn't want to tax Knox any more than needed.

When they got off on Dermont Parade, Knox looked around. "What are we doing here?"

Charlie didn't say anything, just walked towards a shop. Then Knox suddenly stopped, looking up at the sign that read 'Inkarium.'

"This is the magical tattoo parlor." Knox spun Charlie around. "What are we doing here?"

Charlie grinned and walked in. "Hi, Dran. I'm here for our appointment."

A man stepped out from behind the counter, hand extended to Knox. "I'm Dran, I'll be doing Charlie's tattoo today."

"Charlie?" Knox's voice quivered slightly.

A TALE OF TWO HORNS - HANNAH WALKER

"Let me guess, he doesn't know?" Dran led the way into one of the tattoo studios.

"No, it's a surprise." Charlie lifted Knox's hand. "Remember talking about how much you liked the idea of your mark on me? How I mentioned a tattoo?"

"Yes… you're getting it done?" Knox's mouth dropped open in shock. "How? I can't provide a print?"

Charlie reached into his bag and pulled out the paper Max had handed to him. "With this."

Knox carefully took the paper out of Charlie's hands. "This is from when Cora went through an art stage. She wanted to have our prints all along her wall. We did it for her. She has this way of persuading us to do anything. This paper, this is from when we were checking the color of the paints. I didn't know anyone had kept this."

"I happened to mention my idea of getting a magical tattoo to Max, and asked if he had any idea if there was such a thing as a copy of your paw print, or if I would have to wait until you were healed. He remembered doing this for Cora and dug it out of the attic. This is your print, is it accurate?" Charlie suddenly worried it wasn't the right one.

"It's mine, it's accurate. It was only about five years ago, and we don't change prints once we're fully grown."

"Then all we'll need is your scent, which I'll gather here, magically." Dran gestured to the seat on one side of the room. "If you sit there for a moment, I'll collect your scent in a vial and then work on the tattoo."

Still obviously stunned, Knox dropped into the seat. "I don't know what to say."

"I wanted to do this. I wanted to show you how serious I am about you." Charlie crouched next to the seat, resting a hand on Knox's thigh. "I want to wear your mark, have your scent on me, at all times."

"I knew you were serious, but this, this is incredible, Charlie. I don't think you know just how much this means to me."

"I think I have an idea." Charlie pushed up and brushed a kiss across Knox's lips. "Now, sit there and do as you're told."

"Yes, boss."

Charlie watched as Dran gathered various bits of spell-casting equipment together. There was a small golden vial to one side. "That's where the scent will transfer to," Dran explained. "If you can both keep quiet as I do this?"

Both men nodded.

Ocorias tebedi ek mi onphili.

Dran chanted as he used a wand to draw patterns in the air. A fine gossamer mist detached from Knox and spiraled through the air towards the golden vial.

Piari excalia fodeste.

The air around Dran vibrated with power and energy, his magic flaring around him in a vibrant green halo. The mist poured into the top of the vial and a cork magically sealed into the top, trapping the mist inside.

Dran drew another pattern over the vial before tapping the cork three times. He looked over at them both and smiled. "That part is done."

"It was quicker than I thought. It looked easy, although I'm sure it's anything but."

Dran grinned. "It took me twelve years to master the spells needed to perform magical tattoos, and that was considered quick. There's a reason I'm the only tattoo artist in Corent who does this. Yes, there are other shops in Corent, and other artists here, but I'm the only one who can add scent markings to them." Dran turned to Knox. "You're lucky. I'm a customer of Charlie's, and love your work. I was there at the release party. I squeezed you both in because of that. I can only do one tattoo a week, two if I'm careful. I've blocked out all other tattoos for today and tomorrow to get this done."

"I don't know what to say, other than thank you. This is a gift beyond measure. I may be an author, but sometimes words fail me on a personal level. This is one of those times. This truly means more to me than you can possibly imagine. Charlie is… rare, and I worry. Having my mark, my scent on him like this, will give him some protection."

"I'm aware of what Charlie is, and that's the other part of the reason I was determined to get this done as soon as you were well enough." Dran moved over to the stool beside the tattooing chair. "Charlie is a great man and doesn't deserve to worry about being in danger. Doing this for you both makes me feel better."

"Still, thank you. Promise me, if you ever need anything, call on me. If you can't get a hold of me, get to one of my brothers. Tell them I sent you and they'll drop everything to help."

Dran looked stunned. Having a favor in the bank from one of the Vaughns was huge. "Now it's my turn to be speechless."

Charlie chuckled at them both. "I'm not," he teased. "Although, I am nervous."

"Don't be, you know I would never hurt you. It won't be comfortable, but it won't be painful, either." Dran carefully pushed the golden vial into a special slot in a compartment attached to the inkwell on his tattoo gun. "As I use the gun, the scent will slowly mix with the ink. Once the tattoo is finished, I'll perform another spell locking it all into the skin. Once that's done, I'll perform another spell that allows you to keep the tattoo as you shift."

"Wait a minute." Knox leaned forward in his seat. "Are you telling me the tattoo will be visible on both him *and* his beast?"

"I am." Dran nodded.

"Charlie, as much as I want my mark on you, are you sure? Your coat is perfect, pristine white. Are you sure you want to ruin it with my mark on you?"

Charlie bolted upright on the seat. "What do you mean, ruin it?"

"Well," Knox hedged, grimacing at the anger on Charlie's face. "You're pure white. My mark is going to be incredibly obvious, no matter where you put it."

"That's the whole point, you idiot."

"Oh." Knox gaped.

"You can be remarkably dense at times." Charlie flopped back down onto the chair.

"Hey!"

Charlie simply waved Knox off.

"Have you decided what color you want it?" Dran gestured to the pots of color along one wall. "If I don't have the exact color you want, I can create it."

Charlie looked to Knox, who smiled softly. "It's your tattoo, you need to be happy with it."

"Can you do it so it's in Knox's colors? I mean the oranges, creams, and blacks?" Charlie's heart thumped rapidly at the idea.

"You're a Siberian tiger?" Dran looked to Knox.

"I am."

Dran grabbed a book off a shelf to one side. "Can you go through this and find the one that gets as close to your markings as possible, as I'm guessing you still aren't allowed to shift?" He gestured to the cast on Knox's arm.

"I'm not." Knox reached for the book and began flicking through the images.

"Where are we doing this then?" Dran asked.

"I thought at first my shoulder, as that would be obvious in either form, but then I'd never see it if it was there. So, I thought it might be nice to have it on my chest. I can look in the mirror and see it then. I'd like it directly over my heart, please. It seems the most fitting place to be, seeing as Knox owns my heart."

Knox's head jerked up. "You... I... that is... I'm..."

"Look at you tongue-tying the big strong alpha." Dran held up a fist and Charlie bumped his against it.

Knox was unmoving as he stared at Charlie, before he had to fumble to grab the book he'd nearly dropped. "You're too good to me. I don't deserve you."

"I'd like to think we deserve each other." Charlie shrugged.

"You two are cute together." Dran smiled.

"I'm not cute, I'm a big strong alpha, a Siberian tiger. I have massive jaws, paws, and I…"

Both Dran and Charlie were staring at Knox.

"Fine, I'll just shut up, sit here, and choose the pattern that matches my markings."

"Wise choice." Charlie smirked.

Flipping through the images, Knox was humming to himself and Dran beckoned Charlie closer. "It's good to see you so happy. He's good for you, you're good for him. I meant it when I said it was nice knowing you're going to have more protection. I've worried about you for a long time."

Charlie reached out and hugged Dran. "I'm sorry I've worried you."

"Don't be, it's hardly your fault, but you are one of the nicest men I know. I'd hate to see anything happen to you, because you don't deserve anything but total happiness. As for him—" Dran gestured to Knox— "Whether he deserves happiness depends entirely on whether Delicious and Teaks get it together anytime soon."

"Let me let you in on a little secret," Charlie waggled his eyebrows. "I've been typing, Knox dictating, as he recovers. That way he's not behind schedule on the book."

"And…." Dran demanded.

"H.O.T. is all I have to say."

"Yes!" Dran shouted, making Knox look up and frown at them before he shrugged and carried on flipping through the book. "Seriously, finally?"

"Finally. This next book is incredible. I know I'm biased, several times over, but honestly, it's his best one yet."

"Please, tell me it's going to come out soon?"

"I don't know."

"A couple of months yet," Knox answered without looking up from the book.

"Oops, busted." Charlie grinned.

"I'll tell you what, Dran... do an excellent job on Charlie's tattoo, make him happy, and I'll add you to the ARC list. That way you'll get one early."

"Oh, by the gods, are you serious?" Dran pushed back on his seat, standing and moving beside Knox.

Knox finally looked up. "I am."

Dran flicked a gaze at Charlie. "Sorry about this." He turned back around and planted a massive kiss on Knox's lips.

"Hey!" Charlie cried out, although he wasn't really offended. He knew what Dran was feeling, the excitement and anticipation.

Knox patted Dran on the shoulder. "Uh, thank you?" He turned the book around. "This one. Honestly, I'd almost say it was me, not that I can see the face of the tiger, but my stripes are almost exactly like that and the differences are subtle."

"I have no idea where the pictures came from. It's just a collection from a local photographer." Dran shrugged. "But if this is almost an exact match, this is what I'll use." He turned the book around, so Charlie could look at the one Knox had selected. "You happy with this?"

Charlie studied the image. "Hell, you're right, that's almost exactly like your tiger. It's perfect."

"Then lay back and let's get this started." Dran kicked something on the floor and the tattoo gun started to whir.

Charlie stripped his shirt off and laid back, wincing slightly at the cold leather of the chair. Dran quickly chanted and the outline of Knox's paw was superimposed on Charlie's chest. "Are you happy with it there?"

Charlie looked into the mirror Dran held above him. "That's perfect." Not knowing what to expect, he braced himself mentally for pain. It never came. Instead, it was as if there were lots of tiny pinpricks. Not comfortable, but not painful either. Knox was watching the process in wonder as the outline of his paw was tattooed onto Charlie's skin.

Dran maintained a steady stream of conversation as he worked. By the time he was close to done, he and Knox had started on what Charlie was sure would end up a great friendship. There was a lot of laughter, far more than he had expected when he walked through the door. Dran was asking so many questions about writing, publishing, and Knox's books in general. He asked questions about Teaks in particular that Charlie had never even considered. Once or twice, other tattoo artists poked their head around the door, trying to work out why there was so much laughter.

It wasn't long, or at least it didn't feel like it, before the noise of the tattoo gun stopped. Laying it to one side, Dran stood, stretching, and working out the kinks in his back. Knox held up the mirror, so Charlie could see it properly.

"Oh, my gods, that is stunning. Dran, it's truly exceptional. I don't know how to thank you for doing this."

"As long as you're happy? You need to be sure before I cast the spells."

Charlie looked up at Knox. "What do you think?"

"It's perfect, I love it, but that's not what's important. It's how you feel about it."

"I couldn't have asked for it to come out any better than it has. Truly, I'm stunned by how perfect it looks."

"Spell time then?" Dran checked. Both Charlie and Knox nodded.

Dran held a small crystal ball in his hands, rolling it around, chanting words so fast, Charlie didn't have a hope of following what he was saying. A burst of heat rolled over Charlie's chest, followed by a blast of what felt like arctic wind. A featherlight touch ghosted over the paw outline before disappearing. Dran gently rested the crystal ball on Charlie's chest and rolled it over the tattoo. He assumed it left a film on his skin, but when he looked down, nothing was there.

"It's a magic layer, you won't feel anything. It sinks into your skin and protects the tattoo." Dran grabbed hold of a spell stone and began chanting again. This time the spell was much longer and far more complicated than Charlie believed was possible. The spell stone's color fluctuated rapidly. Captivated by the process, Charlie could only watch in awe at the intricacy of the spell. His unicorn watched through his eyes, fascinated by the play of colors in the stone. Damn beast always did love color— that was part of the reason Charlie had multicolored hair, after all. The air around them was thick and oppressive, a visible sign of magic being cast. Charlie didn't realize his eyes had slid shut until a gentle prodding made him jerk slightly.

"Sorry, I forgot to warn you that sometimes happens. The spell is intense." Dran's grin was sheepish as he gestured over to Knox in the chair. His head was tipped back, eyes shut, mouth open.

Charlie smiled and reached for the mirror Dran held out.

"It's all done now."

Charlie couldn't speak, too stunned at what he was seeing. He reached up, about to touch the tattoo before he froze and looked towards Dran, who nodded. He gently caressed the edges first, tracing the outline of Knox's paw before moving inward, tracing a finger over the stripes. It was everything he'd imagined, and so much more. There wasn't an ounce of regret in him, just wonder and happiness about being able to do this for them both.

Dran handed him a glass. "Drink this, it will help with the after-effects of the spell, any residual pain you may feel, and help with the healing. Being magical, you don't need to care for it as intensely as you would a normal tattoo, but still be careful and try not to rub it. But honestly, you shouldn't feel it. If anything strange happens, if anything feels off, then either pop in or give me a call."

"I will. Dran, I truly can't thank you enough for this. It means more than I can possibly express."

234

"I think I can get an idea of just how much it means to you." Dran cast a quick glance at Knox. "You're good together, you know? If you'd have said to me a couple of months ago that you would end up with Knox Vaughn, I'd have laughed in your face. I would never have put the two of you together, but you work. You complement each other perfectly. Seeing you two together, the way you seem to gravitate toward each other, the way his eyes follow you around the room, it's obvious just how much you mean to him. I long for a love like that one day."

"You'll find it, Dran. You deserve to be loved like this. I can't imagine anyone who deserves happiness as much as you."

"Thank you." Dran smiled softly. "How's Matt? Any news on that yet?"

"Nothing. Knox and Carter have both sent requests, appeals for help, information, anything. No one knows anything. The mages and doctors are at a loss."

"Let's hope someone comes forward with something soon."

Charlie nodded, the pain in his chest flaring at everything his friend was going through.

"If you or Matt need anything, you know to call, right?"

Charlie looked at his friend and smiled. "I've always known you'd be there for me. Thank you, it truly means a lot. Both Matt and I appreciate it more than you know."

Dran looked across the room. "You'd better wake up your man."

Grinning, Charlie stalked over to Knox. "Time to wake up," he whispered softly into his ear. "Oh, Knox…"

"Huh?"

"So eloquent," he teased. "The tattoo is done. It's time to go home."

Knox rubbed the sleep from his eyes. "Oh, I must be more tired than I thought."

Charlie just shrugged, not bothering to say anything. Out at the front of the shop, he tried to pay, but Dran quickly waved him away. "I don't need anything for it. I was happy to do it."

"Dran, you're taking two days off. I need to pay you," Charlie insisted.

"You really don't." Dran crossed his arms.

"Please," Charlie argued, but Dran stayed where he was.

"Come on, love, it's pointless trying to argue with a bear. They're one of the most stubborn shifters out there. There's a reason a lot of PAF don't want to work with them." Knox winked at Dran, the bear/mage hybrid laughing, letting Knox know he wasn't taking offense.

"Then I'll do the only thing I can do and keep you in a supply of books." Charlie shrugged.

Dran narrowed his eyes before scowling. "Fine, we'll continue this argument at a later date."

"Why, yes, yes, we will," Charlie teased. Reaching out, he pulled Dran into a hug, being careful of his chest. "Thank you for this."

"You are most welcome. Now, if you'll excuse me, I'm going upstairs to crash into bed and pass out for a bit."

The paleness of Dran's skin captured Charlie's attention. "I think that's probably a smart idea. If you need anything, please call."

"I will." Dran walked them to the door, smiling as he waved goodbye.

CHAPTER TWENTY-TWO

Walking back into Knox's family room, Charlie was stunned to see everyone there. Max winced when he saw Charlie, and Cora wouldn't look at him. "What's going on?" Charlie shared a look with Knox as they took seats on one of the sofas, presenting a united front.

"I'm sorry, Charlie," Max began.

"For what?"

Max hung his head. When he finally looked up, there was anguish in his eyes. "I was talking to Nate about what you were off to do today. Both Carter and Cora overheard. Carter called Tyler in for a meeting."

"It's alright, we were going to tell people anyway. It's not as if I was going to keep it a secret." Charlie shrugged, completely unsure what the big deal was.

Max carried on. "Cora called Evie, who called Matt and Mama Alice, and they all came racing over."

"Why?" Charlie questioned, looking between them all.

"Why!" Mama Alice's roar shook the walls. "You have to ask why?"

"Yes." Charlie leaned against Knox, dumbfounded and oblivious to what was going on. When he looked at Knox's face, he was actually glad to see Knox was as confused as he was. "Why did you race over here? I haven't got the slightest idea what's going on."

"Did you, or did you not," Mama Alice hissed, "Go and get a magical tattoo today."

"Yes, I did," Charlie answered truthfully.

"There is no removing magical tattoos," Alice bit out.

"I am aware of that." Charlie barely resisted rolling his eyes. "Seriously, what's going on here. What am I missing? I thought you all liked Knox, that you approved of us together? You called him 'your sweet boy' when you came to visit while he was on bed rest. What the hell has changed between now and then? Someone help me out here. I don't understand why you're so upset."

"You're not mated!"

"Yet." Charlie could see she was struggling to hold her temper. He caught a startled glance shared between Knox's brothers. "We're not mated *yet*. It doesn't mean we won't be. That, however, is something personal between Knox and I until we're ready to tell anyone else."

"You shouldn't have done that. It was stupid, reckless, irresponsible—"

"Stop. I suggest you stop right there, Alice." Charlie's voice was icy cold as he dropped the honorific mama. "Think carefully and choose your words wisely. You're like a mother to me, granted, but that does not give you the right to say what you're about to say."

Alice ignored him and the warning looks Matt was sending her way. "Your poor mother would be devastated to see what you have done."

"Alice has a point, Charlie," Evie added.

Something inside Charlie snapped. "How dare both of you. You're overreacting, seeing problems where they don't exist, and you damn well know it. I just wonder why. Yes, I chose to get a magical tattoo of Knox's paw and scent. *I* did it. It was *my* choice, *my* suggestion. It wasn't Knox's idea, it was all mine. I did it because I *love* him. I shouldn't have to justify my decision to you or anyone else." Charlie yanked open his shirt.

There were audible gasps as people took in the tattoo prominently on his chest. "This is what I wanted. I did this for me, most of all, but also for Knox. I'd like to think both my parents would be happy for me, proud of me, but you know what? I'm a grown ass man. This is my decision. I'd be having the same 'conversation' with my parents as I am with you. It was my choice, my decision and no one else's. Fuck you all for questioning it, for spoiling something special. Knox—" he turned to face him— "I'm going back to my place to calm down. Give me time?" He grabbed hold of Knox's hand briefly and squeezed. Knox nodded, but Charlie caught a glimpse of the barely controlled rage lurking in Knox's eyes. Charlie stormed out the house without a backward glance, hearing the argument break out behind him.

He'd told Knox he was going home, but he took the longer route back, too angry, and worried if he went straight home, he'd end up destroying things. What the hell had that been all about? The whole thing was absurd. He'd thought everyone got on with Knox, was happy for them both? Why now, why react like this? It made no sense whatsoever. He truly couldn't understand what they were so upset about. All he knew was that he was pissed at them, angrier than he had been in a long time.

As night descended, he forced himself to go home. He didn't want Knox to worry he hadn't returned, go looking for him, and not find him. His temper may have calmed, mostly, but he still didn't understand why Alice and Evie had been so upset. If he was truthful, it had hurt, a lot, for them to turn on him in such a way. Yet, they were family, and he'd forgive them, but he still needed to know why.

"We've been looking for you." The man attached to the voice appeared out of nowhere. Charlie spun around and came face to face with two men holding blades. They'd been waiting for him on his front porch.

"Who are you?"

"It doesn't concern you. It's what we want that does." One of the men ran a loving finger over the blade he carried.

Charlie carefully eased his hand into his pocket, trying to find his phone. There was one advantage to having a magical phone, and that was the extras that came with it. He'd recently changed his emergency beacon to include Knox, as well as Evie and Lane. Finding it, he tapped out a quick rhythm onto the face.

Two, one, one, two. Pause, two, one, one, two, he repeated the code, just in case. Lane, Evie, and Knox's phones would all start blaring. On their screens would be an alert that Charlie needed help and his location. One of the men yanked his hand from his pocket.

"Shit, he sent out an alert. Port! Now!"

The world spun.

Charlie was flung to the floor as soon as he came out of the teleport. Coughing as a thick layer of dirt and dust stirred around him, he struggled to breathe. He had no idea where he was, or who held him. Fighting against the breathlessness, he forced himself to sit up, trying to wave away the dust he was now caked in. Through the haze, he could make out the two men who had taken him arguing with someone else.

"What the fuck did you bring him here for?" the new man demanded, slapping one of the others across the face.

"He used his phone. It was flashing with an emergency broadcast. You're the one who wanted him. If we hadn't ported here, you'd have lost him. I don't see us getting another chance. He'll be heavily guarded from now on."

Why were they after— realization dawned on Charlie. Somehow, some way, they knew what he was. These were hunters, he was sure of it. They'd found out who he was, what he was, and they were here for him. Fighting the rising panic, Charlie tried to think rationally, something much easier said than done.

"I get that, but bringing him here was fucking stupid." The man was growling.

"I thought you wanted him to finish the collection?"

"Finish the collection, Albert? Are you fucking stupid? My collection's only just begun. I've still got his bitch sister and those babies of hers to get. Only then will the family be complete."

Charlie looked in the direction the man was gesturing. There, in a display case, were two horns. What most people didn't realize, was that the pattern of grooves and order of iridescent color on a unicorn's horn were indicators of which family they belonged to. While he couldn't see the colors in this light, the grooves were unmistakable because they formed the basis of his own. He was looking at the horns belonging to his parents. He turned to the side and threw up.

"You know what you're looking at, don't you, boy. You know who they belonged to. I had immense pleasure collecting them, and I'll get even more collecting yours. Of course, I've hollowed them out to get at the latent magic. I'll do the same with yours. I just couldn't resist keeping the shells for my display."

Charlie refused to answer the man. He wasn't going to give him the satisfaction of hearing a trace of distress in his voice. Instead, he forced himself to stay as calm as possible and think. He'd set the beacon off, he knew he had, which meant that his family, no matter how pissed off they were at each other, would go charging to the rescue. The problem was, his phone had been knocked out of his hand. How would they know where he was? They wouldn't, which meant Charlie had to try and rescue himself.

Without lifting his head, he looked around the room he was in. There was one door on the far left-hand side, and a window opposite, which meant a potential escape route on each side. A door suggested he must be on the ground floor, unless that was a balcony. Still, he was a shifter— he could recover from most falls from most of the buildings in Corent. They had to be in Corent somewhere.

Teleporting outside was forbidden without express permission. Anyone attempting it would be magically marked and a retrieval squad dispatched to bring them back. That was something; he didn't want to think about being outside the safety of Corent's walls and potentially falling into the hands of ferals. It was bad enough that hunters had him.

"What do you want me to do?" the one called Albert asked the man who had hit him.

"Just watch him while I sort out somewhere for us to go. We're just on the outskirts of the warehouse district, for fuck's sake. Someone is going to see us eventually and start asking questions. I don't want to still be here when they do."

Charlie heard the door slam. By his reckoning, that left two men with him.

"You'd think he'd be happy we found him. If it weren't for the article in the paper, we'd never have known. Looks just like his mam, that one."

Charlie inwardly cursed. They'd always been careful to hide their beasts, but it had never occurred to any of them that it might be in their human forms that someone recognized them. Not that it mattered now, he'd been taken. That's what he needed to focus on. That and getting himself out of this mess. He hadn't just found Knox to lose him. Fuck that. The man was not getting away from him. He deserved this, deserved a shot at happiness, they both did, and Charlie was going to make sure they got it. Resolve and determination swamped his body. He might not be a fighter, might not be PAF trained, but that didn't mean he was useless. Taking a small breath, he pushed the fear to the back of his mind and plotted.

How had he fallen asleep? It made no sense. His unicorn would never have let him lower his guard to such an extent. He found his answer when he spied an abandoned, used syringe on the floor in front of him. Drugged. They'd drugged him. *I guess that's one way to keep me compliant.* But, it was also a way for them to let their guards down.

Moving slowly, he shuffled until he could see almost the full room. There was only one man left, and he was fast asleep in a chair, his blade laying on a table beside him. Charlie's heart picked up speed. Rather than rush, he waited, letting his unicorn take control. It was hard— the beast was still as groggy as he was from the effects of whatever he'd been injected with. The unicorn perked up his ears, listening, sniffing, trying to check on what Charlie's eyes were seeing. The unicorn was in full agreement. There was only one guard, and he was sound asleep.

Moving cautiously, Charlie eased his body up, moving to kneeling, then crouching, before finally standing. On second thought, he squatted, trying to stay out of sight from the windows. Although, given the layer of dirt on everything, including the windows, he doubted anyone would have a clear view inside. That was probably one of the reasons the room had been chosen. With small and light footsteps, he carefully made his way across the room, praying to all the gods of the para world to watch over him.

By some miracle, none of the boards under his feet creaked with his weight, and he made it safely to the door. His unicorn was right below the surface, trying to share his mind, calling on them both to escape. With an unsteady hand, he gently lowered the lock on the door, holding his breath as he slid the door open just enough for him to squeeze through. Peering out into the dark, he couldn't see anyone about. He considered trying to close the door, potentially buying more time, but it was too much of a risk. Keeping to the shadows as much as possible, he wound his way around the building, only starting to breathe easier when he was out of sight from the entrance.

Like he'd heard, he was in an industrial complex of some kind. It wasn't a part of Corent he was familiar with, and with the buildings as high as they were, there were no readily discernable landmarks he could use to guide him back to safety. He could hear footsteps walking about, but that could be anyone, from the hunters, to a night watchman, to someone out intent on mischief unrelated to him. Ultimately, it didn't matter, he needed to get the fuck out of there. Stumbling slightly, he grunted when he slammed into a wall, scraping his arm. The drugs were still in his system, and his balance was off. He briefly considered trying to shift, but it would leave him vulnerable, and as white as he was, he would make an easy target.

Stumbling around, he worked his way through the maze of buildings, trying to find the way out. Judging by the height of the moon, he'd been out for a couple of hours. Long enough for Knox and his family to call just about everyone in looking for him. Seeing a wrought-iron gate, a thrill went through him. He might just pull this off.

"Where do you think you're going, lad?" An arm wrapped around his neck, choking him. "Thought we wouldn't notice when you disappeared, hey?"

Charlie tore at the arm holding him to no avail. He'd been so close. Frustration tore through him, even as he fought to breathe. When he was flung back into the same room he'd been in earlier, he could have cried. A blow to the back of his head, and Charlie succumbed to darkness once again.

When Charlie came to, he realized it was daylight. How long had he been gone? Knox, his family, must be frantic by now.

"You're awake." A blow to the stomach accompanied the words. "Shift."

Charlie ignored the demand.

"Shift, or I'll inject you with shit that will not only make you shift, but make you wish you were dead."

Charlie steadfastly ignored the demand. When the jab of a needle stung his shoulder, he wasn't surprised. His heart shattered. Not only for what was about to happen to him, but for what Knox would suffer. He would blame himself, they all would. Yet, the way Charlie saw it, this was inevitable. He'd leave the world the same way his parents had, the same way so many of his ancestors had. His unicorn tried to fight it, but the drugs forced the shift, and there was nothing either of them could do to stop it. His unicorn begged him for forgiveness. *There is nothing to forgive. It's been my pleasure having you as my beast.* A single tear rolled down Charlie's cheek as the shift finished and he lay panting on the floor. Such a violent shift had ripped through his clothes and had him rolling around on the floor, leaving his coat a dirty, muddy gray.

Staggering to his feet, he tried to take up a defensive position, but his legs were wobbly, his limbs buckling under the pain of whatever he'd been injected with. When he tossed back his head and let out a plaintive cry, there was a guttural shout.

"What the fuck! He's marked!" The man in charge, the one he still didn't have a name for, was cursing like a minion from the depths of hell. "How the fuck could you not notice he was marked!" His hand became a claw and he sliced through Albert's stomach in one swift move, leaving the man bleeding out on the floor.

"What?" the second of his original captors cried.

"That's a gods damned mark." The man stared at Charlie's chest with mounting horror. When his nostrils twitched, Charlie wondered if he could smell Knox. "Oh fuck."

Charlie was taking that as a yes. When he'd shifted, it had taken more energy than usual, and he was still sweating. It must have increased the potency of the smell emanating from the mark.

"That's Knox Vaughn's scent. I'd know the fucking smell anywhere. Damn bastard hunted us for months." Rising horror covered the man's features. "I'm not having the fucking Vaughn brothers chasing after me. I don't want his horn that bloody much. That's got to be his bloody mate. Fuck this." The man ran, leaving the door wide open. The man looked briefly at his fallen friend and sprinted after their boss, leaving Charlie alone with the man dying beside him.

Unable to cope with the pain tearing through his system, the unicorn's legs buckled, sending him crashing to the floor. With each passing minute, the pain had been increasing exponentially, and Charlie couldn't think, couldn't process. All he was capable of was feeling. A thousand knives ripped through his muscles, shredding them. Something pounded in his skull, and his eyes screwed shut when the light seared into them. Incapable of doing anything, the unicorn screamed, begging for death, for peace, for something, anything to end the horror he was living through. Unable to cope any longer, their minds gave in and they slipped into unconsciousness.

CHAPTER TWENTY-THREE

Someone needed to stop the damn beeping or Charlie was not going to be responsible for his actions. The incessant beep, beep, blip was driving him to distraction.

"How is he?" Wait a minute. That voice… it was… Evie. Yes, that's right, it was his sister.

"No change."

Knox! He was with Knox. Charlie's mind settled at that. Wherever he was, if he was with Knox, he was safe.

"It's been two weeks, Knox. The poison they gave him is out of his system. He should have woken up by now." Evie sounded distraught.

"You think I don't know that!" Knox's roar was full of pain.

Charlie wanted to say something, to let them know he could hear them, but nothing was responding to his commands.

"Do something!" Evie's demand ripped through the room.

"What the fuck do you want me to do, Evie? What about you, Alice? I've done everything I can. I've begged and pleaded with every doctor, every PAF team I know. No one can do anything else. They've done all they can. It's just a question of waiting to see if he wakes up. Waiting to find out what damage was caused by the poison in his system."

"This wouldn't have happened if you hadn't marked him," Alice hissed.

"Actually," a new voice spoke up, one Charlie couldn't place. "It's because Knox here marked him that Charlie survived."

"What are you talking about," Alice demanded.

"Yesterday we caught the man who escaped. He's been persuaded to talk. As Lane told Knox when they found Charlie, those horns belonged to Charlie's parents. These were the hunters who killed them. They wanted Charlie, Evie, and the babies as well. The only thing that stopped them is when they saw the mark after they forced Charlie into a shift. Charlie getting that tattoo literally saved his life. If they hadn't seen that mark, he'd have been dead before Knox found him. I get you're angry, Alice, but don't take it out on Knox. It isn't his fault. It never was."

Charlie finally recognized the voice. That was Sam.

"But…"

"There are no buts, Alice. You're feeling guilty because you argued with Charlie and he left. That doesn't mean you get to take your frustration out on Knox. He hasn't done anything to deserve that. Besides, there's something I want answered. Something I'm sure Knox would love to know the answer to as well. Why were you so against Charlie having the tattoo? Not that he needs it, but do you not approve of Knox?"

"No, I do approve of him." Alice was quick to say.

"Then what is it?"

"It's because that's a permanent mark, and they aren't mated. Knox could still walk away at any time and Charlie would be left with his mark. No other shifter would want him with that," Alice confessed.

Charlie was fuming. Even if that were the case, it was still his damn decision.

"Has it ever occurred to you that Charlie and I have already discussed us mating?" Knox spoke quietly. "We agreed that mating was something we wanted, but decided we needed time to get to

248

know each other fully first before we made anything official. We weren't telling anyone, because frankly, no one but us had a right to know. I know you don't like that, Alice, but it's true. Charlie is a grown man. He's no longer a boy, and it's time you and Evie stopped seeing him that way. He needs to know you support him, that you'll be there for him if he makes mistakes, but that you won't try to control his life for him. He deserves that freedom. Yes, he's one of the rarest shifters out there, but if you carry on treating him the way you've been treating him, not only will you lose him, but you might as well put him on display in a damn zoo."

Charlie couldn't see anyone's reactions to Knox's words, but he could imagine them.

"I never meant to treat him that way." Alice sounded close to tears.

Knox sighed. "I know you didn't, but over time that's what has happened. It doesn't help that Lane is as alpha as he is and that you both see him as PAF and not just a unicorn. Tell me something, though, why do you treat Charlie so different from Lane? Sure, Lane had PAF training, but otherwise, there is little difference between them. What is it about Charlie that has you acting like he can't look after himself? You even stop him running in the forest, only allowing him to run on Lane's property. What sort of life is that?"

Charlie really wanted to join in the conversation, but it was like he couldn't quite break free from whatever controlled him.

The pain in Knox's voice was clear. "Honestly, I think you all need to sit down and sort this out. I don't want Charlie to lose what little family he has, but I will always do what is best for him. Don't get me wrong, I'll always worry if he's out and about without me, but I know just how smart he is. He can and will look after himself anytime he needs to. Think about what I've said, Alice. Because when Charlie wakes up, and it is a when, I won't accept anything else, but when he wakes up, I want this done with. It's time for him to truly live his life."

"I'm going to go. Come with me for a chat, Evie," Alice muttered.

"I'll take you," Sam offered.

There was silence for a few minutes.

"You know, I think you can hear me. Don't ask me why, but I'm almost positive you heard all that." A finger gently caressed his forehead. "I think you're almost awake, so I need you to listen to me, Charlie. I need you to focus on my voice and come back to me. I don't work properly without you in my life. I guess it's been quick, but you're as integral to my survival as the air I breathe. I want you to focus on my voice and use it as a guide to come back. Come back to me, sweetheart. Open your eyes and let me see you."

Charlie fought with everything in him, struggling against the molasses swamp his mind was mired in. It was within his power to make Knox smile again, all he needed to do was just open his eyes. He could do that. He knew he could. He fought, inch by painful inch, through the quagmire, but the brightness grew, and he knew he was getting closer. Knox's voice was like a beacon, guiding him, showing the way home. Because Knox was his home. He was his safety, his port of call, his rock when things became tough. He was everything, and he was his mate. His unicorn woke up, sensing what was going on, and gave Charlie his strength. Together, they pushed forward, covering the last bit of distance to the light.

Charlie opened his eyes, blinking at the brightness that assaulted them. Managing to lick his lips, he croaked, "Knox."

Knox's head snapped up, and Charlie would have gasped if he could. Knox looked ragged. He no longer sported stubble. Instead, he had a full beard growing. There were new lines around his eyes and tiredness radiated out from every part of him.

"Charlie? You heard me?"

"Yes. Water?" His eyes tracked Knox as he poured water and hit the call button. Seconds later, a nurse he recognized came breezing into the room. It was Orin, the nurse who had looked after Matt.

"Good to see you awake and with us, Charlie." Orin began checking him over before moving on to the monitors, scanning the readouts. "Things are looking good on here. Now, can you talk, see, and feel?"

"Yes," Charlie croaked out before sipping the water through the straw Knox held out for him.

"Are you in any pain? I can give you something if you are."

"No." Charlie's voice was a little stronger this time.

"Good, but you let me know if anything changes. The doctor will be here any— ah, there he is. Charlie, this is Doctor Marcus."

"Hello, Charlie." The doctor stepped into his line of sight. "It's nice to see you awake. How much do you remember?"

Charlie searched his mind. He remembered being forced to shift, the hunters seeing his mark and running, then collapsing. After that, he was getting flashes, odd images of events. He remembered hearing Knox's tiger, his roar. Bursts of orange and black, screams and claws. The next thing he remembered was being carried, tears splashing on his face. After that, nothing until he woke up. He hadn't realized he'd been talking out loud.

"We got there just as you collapsed. I called your name, but you couldn't hear me. My brothers gave chase to the guy who ran out first— we were still racing towards you when he ran. Lane ran in with me. We had to fight. My tiger burst free, and let's just say he was pissed." Knox's lips twitched. "That's what you're remembering. After that, I carried you out. You weren't responding, your heartbeat was erratic, sweat was pouring off you. You were so hot, you were like a damn furnace. Lane called Sam and Alfie, they met us and ported us straight here. The doctors took over. You've been asleep for two weeks. It damn near broke me, seeing you in that state."

A tear rolled down Charlie's cheek. "I'm sorry."

Knox brushed it away tenderly. "Hey now, what are you sorry for?"

"Getting caught, hurt, everything."

"That wasn't your fault. You have nothing to be sorry for. The only thing I care about is the fact you're here, looking me in the eyes, and talking. I love you, Charlie. You and only you matter."

"How bad is it?" Charlie asked.

It was Doctor Marcus that answered. "It seems like where one of you leads, the other follows."

Charlie wrinkled his eyebrows.

Marcus chuckled. "You have a cast on your left arm now, just like Knox had. There'll be no shifting for you for a few weeks. Bizarrely it's almost a carbon copy of the break Knox had. You have some bruises, but apart from that, you've been here because of the poison they injected you with. The best we can tell, it was designed purely to force a shift. We haven't been able to detect any other side effects, but we couldn't work out why you weren't waking up and worried that we'd missed something. Now you're back with us, we'll run some tests to be sure, but the poison has already been burned off. You should be fine from now on. My best guess is, your body shut down to fight the poison, knowing being in unicorn form put you in danger."

"When can I go home?" Charlie asked, surprised when Knox stiffened beside him.

"As long as your tests come back fine, I'll let you go home tomorrow, on the proviso that if anything changes, you come straight back." The doctor's eyes held a warning.

"I promise."

"Very well." Marcus nodded. "I'll go and arrange some tests. In the meantime, catch up with your man here, and for goodness sake, remind him to shave!" The doctor strode out the door.

"So…" Charlie fiddled with the blankets. "Is that okay with you?"

"Is what okay with me?" Knox stroked the back of Charlie's hand.

"That if they let me out that I come home with you."

Knox stared at him for a moment. "Is that what you meant when you said home?"

"Yes, of course it was."

"But, that's my place, not yours."

"Knox, wherever you are, that's my home. The building doesn't matter, only you." The last word broke on a yawn.

"Get some rest. I'll be right here when you wake up." Knox leaned down and brushed a tender kiss over his lips.

"You promise?"

"Now and forever, sweetheart."

Charlie wanted to say more, but sleep was calling him.

He was beginning to realize why Knox had been so demented. Staying in bed sucked. Sure, he had a stack of books to read and he might just clear some of the backlog of reading he had to do, but he wanted the freedom to move about, go and check on the shop, everything, anything. But, with guard dog Knox on patrol, he didn't have a chance in hell. Even if he made it past Knox, Carter was always about. He was getting creative about cursing the Vaughn brothers. Bunch of crazy, flea-bitten, mangy-assed, catnip-addicted pussycats. Of course, he didn't say that out loud. He didn't have a death wish. His unicorn was having a fantasy about running around the forest, jabbing people with his horn, his coat matted with blood. The damn beast was in a blood-thirsty mood again. Charlie might just join him.

A cough broke their combined fantasy and he looked up. Knox was leaning against the door frame, twirling something in his hands. "Ready to kill everyone yet?"

"Yes." Charlie went to cross his arms and whacked himself with the cast. "Damn it!"

Knox winced in sympathy. "I did that once or twice." He stalked towards the bed and held out a toy. "I'm hoping you might get the significance of this."

Charlie took the toy. It was a toy tiger, and Knox must have wrapped it in the bow, because it was cuddled around a unicorn. His startled gaze darted to Knox's face. "What are you saying?"

"Want to come cuddle in my box?" Knox frowned for a moment. "Why does that sound like the corniest pickup line ever?"

"I would love to cuddle you in your box if you're both happy to have me there. What about my jailors?"

Knox snorted. "I'm here. Carter knows I won't let anything happen to you. He gave me a lecture about caring for you the way you cared for me." Knox was incredibly gentle as he lifted Charlie out of bed, settling him in his arms.

Wrapping his arms around Knox's neck, Charlie huffed, "I'm not a complete invalid, you know."

"I know that, but right now I need to protect you, care for you, and love you. Let me, let us do that, please? We need it. We're feeling like we failed."

Charlie shook his head. "I don't blame anyone. No one failed, least of all you. Now, take me to your box." Charlie shook his head. "It doesn't sound any better when I say it that way."

Keeping Charlie pinned to his chest with one arm, Knox opened the door to his walk-in closet, walking to the end and opening another door. It was a small room, dominated by a box. This wasn't just any box though. Large and ornate, it was stuffed with pillows of all shapes, sizes, and fabrics. Peering over the edge of the box, Charlie could see a whole collection of toys, from balls to cuddly toys. "Oh wow."

"This is our box." Knox gently put Charlie down inside the box, guiding his hands so he could steady himself on the edge of the box. "Let me shift." He stripped down quickly.

Charlie's gaze heated as he took in Knox in all his glory. The bruising had finally faded and his chest was back to normal, muscles on display everywhere.

"Behave. We can't do anything," Knox murmured as he dropped to the floor of the box. In no time at all, Knox was replaced by his tiger.

The beauty of the beast still took Charlie's breath away. The tiger quickly checked all corners of the box— for what, Charlie had no idea— but soon enough he was satisfied and shuffled down onto his side on a collection of giant pillows. He lifted one massive leg and waited. Charlie took the hint and carefully lowered himself to the floor, shifting about until he could back up against the tiger. As soon as he was in range, the tiger pulled him closer and nuzzled his head. Charlie grinned when a large paw rested over the paw mark on his chest and his back vibrated with the force of the purr coming from the beast. It was obvious how much he approved of the tattoo and happiness, contentment, and comfort washed over Charlie.

He had no idea how long they stayed there, him wrapped in the tiger's embrace, and the toy version of them in his arms, but he didn't care. He would stay there as long as the tiger wanted him to. The heat the tiger was giving off was like a cozy blanket, and it wasn't long before Charlie's eyelids started to get heavy. He didn't fight it, letting them slide shut.

"You have to admit, that is completely adorable." Carter's voice found its way to Charlie's ears. "I should probably tell Knox off for

moving Charlie, but I think that's the deepest sleep I've seen either of them in since Knox went on the mission."

"I'm not asleep," Charlie grumbled.

"It's time for some pills."

When Charlie forced his eyes open, he could see Carter and Tyler grinning down at him. "I'm not in any pain."

"And I'm pleased about that. These pills, however, are to help counteract any residual effects from…" Carter cast a wary glance at the tiger. "Let's just say counteract things. Please, put my mind at ease and take them?"

Charlie reached out a hand and took the pills, dropping them into his mouth before reaching for the bottle of water Tyler held out. "Better?"

"Thank you." Carter leaned over the edge of the box, taking in the possessive positioning of the tiger's paw. "He likes it then?"

"I'd say so. His paw hasn't moved from there since we got in." A loud rumble from behind him made Charlie turn to look as best he could. The tiger was awake and watching him with an intensity that would have been frightening if he was being chased. He reached out and gently ran his fingers through the fur on the tiger's head, smiling as the tiger pushed into the touch.

"I thought they were adorable before, but this is something else." Tyler stared in wonder at them. "I've never seen any of our tigers as content as that. It's obvious you're mates. No one else would be able to stay in such a position. No one else would be welcome."

The tiger sniffed deeply, seemingly satisfied with the results. "That tattoo is something else, you know that?" Carter sighed and leaned forward to give his brother a good scratch behind the ear. "Here's the thing. That tattoo saved your life. I know you managed to set off the beacon, and that was amazing, by the way, but it was Knox that tracked you. He managed to hone in on his own scent, on your combined scent. It was just a matter of finding it to start with. As soon as he picked it up, he was running at max speed. It was all we could do to keep up."

Tyler joined his brother. "Max is feeling guilty, Cora more so. They both feel responsible for everything that happened. Not just the argument, but you being taken. If they hadn't said anything…"

"You all need to stop thinking like that. It's no one's fault. I could and should have been paying more attention to my surroundings. I shouldn't have walked out the way I did. I was angry, and I chose to walk away rather than let it escalate. It did anyway, just not in the way I expected. I don't blame anyone but the hunters who took me. I've lived a long time with the fear of being taken hanging over my head. But you know something? That fear is gone now. I've already been taken, and while it was bad, it could have been so much worse."

All three brothers, whatever form they were in, looked at him in astonishment. "Think about it," he insisted. "I was always sure I would be taken by hunters, tortured hard before I was killed. Yes, I was taken, and it was bad, but I'm here, and what's more, it was only me that was taken. I could have had Danny, or the twins with me. I would never have forgiven myself. So yes, it really could have been a lot worse."

Carter's fist was white-knuckled. "We would have ripped the very world apart to find them, you know that. Not that we wouldn't for you, but all the PAF, everyone would have turned out to find them. Nowhere would have been safe for the hunters. It's not that people don't care about you…"

"I get it, kids, babies are different. They can't do anything to protect themselves. I can."

"You did," Tyler assured him. "Donald, the man who held you, the one who started all this with your parents, confessed everything. He told us that you'd escaped. I don't know how, he didn't say, but you never gave up, Charlie. We are all so damn proud of you. Knox was… I've never seen him like that, and I never want to again. But he didn't for one moment lose faith in you. He knew that somehow you would keep yourself alive until he could find you."

Carter took over, his gaze trained on his brother's tiger. "I've never seen him that bad. I remember what it was like when our parents died. He was distraught then, but he had us to look after, and that kept him going. When he was by your bedside, it was obvious that he wouldn't survive if you didn't. He loves you with all his heart. You make him happy, you give him a home, comfort, peace. I'm sure he's told you all this. But hear it from us as well. He loves you, his tiger loves you. Look at him, he doesn't want to let you go. You are a perfect fit for him, for our family."

Charlie sniffed. "I love him and his tiger with all my heart. Knox is it for me. I knew he was before all this happened. There was a reason I got this tattoo. I wanted it, I wanted the extra connection with him. I hope me being a unicorn, not being PAF, not being an alpha, our differences, isn't something you all hate."

Before Charlie could say anything else, the tiger snarled.

"There's an answer for you, Charlie. Knox doesn't care if we don't approve. He would be with you anyway. We know that. I'm sure he appreciates the fact we all get along, but make no mistake, he'd be with you anyway. Of course, he could just shift and talk." Carter looked pointedly at his brother.

The tiger huffed and stayed exactly where he was. At some point, Charlie must have dropped the toy version of them, because the tiger carefully pulled the toys towards them, lifted it up with a single claw tucked under the ribbon, and placed it on Charlie's chest, next to his paw print. He patted it gently, then went back to resting his paw over his mark and nuzzled into Charlie's neck. Charlie turned his head as best he could and kissed the tiger's head.

"I have never seen anything quite like that." Wonder filled Tyler's voice. "I have never seen a tiger be quite as gentle as he was then. Is that…" Tyler peered closer.

Charlie had the toy cuddled to his chest with his good arm. The one in the cast was lying against the tiger's other leg. Every time he tried to move it, Knox snarled, so he left it there, letting the tiger take the weight. He wondered if he even felt it.

"It's us, the toy version of us anyway."

"It's adorable." Carter sighed. "You really should be in bed, but I guess he's keeping you warm enough, and as long as you're comfortable, I guess you can stay there."

Charlie yawned, but it wasn't enough to stave off sleep. As his eyes started to slide closed, he heard Tyler laughing.

"Yeah, I think he's comfortable enough. Let's leave them to it."

Charlie cuddled into his tiger and let sleep claim him.

Rolling over, Charlie grunted in annoyance at the cast, making Knox chuckle.

"Morning, Sunshine."

"Is it?" Charlie grunted.

"Didn't sleep well?"

Charlie wasn't about to confess to the nightmares he'd had, so he simply grunted.

"If you want, I was going to take you to the shop. I thought you might like to choose some new books." Knox was massaging his head.

Charlie perked up at that.

"I knew that would grab your attention. What do you say?" Knox kissed a path over his forehead.

"Do you really need me to answer that one?" Charlie finally opened his eyes, gazing straight into Knox's.

"Not really. Now, do you want me to help you get dressed?" Knox's hand drifted down Charlie's stomach, toying with the tie around his pajama pants.

"Do you mean get dressed, or…" Charlie licked his lips.

"You choose."

"If I choose, you have to realize I'm choosing a treat."

"I'm unsurprisingly okay with that." Knox grinned.

Charlie watched Knox disappear under the covers. A moment later, his cock was engulfed in heat for a split second. He spasmed.

Knox reared up and growled. "No moving."

"You're just getting revenge." Charlie let his head drop back against the pillows.

"Would I do a thing like that?" Knox teased.

"Yes! Now get to it." Charlie swallowed the last word as Knox swallowed his cock down to the root. He lost himself to the sensations of heat and Knox, letting their connection flare, letting the love they shared manifest in this most intimate way. They seemed to spend half their time being banned from sex, but it didn't stop them having fun. If anything, it had just made them creative. He was allowed sex; this was more to do with the amount of time it would take. They'd never get—

A slap on his thigh dragged him back to the moment. Knox pulled off with a pop.

"If you're thinking this much, I have to be doing something wrong." Knox went back down to his cock, kissing along it as his fingers danced across his balls. Charlie lost himself to the sensations, letting Knox have his way with him, wanting, no, needing this connection. When one of Knox's fingers slipped inside his mouth alongside Charlie's cock, he knew what was coming. He would be coming, there was little doubt about that. Knox's finger shifted to his hole and teased him mercilessly.

"Knox…" Charlie grabbed the lube and shoved it under the bed sheet, ignoring Knox's chuckle, or at least trying to as it vibrated his cock. All was forgiven when a lubed finger pushed inside of him. Letting his legs fall open, he concentrated on the feeling of Knox searching out his prostate, tapping against it, ratcheting up his desire, never once loosening his suction around the cock in his mouth. "Fuck me, Knox. Please, I need you."

Knox pulled off, looking up at him. "You're sure you're up for this?"

"Oh, I'm up alright." Charlie looked pointedly at his cock.

"Not quite what I meant, but I'll take it." Knox leaned down, brushed one last kiss on the tip of Charlie's cock, sucking up the precum there before he kissed his way up Charlie's stomach and chest, detouring to his nipples. Taking each one in turn, he bit and licked, teasing them.

"Damn, that's good, but I need more, Knox."

Knox let the nipple between his teeth go, and carried on kissing his way up Charlie's chest, paying close attention to the paw print. He traced it with his fingers, his tongue following right behind them. As much as Charlie needed Knox inside him, he didn't say a word, letting Knox take as much time as he wanted over the tattoo. Eventually, Knox was satisfied with his ministrations and claimed his lips.

Knox shifted position against him, lining his cock up with his hole. "You ready for me?"

"Always."

Knox slowly pushed forward, inch by torturous inch teasing him, setting his nerves on fire.

"I want to take you so damn hard, yet softly as well. I'm as conflicted as I always am with you. On the one hand, I want you close, protecting you. On the other, there is nothing more beautiful than watching you fly free. You twist me up, yet calm me down. You are the perfect balm for my soul, and I love you."

"I love you too, Knox, more than I ever would have believed possible. You give me courage, strength, and so much more. But right now, you're giving me the urge to throttle you. Damn you, would you just fuck me!"

Knox mock glared, but pulled back and slammed forward. "Like this you mean?"

261

"Exactly like that. Fuck!"

Neither of them spoke again, lost in the moment, the heat, the touch, and taste of each other's skin. Their gazes stayed locked together, neither of them looking away even for a second as Knox pistoned into him. When Knox shifted angle, he grazed Charlie's prostate again, and it was too much. He'd been on edge for too long and he let go, letting his orgasm claim him. His ass clamped down on Knox, tightening so much Knox couldn't move.

"Oh, fuck!" With a cry, Knox followed him over.

Charlie dozed for a moment, trusting Knox would clean him up, eventually, anyway.

"Charlie, we really do need to get up," Knox whispered into his ear. "Don't you want new books?"

"What about tomorrow?" Charlie mumbled.

The covers were yanked back and Knox sprang out of bed. "Nope, it needs to be today."

"What's going on?" Charlie rubbed the sleep from his eyes.

"Nothing is going on." Knox was moving about the room grabbing clothes.

Charlie wasn't so sure he believed him, but he went along with it. If Knox didn't want to tell him, he wouldn't until he was ready.

He was still yawning when the transport mage Knox had hired dropped them off outside his bookshop. Walking in, he shuddered, then smells assaulted him, a feeling of rightness and home settling inside of him. It was a different type of sensation of home than the one he experienced with Knox, but no less potent. Here he was truly himself, in all his geeky glory. He was surprised to see everyone there. Evie, Lane, the kiddos, Cora, Matt, Mama Alice, Sam, Alfie, all Knox's brothers, some of Knox's old teammates, and their friends. The group was huge.

He turned to face Knox. "What's going on?"

Carter stepped forward and handed a parcel to Knox. Knox gently eased Charlie into the center of the room. "Charlie." Knox blew out a breath. "The time since I met you has been crazy, chaotic, full of love and adventure, and you know what, I wouldn't have it any other way. I want our future to be just as crazy, in only the good ways, of course. I've never met someone as selfless as you, as prepared to go out of their way to help others. Your ideas for my book, your suggestions took the next one in the Davidson series to another level. Therefore, you should be the first to see this." Knox held the wrapped parcel out to him.

Charlie took it, seeing Knox's hands shaking. "What's going on?"

"Open it up, Charlie."

Charlie braced the parcel on his cast, peeling off the paper, aware of everyone watching him. His eyes lit up. It was an ARC of *Fireman's Inferno*. "Knox, it looks amazing."

"Open it, Charlie." Knox's gaze never left his.

Charlie opened the cover, looking at the blurb, the copyright, and then the dedication.

I never once believed I would find a love that could redefine who I am, or that I could find a partner who could make me see the world through fresh eyes. I was sure it wasn't meant to be.

I was wrong.

I've fallen in love with an incredible man who makes my heart soar and my soul sing. This is for him –

Charlie, I love you with everything that I am. Will you marry me?

Charlie's finger froze as it moved across the page. His gaze shot up and locked with Knox's. "Is this... are you serious?"

Knox dropped to one knee in front of him. There were gasps all around them, but Charlie didn't break his gaze from Knox. Holding out a box, Knox opened it to reveal a platinum ring with a rainbow-hued diamond set in the middle. "Charlie, as the dedication says, I love you. You make my soul come alive, you light up the world with your presence, and I want to spend eternity with you. Will you do me the greatest honor of agreeing to be my mate, of becoming my husband?"

A tear tracked down Charlie's face, even as a smile broke free. "Yes."

As soon as the word left his lips, Knox was on his feet, lifting him and spinning him around. "I love you. You are my everything."

"No, Knox. You are mine."

MEET THE AUTHOR

Hannah Walker is a full-time mum to two gorgeous teenage sons, and shares her home with both them, and a very supportive husband. They have always encouraged her to follow her dreams.

She has always loved books from her childhood years reading alongside her father, inheriting his love of Sci-Fi and Fantasy. She has combined this with her love of MM romance to write her series: Avanti Chronicles, Elements of Dragonis, and Demonic Tales. She loves writing about a complex world where the men love, and live, hard.

Welcome to the world of MM Sci-Fi.

UPCOMING BOOKS:

Demons Don't Duel, Demonic Tales book three.

Bray's Balance, part of the Avanti Chronicles.

A new sci fi series.

A new Standalone in the Spoils of War world.

A standalone in the Dragonis world.

OTHER BOOKS BY
HANNAH WALKER

The Avanti Chronicles

Corin's Chance

Tate's Torment

Delphini: Damage Control

Once Upon an Ocania

Dax's Desire

Bell's Beloved

Mission Most Mysterious

Delphini: Situation Critical

Hunter's Hope

DEMONIC TALES

Demons Don't Dream

Demons Don't Date

Elements of Dragonis

Booker's Song

Seeker's Portrait

Summoner's Dance

Spoils of War

Made in the USA
Columbia, SC
28 December 2017